Praise for Karl Va

CU00403379

"Karl Vadaszffy's *The Missi*
debut mystery, spare and fast-paced with a terrific ending. I
wouldn't be surprised if it spawns a DS Kate Nielsen series."

Glenn Cooper (*Library of the Dead* and *Book of Souls*)

"A thriller to make your pulse race. Desperation and
frustration stain the pages – a cracking good read."

James Becker (*The First Apostle* and *The Moses Stone*)

"Karl Vadaszffy delivers a real treat in *The Missing*, a thriller
written with the passion and intensity of a master storyteller.
Mystery, action, a flawed but determined protagonist, this
book has it all. I'm a fan of Karl's skill."

Matt Hilton (*Dead Men's Dust* and *Judgement and Wrath*)

"A mystery that grips, provokes and most definitely causes
the spine to tingle. Nothing is as it seems in this suspense-
laden tale, the pith darkening on each exquisitely written
page. *The Missing* moves at a relentless pace, taking the
reader on a journey into the twisted mind of a very dark
soul. A spellbinding thriller."

C. M. Palov (*The Templar's Quest* and *The Templar's Code*)

"*The Missing* plunges you into a nightmare scenario worthy
of Harlan Coben at his best. However, this is more than
a suspense novel, it is a perceptive and intriguing human
drama. All the interactions ring true and the characters –

even the monsters – are always believable."

Elly Griffiths (*The Crossing Places* and *The Janus Stone*)

"*The Missing* is a fast and compelling book, by turns tender and brutal, with a pounding sense of approaching crisis. The author's command of the scenes is impressive."

Patrick Lennon (*Corn Dolls* and *Steel Witches*)

"*The Missing* is a nightmare of a book, triggering a reader's darkest fears and keeping him in a state of tension from the first page until the last."

Thomas Perry (*Strip* and *Silence*)

"Karl Vadaszffy is just the sort of writer we should encourage – young, ambitious and creative."

Michael Dobbs (*House of Cards* and *Winston's War*)

"A remarkable book that makes compulsive reading. *The Missing* is raw and brutal, balanced with an overlay of tense paranoia."

Quentin Bates (*Frozen Out* and *Cold Comfort*)

THE MISSING

Karl Vadaszffy

PEACH PUBLISHING

Chapter One

"What's it like?"

"Scary."

"Scary?"

"Yes," I say. "Really scary."

My knuckles grip the leather as tightly as I can. I know how lucky I am, so I have to keep the journey steady and safe. Beyond my hands that sit on the leather steering wheel, the dashboard gleams from the early-morning clean I gave it. Then there's the road – a winding three-lane carriageway, arched over by occasional pedestrian and vehicle bridges. To my right, a concrete bank and, risen behind it, the electricity cables of the railway line. There's graffiti on walls. To my left, fields on which farm animals graze, and further in the distance there are hills.

We're on the M1.

It's only been three weeks, but it feels like a lifetime. The greatest happiness I've ever known. I turn my head towards Jennie for the longest glance I can sneak while driving. Her flowing brown hair, her dark eyes, her olive skin. Her features are a maze in which I get lost.

The sunshine is strong today. I've got the roof down on the Mazda soft top. It's taken me three years of saving to get this close to it, so I savour each moment I'm in control of the wheel and comfortable in its beige leather seats. The wind brushes against our heads, my short hair unfazed and Jennie's locks taken in the breeze's stride. She looks so graceful; she should be on a catwalk. I have to look at her to remind myself that she really is by my side.

"What do you mean, really scary?"

Even though there's insecurity in her eyes, she smiles at me, perhaps to cover embarrassment, her lips drawing apart, revealing her pearl-white teeth. I've been fighting to keep the play and what happens in it a secret since we left her house. It's really fear-inducing: *The Woman in Black*, a show I've seen three times, but Jennie hasn't even heard of it.

"It's scary," I tell her, "and you'll jump, you'll scream, but it's so worth it."

"Scream?"

"Depends how brave you are."

"You know I'm not."

"It's worth it. The beauty of it, though," I explain, "is because it's a play you don't think it'll work. They're only actors and you can see the whole stage. But even so, somehow your backside flies out of the seat."

"Oh God."

"You'll be fine."

She reaches into her handbag, removes a pair of sunglasses and draws them over her eyes to shade off the rays. Now the movie star in her comes out. I put my hand on hers.

Over the past three weeks I've felt it – bliss might be the best word to describe what's consumed me. Jennie came into my life and gave me everything I ever dreamed of: happiness, fulfilment, excitement. At a time when I was doing nothing more than standing still, when work was all that mattered and I was always alone, she brought me back to life.

I'll never forget the day we met. Rushing through the crowds around Covent Garden, I was making my way to Long Acre. I'm an estate agent in London, even though I live north of the city, in a small city called St Albans. I was on my way to meet a couple – potential clients who had taken an extended lunch break to meet me in Leicester Square. Round a corner and that was when I collided with her, and the coffee cup she was carrying fell to the floor.

"Shit," I said.

"Yes, shit," she responded.

"Oh, shit. I'm so sorry."

"It's okay," she said, and I looked into her beautiful eyes for the first time. And that was when, seeing the concern on my face, she smiled. Just like that: a simple smile and I relaxed.

She placed her hand on my arm and repeated she'd be fine. Then she started to move on and I felt worried I'd never see her again. A tightness in my stomach told me not to lose her. I thought of nothing else, not the potential clients, not the money I could make on commission, just her.

"No, don't go," I said. Then, realising how vacant I sounded, I indicated the empty cup on the floor. "Let me get you another."

"Really, it's fine," she said, and started to go.

"Please, let me. I couldn't possibly live with myself if I knew I was depriving you of a necessary caffeine kick. And it's always necessary, believe me." It was a poor attempt at humour, but it got her to think about it. "It'll only take a minute." Still thinking. "Please."

And with another smile she nodded. That was the first time we walked side by side, the first time I felt like I belonged with her, only inches apart, like we are now.

I turn to her again and she smiles and says, "I probably won't be able to sleep after this thing."

"Don't worry, I've already thought of that," I say. "I'll make it up to you. Afterwards will be the best part." I don't want to say any more, so I stop. I break into a smile and then a laugh.

"What's so funny?"

"Not funny. Just can't believe it. One minute we're strangers, the next I'm buying you coffee and we've got a date. It's almost unreal."

"It's our story. Maybe we'll have kids to tell one day."

It wasn't long after I'd bought her the drink and persuaded her to have it with me in the coffee shop rather than take it out that I realised this could be the woman of my dreams. Drink led to talk and talk led to dinner. And it hasn't stopped since.

The traffic in front of us slows down, so I have to let go of Jennie's hand to change gear.

It was the night of our third date when I knew she was the one. We'd had dinner at a restaurant in the Strand and then a romantic walk along the Thames, a light breeze pressing against our backs. Down to the Tate Modern, then a glass of champagne as we sat on the grass outside, and a walk back to Piccadilly, where I'd booked a hotel. Once there, we dimmed the lights and lit the candles, filled the bath with bubbles and surrounded it with scents and more candles. We bathed, naked together for the first time, the thrill of the introductory touch electric. It couldn't have been better: this was perfection.

After bathing, I carried Jennie to the bed and placed her on it. The scented petals we'd placed on it tickled her back. We kissed and then made love. It was the deepest, purest lovemaking I've ever experienced.

Afterwards, we held each other, listening to the sound of our own breathing.

Now as I drive, my attention keeps being drawn to Jennie, even though my mind is wandering. The reason is simple: there's going to be more to this evening than the theatre. After the play, after I've comforted her, we'll be at dinner, a glass of wine in hand. I'll tell her I love her and I'll ask her to be with me forever.

"I can't wait," I tell her. "You'll love it."

Perhaps it's the nerves, but I need to pee. I notice that

4

London Gateway services are only a mile off. "Got to stop to use the loo."

I take the exit and head up the ramp, onto the bridge, over the motorway, then straight ahead. Turn into the car park and head towards the building. I park close to the entrance.

"I'll wait," she says when I ask if she wants to come in.

"I'll be quick."

I kiss her on the cheek, shut the door and trot into the building. I follow the signs and enter the toilets. Once in, I relieve myself, wash my hands and leave.

Just as I'm about to exit the building, I see a coffee stand and I'm transported back to Long Acre. Jennie's body meeting mine. I stop. There's no queue, so I take the dozen or so steps to it at a jog.

The guy behind the counter asks me what I'd like.

"Latte," I answer: the drink Jennie spilt as we knocked into each other. "And I'll have a mocha. Both tall."

While the drinks are being poured, I turn around and picture Jennie sitting in the car, the sun illuminating her. The visor is down and she is reapplying her lipstick. Her hand brushes through her hair. Dozens of guys who pass the car see her and take a second glance.

The drinks are ready. I hand the barista a note, take the change and drop a couple of coins into the tip box. As I turn, there's a woman behind me, but I manage to sidestep her. Today I'm more careful.

I move to the automatic doors. They take a moment to open. When they come apart, I edge through and some of the coffee spills onto my hand. The scalding heat makes me stop. I bring my hand to my mouth.

Licking it off my hand, I resume walking back to the car. I have a full view of the car park. My eyes move towards the Mazda. As my eyes land on it, I come to a halt again. More liquid spills over the rim, but this time I don't react.

I look from left to right and back again. I look near and far. I look behind me. I do a three-sixty, scanning every direction. I turn back to the car.

Jennie isn't there. There must be a simple explanation – she's likely changed her mind and gone to the loo, or she's in the shop buying something – so I continue to the car and, when I reach it, put the coffees on the ground next to the curb. I look all around me in case she's stretching her legs somewhere. I open the car door and stand on the trim of the interior. From here I can see over cars and into the distance.

I can't see her.

I'm surprised that Jennie would leave the car unlocked, but there aren't many places to go – a hotel in the distance and a petrol station behind me – so she must be in the building. I pick up my coffee and lean against the driver's door, taking a sip every few seconds, waiting for Jennie to emerge from the building.

Five minutes later she hasn't come out. Maybe she's not feeling well and needs my help. That's possible. I lock the car and head back to the building.

I re-enter, sipping the coffee. Through the automatic doors, a right turn and I'm outside the entrance to the toilets. I wait for someone to come so that I can ask them to check for Jennie. But no one comes, so I take the opportunity to look in the newspaper shop that's to the side of the toilets. I look behind all the units in case Jennie's there. I don't find her.

So she must be in the toilets. I hope she isn't in there feeling unwell – I don't want this evening to be ruined. I leave the newsagent and call after a lady I see approaching the toilets. "Sorry," I say to her, "but could you check to see if there's someone called Jennie in there? I think my

6

girlfriend might be unwell."

"Sure," she says. "Just a mo."

It's only thirty seconds or so before the lady comes back out. She shakes her head and goes back in.

Jennie must be at the car then. Something I can't identify tugs at my stomach, but I shrug it off. She'll be there. Where else could she be? I take a large mouthful of my mocha and make my way towards the exit.

There's a sharp wind as I emerge. I look at the car and stop in my tracks when I see Jennie still isn't there. I recognise the tightness in my stomach as nerves. I haven't felt like this since the hours approaching our first night together.

Could Jennie, somehow, have worked out my plans to propose later? Have I scared her off? For the first time, I'm unsure of what to do next. Coupled with the possibility that Jennie might have run away from me, I feel confused and worried. But that can't have happened; surely that's impossible. We're happy together. I was positive when I decided to propose that Jennie would jump at the chance and say yes.

So maybe she is inside. Maybe the woman didn't look properly.

This time I run back into the building, dropping my coffee into a bin en route. There's no one around to help. I don't wait, and go in myself. When I enter, I see a woman applying mascara in front of the mirror. She steps back.

"It's okay," I tell her, slightly out of breath. "I'm looking for someone." This doesn't calm her, but I'm focused on finding Jennie, so I ignore her look of alarm. "Jennie!" I call out. "Are you in here, Jennie?" I move to each cubicle and knock on the doors, calling her name each time.

Someone answers, "No," but it's not Jennie's voice.

Now I really don't know what to do. She isn't anywhere and she wouldn't have just left: she can't really be scared of marrying me and she's not playing a joke on me. Surely.

I feel uncomfortable; there's sweat under my arms and down the centre of my back.

If she's not at the car and not here, then where is she? A sudden dangerous thought comes to me. What if something's happened to her?

Two more women come round the corner, but I run past them and leave. I hear an eruption of voices as soon as I'm out of there, and run over to the fast food area. Several families sit at the tables and there's a short queue. But there's no sign of Jennie.

Maybe she's back in the car waiting for me. I hope.

I hope to God. I run back out of the building, but the second I emerge I see she's still not there. She's gone. Gone I don't know where. The sun's gone too. The day feels fucked and I don't know how to make it better. I rush back to the car. As I'm about to reach the tarmac, I feel my feet knock into something. Something wet. I look down, see I've knocked Jennie's coffee over, and trip. I manage to put my hands out to cushion the fall, but they scrape along the gravel as I hit the ground. The blow takes the wind out of me and I can't breathe. My hands are bloodied, my trousers torn.

I get up and lean on the car to get my breath back. I notice that my hands are trembling. I shake my head and try to think. Try to work out anything I've not noticed. Anything I've not seen and done. What the hell should I do? What should I think?

"Phone," I say to myself, realising my next step. I remember the phone in my pocket and the phone Jennie always has on her. I use the speed dial to access her number. I wait for the ringing to start. The connection takes forever.

It rings. Finally it rings. We'll be able to sort this mess out. She'll pick up and there'll be some kind of silly explanation and we'll laugh about it later on.

But after the third ring my heart beats faster, and by the fifth ring I start to doubt. At the seventh ring, I expect her voicemail, but I don't get it. Why not? Her voicemail always comes on at the seventh ring.

"Answer me," I say to the phone. "For fuck's sake, answer!"

It cuts off, so I dial 999. I don't even think about it; it's like I'm on automatic pilot. I don't know what to say when they answer, but I know I need help.

The operator asks what service I want and I tell her I want the police. Within three seconds, I'm connected. The man on the end of the line asks what my emergency is.

"My girlfriend," I tell him, "she's gone. I don't know where she is. One minute she was here, the next she was gone. I've looked everywhere."

The man asks me to slow down. He asks my name and I tell him. He asks where I am and I tell him. He asks when I last saw Jennie and I tell him. He asks if there is no other logical explanation and I tell him, "There can't be. Maybe somebody's taken her. She was here."

He tells me he'll despatch officers to me right away, so all I can do is sit and wait.

My mind wanders. Initially I try to shrug off the concerns I have, but when Jennie still doesn't show up I can't help but think of her in pain, calling out my name. What if she needs my help? What if someone's got her?

I can't sit still, through the concern tugging at me, while I wait for the police, so I charge around the area, straight over to the hotel, into its foyer, then back and behind the services to where the petrol station is situated.

Fifteen minutes pass before I'm back at the car, despondent. Jennie's nowhere. Just as I reach the Mazda, I notice a police car pulling into the car park and I flag it down. The officers take a few moments to get out of the car – moments that feel longer than they likely are – and I stand next to the passenger door of the police car, shuffling on my feet.

"Mr Simmons?" the driver says as he gets out.

"Yes, John Simmons," I say. "My fiancée – girlfriend – I was going to propose tonight – Jennie Michaels – she's was with me and now she's gone – I've looked everywhere." I'm struggling through what I need to tell them and I'm made even more anxious when I see how unconcerned they look. "You've got to help me find her."

"We will, Mr Simmons, we will," the driver tells me. "Now, Jennie Michaels you say her name is?"

"Yes."

"And her address?"

"4 Sanders Road, St Albans."

"Description?"

"Medium-length brown hair, down to just below the shoulder blades, slim, five nine, tanned skin. She's wearing dark blue jeans and a cream shirt."

They're still not moving. I can't stop myself from becoming more agitated.

"I tried calling her. She's got a mobile on her, but even the voicemail function's been switched off. It's always on."

"And what's the number?" the officer asks.

I tell him.

"How long have you known Miss Michaels?"

"What's that got to do with anything?" I snap, only realising after I've said it that it came out all wrong.

"Do you have a problem answering my questions, sir?"

"No, of course not. I'm sorry. I just want you to help me find her."

"Then answer our questions so that we can start."

I'm sure the second officer, the passenger, snorts a laugh. I look at him but don't say anything. Then to the driver:

"Three weeks."

"That's a very short time to get to know someone and then go and propose," says the passenger officer.

"Not for us," I tell him. "We're very happy together."

He nods his head. "Of course you are, sir." The git exudes sarcasm, but I need them and their help, so I resist the temptation to answer back.

"Your address and phone number?"

I tell him and give home, work and mobile numbers.

"I'll be a few minutes," the driver says to me before turning around and getting back into the police car.

The other officer and I stand in silence for a time. I keep switching my glance between the officer in the car – he's speaking on a radio – and the one next to me. The one by my side doesn't say anything, but he keeps looking at me. Even when I'm not looking at him, I can sense his eyes glued on me. I want to move away from him, want to get my head clear.

I'm brought back to what's in front of me by the officer's voice. "Did Miss Michaels go inside, sir?"

"Yes... No... At least I thought she had when I came out and she wasn't in the car." Nothing makes sense. "I don't know," I concede.

"Did you speak to anyone? Anyone who might have seen her?"

"No. Yes. In the toilets." With my hand, I wipe the sweat from my forehead. "What if she's been taken?"

"If anything's happened, CCTV will show it to us."

"I hadn't thought of that." Hope – I feel hope. "Go and look. Please." He doesn't move. "Please," I add, louder.

"You'll have to be patient, sir." He crosses his arms and steps back, making it clear that he won't be rushed.

Our conversation is ended by the sound of the police car's door closing. The officer comes over to us and whispers

11

something into his colleague's ear. In response, the officer's eyebrows rise.

Something's wrong.

"What?"

The driver says, "You are aware, sir, about all the kinds of trouble you can get into for wasting police time."

"What?" I ask. What are they talking about?

"Wasting police time is a criminal offence."

"I know. What do you think I am?" My heart could explode. I'm struggling to catch my breath. "Just what are you saying?"

"Stop it, sir." The passenger officer. Sarcastic bastard. I called them – I need them and they're acting like this.

"If someone's taken her, they're getting away from us."

"If?" The sarcastic one again.

"You've got to find her. This is serious!" I almost take him by the lapels of his florescent jacket. Fucking fool!

"We'll do no such thing. Unless you want to give us a mobile phone number that's recognised, that is."

"What are you talking about?"

"The mobile number – Jennie Michaels' mobile number that you say you rang earlier – is a number that's not recognised."

No. No. "Impossible. No way." I remove the phone from my pocket and again use the speed dial to call Jennie's number. "No way," I repeat as I wait for the ringing to begin, to prove them wrong, to show them they're putting Jennie's life on the line by playing games with me.

Stupid phone is so slow. Their eyes are fixed on me as I wait for the ringing to begin. I want them to stop staring. I want to scream at them to fuck off. But I need their help, so I can't.

A drop of sweat slides to the end of my nose. I wipe it with my hand before I hear the tone. The three beeps and then the automatic voice. I take the handset away from my ear and look at the screen. Numb.

Number not recognised.

No. "But that's not possible," I say. "I rang it half an hour ago."

"Of course you did."

They both look thoroughly pissed off, but all I can do is shake my head; I can't answer them, can't plead with them to believe me.

Confused. Who's doing this to me? What's going on? I don't know. My mind feels like it's buzzing. Like I might faint. Have to sit down. I open the car door and fall into the passenger seat – Jennie's seat – and my shoulders hunch forwards like I've been punched. I feel the shape of Jennie's body beneath me as if she's left a mark on the seat. The officers are speaking to me, but I don't hear them. I only hear a reverberating noise. There's nothing else in my head. Nothing.

One of the officers clicks his fingers in front of my eyes to get my attention. I don't know how long I've been out of it. In all likeliness only seconds, but I feel like I've been in this seat all day.

"You're in trouble, you know that?"

I nod my head. I can't speak. I've given up trying to explain, trying to tell him he's making a terrible mistake, that he's putting Jennie's life in danger. But even so, my mind races with its own thoughts. What will happen to Jennie if they don't help me? What will happen to *us*? He tells me I'll hear from the police; that I'll probably end up in court.

I couldn't care less. I can only think of Jennie. Of her helplessness right now, wherever she is, and the helplessness I feel.

"You'll be hearing from us very soon."

I manage to stand up as the officers leave me, small as an ant in the middle of a field, and I really have no idea what my next step is. Where should I go? I'm like a toddler who has wandered off from his parents in a supermarket, only there are no adults who will look out for me and make the pain of disappearance disappear.

I walk round to the driver's side and get in. My body crashes into the seat, heavy as lead, and my head droops forwards on impact. My hands slap onto the steering wheel. My knuckles once again peer over the top of its leather cover. I look at my hands, grazed and bloody. I want to grip the steering wheel but am without strength. My chest pounds up and down and my breathing is loud as I suck in all the air I can.

"Where are you, Jennie?"

I turn to my left and picture her beside me. In my mind, she smiles at me and asks why I keep looking at her. I smile back. I don't have an answer; it's just that she's so damned beautiful. I picture but don't see. Because she's not real any more.

I start the engine and pull out of the parking space without a clue about where I'm going. I'm in the dark and I'm scared. Just like the lawyer is in *The Woman in Black*.

I realise that's where I should be going. If she went anywhere – if this could possibly be a joke – maybe she went there. Maybe I'll turn up at the theatre and she'll be standing outside, laughing at me. Maybe we'll hug and everything will go back to the way it was before. Maybe I'll propose and she'll say yes.

Or maybe she has run off from me. Could she, somehow, have known about my plans?

I pull back onto the M1 and dial her number again. By the time I reach Brent Cross, I've dialled it almost thirty times. Each time the result is the same: *Number not recognised.* I don't know how long this journey is going to take and, although I cling to the smallest piece of hope, I dread the moment when I arrive at the theatre, for if as I suspect she's not there I'll be stuck again and won't know which way to turn.

Chapter Two

Sarah Elson woke up ready to follow her regular routine. The alarm clock rang at six fifteen and she was up and in the shower by six thirty.

At six fifty, she was out of the shower, towelling herself dry. The mirror in her small en suite bathroom was covered in steam. Once her body was dry she wiped the steam off the mirror with the towel, which she then placed on the sink. Her teeth were next, then moisturisers and other creams. Although she didn't need to do much – she was, her mother said, blessed with natural beauty – at only twenty-five years old, Sarah had already begun the age-old process of trying in vain to stave off the signs of ageing.

She went to the kitchen, filled the kettle and made herself a piece of toast with strawberry jam. She couldn't face more than that so early in the morning.

She took the coffee back into the bedroom where she got dressed. She put on each item of clothing with care. Lifted her brown hair high enough so that she could swing her blue jacket round and onto her shoulders before the hair fell back into place. Then it was time to finish the toast and coffee, which by now had reached the temperature she preferred.

She left the flat at seven twenty and walked down the stairs from the second floor. It had been sunny for the past week and this morning was no different. From her handbag she pulled out a pair of sunglasses and, with a twist of the neck, swung her hair further behind her back.

She had no idea, of course, that as she walked along the main road to the bus stop her every move was being tracked.

It had happened for the past five days, sometimes from only a few feet away. She was being watched. He was getting ready. She would be his first.

Sarah only had to wait three or four minutes before her bus arrived. She found the last available seat. She removed a book from her bag and entered a fantasyland in which all men were muscle-bound heroes and bad guys were always punished.

It was a ten-minute ride to the train station where she boarded her train to work. From there it was another thirty minutes, possible delays excluded, followed by a fifteen-minute walk, before she arrived at the office in which she worked.

In the office she sat behind a desk all day, typed, joked with colleagues and put on a fake smile, despite feeling pretty glum about what had become of her professional life, all the while counting down the minutes till lunchtime arrived.

When it came, routine was followed again. She left the building, down three floors in the lift, and exited into the stream of the passing public. At the end of the road, she entered a coffee shop. She ordered her favourite drink and a croissant. Enough for lunch. The same as every day. She sat on a stool at the side counter, eating, drinking and reading her book. She'd almost reached the final chapter. It'll soon be time to pick up a new one, she thought.

On a stool, sitting by the opposite counter but facing her, he sat. He'd been waiting for her all morning, and the chance to watch her from such close proximity excited him. His eyes stayed focused on the back of her head; on her luscious black hair, which shined in the daylight. He wanted to touch it. He wanted to put it in his mouth, to feel her. He imagined what it would be like to touch her skin – had imagined it for a five days now. If he had one virtue it was patience, and this game was new to him, so he wanted to get it right. After finishing her chapter, she closed the book and placed it in her bag. She took a final sip of her coffee as she stood up, threw the bag over her shoulder and left, not noticing the man who also stood up and inconspicuously followed her out. You wouldn't notice; no one would. This was London, after all.

He walked behind her all the way down the road and came to a stop a few feet before the entrance to her office. She stopped too and looked at the ground. He had observed her do this several times since he chose her. He thought she looked sad. He often thought, despite her beauty, that she looked unhappy.

But he didn't care about that; he only cared about what they were going to feel tonight – that was when it was going to happen. It was because of the beauty that he'd selected her, and he couldn't contain himself for much longer, so strong was his sense of expectation. Soon he'd be able to lay his hands upon perfection, for that was how he viewed her. He'd actually be able to feel her warm, soft skin upon his own, feel her breath opposite his, look directly into her eyes as she looked into his.

She returned to her desk for another four-and-a-half hours. Barely broke into a smile as the fatigue of another monotonous day wore away at her. Ignored all the girly gossip, all the flirtatious guys who approached and propped themselves on her desk. Simply nodded in acknowledgement and feigned interest while thinking about her forgotten dreams and lost aspirations.

Dreams that would never be able to come true after the night that was to come.

Never say no to a drinks invitation, she'd been told on her first day working for the company. Never. So of course she'd accepted the invitation from a small group of colleagues – three girls and two guys – when one of them approached her desk ten minutes before it was time to go home and asked her if she'd like to join them for a cocktail. The truth was, although politeness and the ability to learn from her superiors had led her to accept, she loathed the idea because she had nothing in common with the people with whom she worked. They were happy to sit at a desk, drink away their earnings and sleep around with everyone else in the office. But she hadn't followed their examples. She still believed in herself. She still expected more of herself.

She worked for a newspaper, but not in the way she'd hoped when three years ago she left university, determined to make a name for herself in journalism. Since then she hadn't managed to get past being a sales agent. She hadn't realised how competitive things were, just how many people were willing to use anything – things way beyond talent – to get what they wanted. And she would never be one of those people.

So she'd stayed put for three years and her disappointment had only grown stronger.

Five thirty and it was time to get the drinks in. Her colleagues were by her desk, dressed and ready, before she'd even had time to switch her computer off. And she dreaded what was to come.

A short walk and they were there. A pub in St Martin's Lane and a booth. One of the men, a guy named Adam, said he'd get the first round in. *Round* meant more than one drink. More than one drink meant getting home late, something she hadn't planned on and hadn't wanted to happen.

But half an hour and two rounds of cocktails later, her mood lightened up, she loosened up and she started to relax. She'd forgotten how alcohol softens you up. And she felt good for it. Within no time at all, she was speaking more loudly, she was saying things she'd never dreamed of saying to them and she was flirting. She didn't know what she was doing, nor did she care, possibly for the first time since starting to work in London.

When she'd emerged from her office building, he'd been waiting for her. His excitement had peaked and he didn't know if he'd be able to contain himself during the journey home, so close together would they be. He anticipated that she would be amazing, unlike all other women; he'd seen so much in her that he craved.

He planned to use her as his way out, to escape the pain of his past, the misery of his present, as the means by which to start afresh for the future. She was going to be placed on his pedestal.

But when he saw her step out with five other workers and fail to bid them farewell, he encountered a wall of frustration. He'd waited all afternoon and was ready to begin. He desperately wanted their time together to commence. So he was infuriated when she took a left instead of her usual right turn and entered the bar.

Now he sat three tables away from them, waiting. The calmness of patience had returned – a scotch on the rocks had helped – and he was biding his time.

She was a beauty. She would be the one to prove to him there could be more to women, beautiful women especially, than he'd seen so far. Depth, sensitivity, normality.

He watched her more closely than ever before, watched her smile and giggle. Those teeth. Felt a sense of pleasure, of pride.

But then it wasn't long before he could hardly believe what he was watching: she was laughing uncontrollably. Knocking back the drinks. Things were starting to change; he could see his plan was failing. The alcohol would ruin everything; he wanted her to be fully conscious when he did it, wanted her to know what he was doing, wanted her to recognise his features as he took her on a journey she'd never dreamed of, wanted her to feel the connection too, and wanted her to be a real part of it.

As he saw the contents of each glass disappear, he was transported back thirty years. He winced as he saw his father consume glass after glass, each one coming down with a thud as they connected with the coffee table. His father topped up, continued to get smashed.

The son watched, his needs uncared for, his only purpose to be a sponge absorbing the insults that his father dished out. The subject of those insults was his mother, out of the door three years prior. The sadness he'd endured in his mother's absence and the tears he'd initially shed had dispersed and hardened into feelings of bitterness; his old man's words had resonated within him and changed the way he thought and felt. He'd learned – been trained – to hate the woman who was his mother, absent, nothing more than an unpleasant distant memory.

In turn, he'd developed similar feelings for the man who sat before him, the man who chugged back the whiskey, the man who belittled and berated the woman who'd bore a son fourteen years before. A clang, the bottle open, the liquid poured, the glass in hand. "Bitch, she never cared about you. About us. What kind of woman, what kind of whore, abandons her son and husband?" Down in one, then the clang again, the bottle, pour, hand. "Fucking whore never cared. Leaps into the arms of any man who'd take her. Not to you, boy, her only fucking child, but to a man with a wad of cash, she's there eager, spreading her fucking legs."

He was still thinking of his mother when, in the pub, he saw the touching begin. He saw Sarah Elson change: she became a flirt, just like the other three women, the opposite of what he'd expected. Her fingers lingered on the guy's arm. Adam, he discovered, was the guy's name.

His hopes started to deflate. Then anger: that things were becoming too similar to the things he'd tried to forget. And he'd failed miserably, would never be able to forget, was kidding himself that he could forget. It was too much to escape from.

He started to feel dizzy, couldn't differentiate what was in front of him from what was in his memory.

He saw an eleven-year-old boy, home early from school. He'd felt ill, so he'd decided to play truant. Even at such a young age, he hated authority and he knew that if he said he felt ill, he'd be told to put up with it, when all he wanted was to fall into his bed, close his eyes and recover.

He unlocked the door and walked in, taking his shoes off and removing his coat. He put his bag on the floor by the front door and went into the kitchen. He reached into a cupboard for a glass, filled it with water from the tap. Then up the stairs, where he heard noises. Sighs. Short, sharp whimpers. Other noises too. He moved along the corridor, edged forwards the door from behind which the noise was coming. And that was the first glimpse he got of the personality his mother had managed to keep hidden: she was on her knees and leaning forwards onto her arms, a man he'd never seen behind her and also on his knees, thrusting hard, covered in sweat. The man looked up, when he heard the young boy start, and shouted, "Shit." The child ran before his mother and the man had the chance to become disentangled.

When he returned, his mother didn't say a word to him. They made eye contact; he recognised a warning glance, but that was all. And he kept their secret tucked away. But it always lingered in his mind.

Metres from him, Sarah and Adam had their tongues stuck down each other's throats. Seeing this made his blood boil to a new level. Somehow Sarah had become like his mother. Like the fucking whore. It became his father's pet name for his mother when, five months later, she'd packed her bags and got into the car of a man – not the man he'd seen fucking her, but another man, younger. Despite his confusion, his fists clenched as he watched her take off, tears streaming down his cheeks, and again, right now, they clenched as he kept his frozen glare on the couple before him. He took the unopened packet of nuts he'd bought, squeezed, popped it, and ground the nuts into dust.

Sarah's hands were exploring Adam's body, her nails tickling the skin between shirt buttons, his hand squeezing her arse. "You're going to fuck him," he mumbled to himself. "Dirty whore." Still dizzy, he started to feel the hate return; she'd brought it back to him.

His heart pounding, he got up and walked out. Fresh air.

The moment was gone; he felt nothing for her any more. Now she was an object, a piece of sexed-up meat. He only wanted to hurt her. Destroy her for destroying his hopes.

Composed, decided, he went back in; he'd wait for his opportunity.

The other colleagues faded away and Sarah and Adam moved to a table on their own where they continued fondling each other.

Soon enough, they were leaving. He had to get moving when he saw Adam hail a bike pedal cab outside the pub. He feared he'd lose them. The sloth-like necessity of watching had dulled his senses. It took him a moment to react and move into position. He was relieved that it wasn't a black taxi; he could keep up on foot with a pedal bike.

Traffic was heavy that night, so at times all it took was a trot to keep apace with the bike cab. One or two close calls for the bike with overzealous drivers in real cars made an unexpected queasiness fill his insides – an accident of some kind would ruin his plans.

It was fifteen minutes before the bike cab pulled over and the drunken couple stumbled off it. They entered Oxford Circus tube and he followed, not bothering to keep his distance, for he knew they'd never realise he was there because they were so drunk and there were so many people around. Almost placed his hands on their shoulders at one point.

They boarded a train, got off at Euston and transferred to an overline train.

Not long later, as Adam and Sarah Elson emerged from the station, it was raining outside. The moon's reflection glowed in the puddles. He walked behind them, a little more cautiously now for they were completely alone, the three of them.

As they stood outside Adam's house and as Adam tried to find the door key in his pocket, their observer stood on the other side of the road behind a parked car. They didn't see him; wouldn't see him coming if he chose to. They merely saw each other, and before Adam had found the key Sarah Elson was all over him. She surprised herself, couldn't really believe she was taking charge and pushing her body into his. She felt his hardness on her hip and rubbed against it. He breathed deeply, found the key and opened up. The second they were inside, their kissing recommenced and became wilder, more passionate. They didn't even wait to get upstairs. They started to pull the clothes off one another at the bottom of the stairs and, half naked, he picked her up and carried her into the living room, placed her on the settee and went down on her.

Outside the drizzle had turned into a downpour. As soon as the front door had slammed shut, he'd approached the house and walked down the path. While trying to peer in through the misted glass of the front door, a light appeared in the front room, so he took three steps to the left where there was a window. There were nets but no curtains drawn. He peered in, cupping his hands around his eyes, water covering him. A standing lamp in the opposite corner of the room had been switched on. On the left of the room was the settee and, upon it, she was lying, naked, and Adam was eating her. Instinctively, he touched himself. She looked gorgeous, the body he'd imagined all along, the one he'd get later; she would be his for the purpose of the thrill. He watched as she writhed around, her hand pressing Adam's head closer in, and his tongue ran along his teeth.

Adam entered her. Beyond the window, he dropped to his knees, his penis in his hand. This would be a taster for him, a warm-up of sorts. As he used the fantasy of watching them fuck, his mind flitted between her body on the settee and the thought of his mother and the man he'd caught her with – thrilling and sickening for him at the same time. It was only seconds before it was over for him, but Adam kept on, faster and harder.

Satisfied from part one, he returned to the other side of the road to await the start of part two. He'd now seen what was there for him on the other side of her clothing, so a longer wait would be no hardship. There was only one use for her. Patience – for him, killing would be nothing more than a waiting game – and then he would take, the way he'd planned.

*

When Sarah Elson woke up the following morning, she was lying on the sofa across Adam's naked body. With her senses back to normal she regretted what had happened, not that she could remember much about it, but with the sight before her eyes it was pretty guessable.

She couldn't believe she was about to do it – even though

she'd surprised herself several times in the past twelve hours – but she decided to head out without waking Adam up. Leaving him on the sofa, she picked up her clothes, quickly dressed and left the house.

She was greeted by sunshine as she came into daylight, but she shivered. All she could think about was the other workers finding out. Not that it would take much guesswork: she'd left with him, and she and he had been all over each other in the pub. At least today was Saturday and she wouldn't have to face up to things until Monday morning. She could get away with feigning ignorance until then.

When she stepped away from herself, as she often did, and took a look at the bigger picture, she saw that *she* was leaving Adam. Walking out on the one-night stand. She'd always pictured a man doing that to her if she were ever foolish enough to put herself in such a predicament, not the other way around. And with the odd reversal of fortune in mind she smiled to herself. Sod it, she thought and meant it.

She couldn't concentrate on her book during the journey home and found herself having to re-read passages the second she'd finished them. Thinking about it, she didn't believe in the innocent heroine any more, nor the heroic adventurer who comes to rescue the damsel in distress. And as she exited the train when she arrived back at her station, she dropped the book into a bin. Perhaps it was time for something different.

Her block came into view as she was a street away from home. Her mind still lingered on the night before – she wondered exactly what she'd done, but she doubted Adam could remember either, they were so wasted. It didn't take long before her fear of consequences was gone. She didn't care. There was so much more to do with her life and she was going to do it. She was going to get her portfolio of writing out there and someone was going to discover her. Hell, she might even try her hand at writing a book. If the trash she'd been reading could get published, there was no reason why something she'd muster up couldn't be. She could at least string a sentence together, which was more than most of the romance writers she read could do.

Yes, she would do it. She was determined for the first time since leaving university and starting work.

She unlocked the security door to the building and heard it bang shut as she mounted the first set of stairs. Feeling human again, she skipped up two steps at a time.

She reached her floor and was forced to stop. She drew a short breath. Her door: it had been prised open. Bits of splintered wood hung from the wall. Now she felt uncertain, didn't know what to do. The security door downstairs brought a degree of reassurance to her. Whoever did it, she thought, had probably taken off with what they wanted hours ago.

Slowly, she pushed the door open. The contents of the hall cupboard lay strewn across the floor. Several pairs of shoes, newspapers and magazines lay tangled together. She heard no noise yet still called out, "Hello?"

No answer, hardly a surprise.

With her heart beating too quickly for comfort, she stepped forwards and rounded the corner into the lounge. A solitary dining chair sat in the middle of the room and was surrounded by the things that had once been in her units and cabinets. All over the floor. The place was a mess. She turned and went into the kitchen where she found all her appliances smashed to pieces on the floor. And then she tried the bedroom.

Perfection. That wasn't expected – not a thing was out of place. The bed was still freshly made; her shelves filled as before; her units holding the usual stuff on display.

Then the television in the living room came on. The sound of voices – *Football Focus* – made her jump and gasp, and goose bumps covered her from head to foot. Instinct made her move towards the living room to take a look. To see if a freak of nature had somehow managed to turn the television on. She hoped it had.

"Hello?" she called out again as she approached.

She crept towards the noise. And then she saw him – not a freak of nature but a freak. He looked normal, but by being here he was anything but normal. Sitting upon the solitary chair, he stared at her. She froze, unsure of what to do. He didn't move and she was near the front door, so she leapt towards it. But it was no longer open. She grabbed it and pulled, but it wouldn't budge. Now she shrieked, realising. Shrieked for all her worth and pounded on the door, pleading to be set free. Tears appeared; she couldn't stop them. They fell with the force of a waterfall as she realised that no one was coming to free her; that there was no way out; that there was no hero to save her.

Knowing this, she turned around. With slow steps she made her way back into the lounge. As the wall disappeared and the entryway opened up, she brought her eyes in line with his. He still sat on the chair. Hadn't moved a muscle. Hadn't said a word. He just kept his eyes on her, his head tilted to the right.

Tears streamed down her face and she tried to work out the best way to plead for her life.

Before she could speak, before she could beg, before she could ask what he wanted, he said his first words to her: "The bedroom's ready."

She shuddered because she understood fully.

Then, thinking of his mother, thinking of how Sarah Elson had devastated him by turning out exactly like her, he added, "You fucking whore."

Chapter Three

The dash to the Fortune Theatre has paid off. I've got here in about forty minutes. Traffic on Finchley Road was heavy, but I managed to weave in and out of it. I'll probably find a bus lane infringement penalty notice on the hall floor in a few mornings' time, but I don't care. I'd go down a one-way street the wrong way if I knew it would get me closer to finding Jennie.

Groups of people are milling around outside the theatre. There's still twenty minutes to curtain up and I go to each group, describe Jennie and ask them if they've seen her.

They shake their heads; no one can help me. No one looks that bothered either.

I hang around, hoping against hope that she'll turn up. I question everyone I can and even start giving out my business card. "Contact me," I say, "if you see her."

Some agree to keep an eye out for her and I start to receive a few words of comfort. But I get the impression they're just trying to get rid of me. I won't let my lack of success faze me though. I can't. Have to keep moving, asking anyone, everyone, about Jennie.

As show time approaches, I go to the box office and ask for the theatre manager. Presumably because she sees how flustered I am, the assistant doesn't ask why I want to see the manager; she just picks up the phone and makes the call.

Within minutes, which I spend shuffling near the door, peering out and looking for Jennie, praying she'll step out of a taxi, the manager appears. He has the kind of face that says he's switched on and ready to listen. He tilts his head towards me, his ear sticking out in my direction, as if mine

31

are the first words he's ever heard and he's hanging onto them.

"I need your help."

"And how can I help you, sir?" he asks.

"My girlfriend, she's gone missing. We were supposed to come here this evening, but she disappeared at the services on the motorway. London Gateway. Do you know it?"

"Yes, sir."

"I'm praying she's come here. That she's... that she's just playing a trick on me. I don't know." As I speak, my voice rises and I struggle to get the next word out. It is gratifying, though, to see that I am getting through to someone, albeit only a theatre manager. "Please," I beg him, "let me look in the auditorium. She might be in there waiting for me." I point and am already halfway down the stairs, and without saying anything he concedes.

"Make it quick," he says when he catches up with me. Then he takes me by the arm and leads me into the auditorium.

Everything is red and for a moment I have to remind myself that I'm not here to watch anything, that I don't need to look for my seat; I'm here to find Jennie. As the entrance to the auditorium is at the back of the space, I leave the theatre manager standing in the doorway and walk down the side aisle to the front of the stalls from where I get a better view of everyone, from where I can start my search. I scan each row in the stalls, pleading in a whisper for Jennie to be here, but I can't see her. It feels useless. I jog back, pass the theatre manager and enter the bar. Again, Jennie isn't here. My head starts to spin and I feel nauseous, but I have to continue my search.

The theatre manager must see the colour of my skin change because he asks, "Are you all right, sir?"

"I need... I need to see... upstairs. Please."

"Sir, I think you've done enough."

"Please," I repeat. "She might be hidden up there."

"Not without a ticket she won't be."

I think I might pass out.

"Listen," he says, taking me by the shoulder. "You take a seat here and I'll put a call out for her on the pager system." When he sees that I'm about to protest, he says, "It'll be heard in every corner of the theatre. If she's here, she'll hear it. And if she hears it, she'll respond to it." I don't look so convinced. "Won't she?" he presses.

After a few seconds, I nod my head. "Yes," I say, "I suppose she will."

As he leaves me, he whispers to the barman, who is by my side almost as soon as the theatre manager has left. He hands me a glass of water. Tells me to drink it.

"Thanks."

"You okay?" he asks.

I can't speak. I can only shake my head. I feel my temperature rising, so I ask the barman where the toilets are. They're only feet behind me, so I leap up and I'm in there.

I lean on the sink for a second, then turn the tap on and scoop half a dozen handfuls of water over my face. I look into the mirror and see my eyes. I stare into them and try to regain my composure, discover some kind of determination. I have to remain calm.

A few minutes later, I go back into the bar. I hear the final warning bell that tells the audience the show is about to begin. Jennie and I are supposed to be in there. So it's ruined. Everything's ruined. It's not going to scare her and I'm not going to be able to provide her with comfort. Wherever she is, I'm unable to comfort her and that kills me.

The theatre manager reappears and stands beside me. "No luck," he says. "Sorry."

33

"Thank you," I say. He waits for more from me. "So I guess I'm stuck."

"Look," he says, "if you're really worried, call the police. They'll have to help you. Or have you tried calling her family? Have you checked her home?"

I shake my head. "No, I haven't tried her home yet."

Seeing that I'm not moving, he says, "Listen, the show's got to start and I'm needed in the auditorium. I know you've got a ticket, but I've got to ask you either to take your seat or vacate the theatre so that we can start. There's a lot of people waiting. The actors are ready."

Without saying anything else, I stand up and leave, starting the climb to the foyer. Outside the theatre I sit down. I need some time to think. Think clearly.

I watch streams of people moving in every direction. Some couples hold hands and I feel a sense of longing; some are alone; others are in groups. Some are arguing, some laughing, some confused and staring at maps. At the moment, I don't belong in any of these groups. I'm part of a pair, but right now I'm alone. And if something's happened to Jennie that means she's alone too. And probably afraid.

I grab my phone from my jacket pocket. I select the contacts list, scroll down to find a name – anyone who might know where Jennie is. Now I realise just how much I've kept her to myself. I've not shared her with anyone else. As I look at the names, I don't see anyone who knows Jennie, much less where she is. But Mum. Mum knows about her. I remember calling her. It wasn't that long ago and I said, "Mum, I want to tell you all about a girl I've met, Jennie." Mum's voice will calm me, help me focus and sort out what I should do next.

I dial and, after three rings, she picks up. I interrupt her greeting. "Mum, it's John."

"Oh, John, how nice. I was just thinking about how

nice it would be if you were to call. See, we must have a clairvoyant link."

Her attempt at humour isn't funny, not now. "Mum, I'm in trouble. Well, I'm not, but Jennie—"

"Jennie?"

"Jennie. My girlfriend, Jennie. I told you about her, remember? I've been seeing her for three weeks."

"Oh, but my boy, you haven't called me for, oh, I don't know, almost three months now. That's why I was thinking it would be good to hear your voice. It's been so long, you see. But I understand – you're so busy with work."

"No, don't you remember? You must. We spoke just over a week ago. I said, 'Mum, I want to tell you all about my new girlfriend, Jennie'. Don't you remember that, Mum? You must."

"No, John, my boy. I really don't. Maybe you said something several months ago and I've forgotten, but—"

"No, Mum," I snap. Why does she have to be forgetful like this again, now of all times? "It was about ten days ago. I'm telling you."

But she persists. "No, John, it's been three months. I wish it were more often than that, but it's always about three months."

"Oh, Mum," I say. The words are stuck and my head's starting to ache.

"John," she says softly in a soothing motherly voice, "are you all right? Is there anything I can do?"

"No, it's nothing," I say. "I'm fine. And how are you feeling?"

"I'm okay. You know how it is."

"Yes, yes I do." I hear her breathing, but she doesn't speak. There's a quiver in her breath. "I'm sorry I haven't called more often." I hate to think I upset her when I don't call. Even though she is the way she is, what with her memory and pain and medication, I don't want to add to her worries. She raised me well.

"That's okay, son. You have an important job. Besides, your brother keeps me going. I see him every week, you know."

"Yes, Mum, I know."

"Now tell me about this girlfriend of yours. Is she pretty?"

"Is she what?" Her question takes me aback.

"Pretty, John. Is she pretty?"

"Oh, yes, Mum, she's pretty. Yes... So incredibly pretty."

"Oh good, I'm glad. You deserve a pretty girlfriend. You're such a nice, handsome young man. And my nice, handsome young son must bring his pretty girlfriend home to meet his mother soon, you hear?"

I hold the handset silently for a moment. Clutch at it. I don't know what to say, but I need to be positive. "Of course I will. Very soon."

"You come by soon, okay dear?" she says.

"Yes, I will. Soon."

I press the *End Call* button. I'm on my own. There's no one else to call; no one to help me. I think of the people I should tell and realise I don't know Jennie's family, don't know how to reach out to them. What will they go through when they can't get hold of her? Jennie once referred to a brother, but I can't even remember his name. I'm annoyed with myself for never asking her about family, frustrated with her for never telling me. Why didn't she say more about them? Or her friends. She mentioned a Michelle, no more than that, but I never met her. Never met any of her friends. Three weeks is a short time and we wanted to spend every minute of it together, not with other people.

Jennie did tell me she'd moved around a lot since she was a child, mentioned a bundle of towns and cities, some I'd heard of, some I hadn't. But I don't remember what they were. I think Liverpool was mentioned. Beyond that, though, I haven't a clue. It was too much to take in – the moment, just being with Jennie and feeling so lucky to have her in my life, prevented me from taking everything in.

Whatever I know or don't know, I'm sure that being positive is the most important thing. Be positive and proactive and find out what's going on.

So what next?

The theatre manager's words come back to me.

Jennie's home. That's what's next.

Chapter Four

"Please."

Never-ending sobs.

Until death.

"I'd wanted you since the first time I saw you, you know that? And then you blew it by going and screwing that fucker."

Sarah Elson's eyes widened; he knew what she'd done.

"You're supposed to be my first, the way I'd planned it, and then you turn out to be a fucking whore. I've waited since she left and then the other one… they, fucking whores, like you. How dare you."

Bound by the wrists, brown tape over her mouth, a bruised cheek, tears still in freefall, Sarah was positioned on the dining table chair, now in the bedroom. He'd given her clear instructions not to turn around. She'd obeyed. Even though he was somewhere behind her, even though she desperately wanted to see what he was doing and even though she wanted to defy him, appal him, tell him to fuck off and die, she kept as still as she could, with only the occasional shudder the proof of a beating heart. She kept her eyes fixed on the bookshelf in front of her, fixed her eyes on the same book spine, didn't falter in her focus. She found some kind of reprieve in the title's font, but it wouldn't help her for long.

She had heard the cracking noise made by his knees as he lowered himself to the ground. She had heard the zip of his trousers opening. She had heard his breathing.

But now all was silent.

Her neck started to twitch, her body was covered in goose

bumps and her hair moved because of what she assumed was a breeze connecting with her neck. And then, when she heard a sigh, she realised that it wasn't the wind that was moving her hair; it was his fingers – the fingers of his right hand, while his left gently brushed over the skin of her neck. The sound of his breathing got louder as he leaned towards her ear. She felt his breath against her skin.

And that was when she turned to face him. She looked the devil straight in the eyes. Confronted him. Desperately tried to show him that she wasn't scared, petrified, despite her tears that indicated the contrary. She looked deep into his eyes and tried to recognise something – something human, anything that gave her a clue about what he was planning to do with her, anything that suggested she might find a way out of this. Somehow.

Anything she could appeal to.

Even though he looked like a normal human being, she saw nothing, just cold, vacant eyes. The eyes of a monster, and she knew.

She saw his hand, just before the other hit the side of her face. Her head snapped back. Her jaw went numb – so much so that she was sure, or as sure as she could be in her daze, that it had been broken. He stepped round to face her, grabbed her by the sides of the head with both hands, and said, "You were so beautiful. I thought, just thought, you might show me that women can be different. That they can be fucking decent. I was almost sure it was going to happen. I had… confidence in you. Everything I saw made me believe. And then you blew it, like every woman in this sick world." A long pause. "So fucking beautiful."

His right hand crossed in front of his body, bent towards his shoulder and whipped her, striking her cheek with the force of an articulated lorry. Now her head snapped the other way. He grabbed her by the nose.

He smiled. "Not any longer."

He hit her again, on the face. She felt the bone at the top of her nose collapse under the weight of the blow. The chair was knocked back and she landed heavily on the floor.

"You were beautiful."

Her eyes were closed; no tears got through now. None whatsoever.

She managed to force open one eye the slightest amount and she saw him standing over her, like a tiger stalking its prey. She could make out his figure – naked, it was – before he leaned forwards and started pulling at her trousers.

They came off with ease and he entered her. He made a lot of noise. She whimpered.

When he was finished – at least, she thought he was finished – he said, "He stained you. Ruined you for me. Not pure, not the way you're supposed to be." His voice rose higher. "It's not how it was supposed to be!" He hit her again. "It was supposed to be different!"

He wasn't finished. In fact, he was only getting started.

Chapter Five

After sitting in traffic for almost an hour and a half, I've arrived at Jennie's house. I get out of my car and move to the gate. She doesn't have a lawn; just a bush and a small path that's about five feet long. I open the gate and go to the front door. Daylight has gone and the night air is cool. I cup my hands in front of my mouth and blow warm air on them. I knock on the door.

I'm not feeling patient any more, so I knock again when an answer doesn't come promptly. Knock loudly. Hit it again. There's a doorbell, so I ring it. Five more times after my first attempt doesn't garner a response. "It's me, Jennie. Come out!"

When I realise she's not coming out – that she's either hiding from me or she's been taken, or even worse has happened, God forbid – I become consumed by a greater worry, but I know I have to suppress it.

I go to the front window and pound on it. I try the side gate, but it's locked. I'm not athletic, but I've got to give it a go. I'm tall enough, so I can reach the top of the gate without a problem. It's not smooth – full of splinters. With my arms up in the air and my hands gripping onto the top of the gate, careful of the splinters, I push up from the ground. I manage to get my feet as high as the gate's handle, dangle for a moment, realise that my upper-body strength can't take me another three or four feet up and then over, and have no option but to let go.

I think about kicking the door in. Or maybe I should smash a window, get in that way. I peer through a gap in the fence, squint to get a view. I can make something out. Just, through the slightest of gaps where the wood is splintered, I can see it. It's a light.

"Jennie!" I shout again. "Jennie, it's me!"

I wait for a response, but one doesn't come. I look at the gate. It doesn't seem that high. I should be able to find a way over it at my age. I really must get in shape. Either way, I'm determined to do it. From the side of the gate where the fence is, I take a three-step run-up towards my target, throw my hands high into the air and jump. I catch hold of the top of the gate again, but instead of being able to kick myself over the gate, which is how I imagined it would happen, I fall back onto the concrete. My back jolts as I strike the ground and I can't move. And my hands are bleeding again.

I stare up at the stars. That's it. This fucking gate isn't going to beat me. Whatever's happened to Jennie isn't going to beat me either.

I lean on my elbow and see the mobile phone that has fallen out of my pocket. I pick it up and dial the police. They've got to help this time; I have to convince them.

"Listen," I tell the person who answers, "my name is John Simmons. My girlfriend, Jennie Michaels, disappeared from London Gateway services earlier today. Now I'm standing outside her house and she's not here. But there's a light on. She's either been taken or she's in there and hurt. So I want the police to come here and break the door down, or should I do it?"

He asks for Jennie's address. I tell him, then I'm put on hold.

I fill the time waiting by pacing in front of Jennie's porch and I fight off the pain from the fall. I won't succumb to anything that could get in the way.

"Mr Simmons," a voice says, the line coming to life.

"Oh, yes," I say. "Yes, this is John Simmons."

"Mr Simmons, my name is Supervising Officer Matthew

Joynes. I oversaw your first call to the centre earlier today. I've also spoken with the officers who met you at London Gateway. And I'd like to repeat what they told you this afternoon: that wasting police time is a criminal offence."

"But I'm not wasting police time!" I shout, suddenly infuriated. "I'm doing your bloody job! You should be here trying to find Jennie. Instead, I'm here at her house doing what you should be doing. She's not here, but there's a light on. She lives alone, for Christ's sake! So you should be knocking her bloody door in. Don't you see? I've just come from the theatre where we were supposed to be going tonight. She's not there either. And she was with me before I called the officers. She was with me and then she was gone!"

"I understand that, sir, but you really haven't told me anything that sounds a concern."

"What? That she was there one minute and gone the next. Do you really think I'm making this up?"

"Well," he says, "the mobile number you gave the officers, the one you said could be used to contact this lady, doesn't exist. It does make what you're saying sound somewhat suspect."

Why doesn't he see it? Why doesn't he help me?

"But I'm here. I'm here at her bloody house. Come down here and take a look for yourself if you don't believe me."

"What's the address, Mr Simmons, and what's her full name?" he asks, breathing loudly.

I repeat the information I gave the other person only minutes ago.

I breathe a sigh of relief when he tells me to hold. Finally someone is going to help sort this mess out. Finally someone is going to help me find Jennie.

He's gone for what seems like an age. I'm cold yet sweating. Everything is flying around in my mind when the phone beeps. I look at the screen: low battery.

"No," I say. "Fucking phone, no."

Moments later, the officer is back on the line. "Mr Simmons?"

"Please," I say, "come quickly. My battery–"

"Mr Simmons, I repeat to you that wasting police time is a serious criminal offence. I am now going to pursue this matter further."

"Pursue it," I tell him. "Please, pursue it. Come down here and pursue it. Arrest me if you want. Then at least you'll be here and you can look for Jennie. You can tell me who's in her fucking house!"

"Mr Simmons, no one named Jennie Michaels lives at that address."

It's like he's punched me in the stomach. Did I hear him properly? "But that's not possible," I tell him. He's got to be lying. I collected her from here this morning.

"Mr Simmons, I suggest you hang the phone up now or–"

"No!" I shout. "You're lying! I was here this morning. I was. You're wrong. You're wrong! Why are you doing this to me?" Why? Someone's playing with my mind. What have the police got against me? Why is he doing this? Why is *she* doing this?

"Unless her name is Wong, Mr Simmons, you are very much mistaken."

And then he hangs up on me. The phone makes its final sound before the battery dies.

Who are the Wongs? Where is Jennie?

Now I'm here alone, without contact with the rest of the world. I don't know a thing, I don't know where Jennie is or who she is any more, and my one means of contact has gone. I want to throw the phone to the ground and smash it, but I don't. I know how much I need it: I need to charge the bloody battery.

I step back, taken aback. I'm coming unravelled, but I know I have to hold it together. There's got to be an explanation – I know Jennie. She hasn't run away from me, she hasn't lied to me; she's been taken, I'm sure of it.

Home – there's nowhere else. I back down Jennie's path without noticing the voices behind me. I turn to walk out of the gate and see a Chinese couple standing there. They're in their forties, but she looks older than him, plump, while he's thin and looks gaunt, like he hasn't eaten for years and she has her fill every day. I look at them, don't move, don't speak, don't do anything; just stare at them with pleading eyes.

The man eventually speaks. "Can we help you?" he asks. He has no accent despite his foreign appearance.

"Jennie?" I say, but he doesn't seem to understand me.

I walk past them. They turn and follow me with their gazes. A few feet along the pavement I stop and turn to them.

"Is everything all right?" he says after I still don't speak.

I shake my head. Scrambling for words, searching my mind, I say the only thing I can think of, hopeful to get an alternative answer to the revelation the police officer sprang on me. I need to be told for sure. I won't believe it unless I hear it from this man's mouth.

"Does Jennie live here?" I ask him.

"Jennie?" he says.

"Jennie Michaels," I say, losing patience.

"Only we live here," he says, shaking his head. "Just the two of us."

I gasp for air. "How… how long have you lived here?" I manage to say. This can't be happening. I don't want to hear his answer.

Then he hits me with it. "Two years," he says.

Chapter Six

The second was going to be easy. He had no expectation, not any more. He just wanted to hurt.

After his mother left, he spent the next six years sitting next to his old man, listening to him bitch and moan, listening to his anger and aggression. The father never tried to console the son who felt pain. In fact, all he did for the son was make him watch: watch his father drink litre after litre of spirits, pass out, wake up and start what was a routine again.

After six years of the same, he tried to start a new life for himself, but it was a life with no ambition. He was seventeen and he got a job putting boxes together in a factory. Lousy work, he knew it, but he didn't care. He was out of the house, away from the old man, away from the booze and the swell of rage; that was what mattered. The chance to save and then escape.

He spent each day standing in line, moving his hands automatically, not talking to a soul. His interest in the opposite sex had developed and, while he connected the sides of boxes together, he snatched glances at the slim and tanned legs that walked past. He craved them, but he had no idea how to approach women. It didn't take long for the quick glances to become long stares.

He waited for them to speak to him. They didn't.

The hate he felt, at first for his mother, now for every girl who ignored him, and all women like them, never left him; although he resisted for years, it only grew in intensity.

So eventually he came to hurt. It hadn't started like this; it had started with him wanting to find and take purity, the desire to prove that beauty and purity can mix. Unlike anything he'd ever seen. Sarah Elson was going to be the one. But she turned out to be anything but, and his hopes faded.

What he'd thought for thirty years had been right, he realised.

Rachel Price was the opposite of what he thought Sarah Elson was. She flaunted her appearance and had the confidence of someone who recognised their good looks.

Every morning at six thirty, she jumped out of bed, her energy thriving. She jogged out of the bedroom and into the bathroom of her two-bedroom house, rinsed her face with two handfuls of cold water, applied extra water to her eyes, and started her daily stretches. Still jogging, she moved into the kitchen. She ran the cold water tap, took a glass from the cupboard above the sink and filled it. Taking a brief pause from jogging, the twenty-three-year-old sipped down a quarter of the glass. She resumed the jog, then less than a minute later stopped and sipped again. This was her routine.

When the glass was empty, she left the kitchen, removing her pyjama top. Underneath the top, she boasted a muscular and slim physique. As she went into the bedroom and flung her top onto the bed, she performed a couple more stretches that sent her arms behind her head. Next, off came the pyjama bottoms. She kicked them onto the bed and bent down to stretch her hamstrings.

Then from the drawers at the end of the bed she pulled out her running clothes – sports bra, underwear, jogging bottoms and sweatshirt. Once socks and trainers were on, she jogged down the stairs, then continued on the spot in the hallway, and she stared at herself in the mirror that was on the wall next to the front door. She liked looking at herself: the way parts moved up and down; the way her black hair moved over her forehead, her ponytail swinging from side to side; the way her body curved. And she liked knowing that, when she left the house, men who saw her would like looking. Rachel Price liked the attention men gave her; liked it too much.

She jogged down a small side street and onto the main road, past a row of shops. She jogged particularly slowly as she passed the newsagent; she knew that the men who were up early for work and buying the day's newspapers would peer out of the shop. She liked the builder types, the ones who whistled, who weren't afraid to show they liked what they saw. She liked her men upfront and bold.

At the end of the row of shops, she crossed the road and headed towards the park. Into the park and the jog became a run. The run became a sprint as she passed the swings.

At the end of the park, there was some woodland. She went into it. The ground was wet this morning. Trees, bushes and weeds. She kept running, hated to stop, hated to feel like she couldn't hack it. Hated to feel like she'd lost. Kept running as she got deeper in, as it got darker. Always got a chill that far in. Kept running, despite the stitch. Kept running, despite the teenagers hanging around up ahead. Kept running.

Three minutes later she was in deep enough. Alone, and she always felt it, despite her confidence. She turned back and began the home straight. Back, and back through the woods. Teenagers gone. Emerged from the trees and went back into the park, past the swings and then the shops, and along the road towards her house. The bus stop, then the left turn into her road. Outside her front door. The key in her hand. The lock opened. The door pushed in then pressed shut. Her trainers kicked off.

Jogging on the spot continued for a moment and then stopped. She dropped her clothes onto the floor and walked into the bathroom, the same as every morning.

Showering was always quick and she was soon back in the bedroom, the body lotion bottle in her hand. As she cupped her hand and squeezed the contents into it, she looked at herself again – looked in the mirror as she ran the lotion over her skin. Her fingers were cold. Looked in the reflection of the mirrored wardrobe and smiled at the success of what she saw. Looked in the reflection that suddenly moved. Screamed as she saw the wardrobe open to reveal him.

Chapter Seven

I'm still in my car outside the Jennie's house. The Wongs stayed on the path for a time, expecting to see me leave, visibly puzzled when I didn't. They gave up and went in about half an hour ago. Probably think I'm mad sitting out here. But I can't move yet. I know I need to get home – have to charge the phone – but I must get things straight, get my thoughts together. Because this isn't the Wong residence; Jennie *does* live here, of that I'm sure. I met her here this morning – watched her come out of the front door.

Or did I? Maybe I only saw her standing in front of the door. The more I try to picture her this morning, the more the memory becomes indistinct. I picked her up. She was there. Did she come from inside? Or was she already outside? Was it a trick, a deception? Am I supposed to be confused?

The frustration of not remembering makes my head feel like it's about to explode. It's spinning. I can actually feel it telling me that there's too much thought bouncing around in it. It's telling me to leave it alone; and that's exactly what I want to do. I don't know what to do or even if I want to do anything, but the good in me won't drop it, no matter how drained I feel. I have to save Jennie, do something. I can't just give up.

I've never been inside Jennie's house, that much is certain – never had reason to. She always came to my place or we went out. We've done so many things together. We've been bowling, ice skating, dancing; we've dined in the finest restaurants; we've seen movies and listened to music and been to concerts. Picnicked in Regents Park, which was beautiful. And the theatre, where today I was going to introduce Jennie to the scariest play in the world. For the briefest of moments, I can see the look on her face that I've imagined since booking the tickets – her jumping out of her seat; me hugging her and telling her it's all right – and it makes me smile. That was meant to be us and it was going to be another perfect evening. And I can still see the look on her face as we eat dinner, as I pull the ring out, as I tell her I love her, that I need to spend the rest of my life with her and that I'll always be there for her.

My smile disappears when I realise the most chilling thing of all: it may never happen.

Yes, I can see it all – including things that haven't happened yet – but I can't bring my mind to picture what happened this morning. Why is that? Why can I see the future but fail to visualise the most recent of events? To see what I saw when I drove into this very road, pulled over, greeted Jennie. I can't see a bloody thing.

But what about all the other times? All the times I've collected her from here – at least half a dozen occasions, it must be. We didn't always meet out. We didn't always meet after work. I collected her from here. But I can't see any of the times when I did. I can't see her stepping out of that house, the place right in front of my eyes as I turn my head and look at it. I can't see myself knocking on her door. But she lives here; I believe that much. Why would she have asked me to collect her from here if she didn't?

Those crazy Chinese people must have been lying to me – perhaps they're in on it. Perhaps they're standing in the front room now, hiding behind the curtain, peeking at me. Laughing at me. Perhaps Jennie's got them in on it; maybe she's in there with them. Because if they weren't in on it and if they were speaking the truth, that would mean Jennie had lied to me. Why would she have misled me? Why would she have done that? Doesn't she know what it would do to me? And why would I not notice the simplest of things, not remember?

I don't have any answers, but my mind fills with thoughts of danger and trickery. I've read enough stories and newspaper articles. The more I think about everything, the more questions I come up with. And they're uncomfortable questions, so uncomfortable that I want them to stop. If I close my eyes, will it all go away? I want Jennie to be found. I want her to be next to me right now in this ridiculous car. This car that I've dreamed of having for years. I want Jennie by my side. I always thought this car would bring me happiness, but I was wrong. I'd trade it for her in a heartbeat. Take the fucking thing away. She brought me happiness, not this car. No object could ever do that; not in the same way Jennie did.

I can't take it any longer! I grab the steering wheel and shake it hard, so hard that my body shifts in the seat. I want to pull it off, I'm shaking it so hard. Then I bring my fist down upon it. I hit it again and again, until my hand is throbbing. I've lost control momentarily, a necessary release, but I pull myself together just as quickly. Hitting the steering wheel has given me a sense of calm. Now it's time to move.

Home.

Chapter Eight

Rachel Price's hands and legs were bound to the bedposts that surrounded her. She was naked. He'd used dozens of pieces of duct tape to stick her legs to the bed so that they were spread wide apart, so wide that she had cramp. The pain was agonising, it had made her vomit. Remnants of last night's dinner were all over her naked chest.

He stood at the foot of the bed, watching her. He looks like a normal guy, she reckoned, or hoped, amid the chaos in her mind, able somehow to summon together that one cohesive thought. He was slim, had short dark hair and a narrow face. His head was pointed downwards, which meant that he had to raise his eyes to look at Rachel. Perhaps he was bowing his head in shame. Perhaps he knew that the tilted angle enabled an evil glare to come from his eyes. Either way, Rachel couldn't read him. He kept motionless.

"The first one," he said, "she was beautiful. Should have been my queen. I'd waited patiently. So patiently. Even though I wanted it to happen sooner, I waited. But she turned out to be a slut, just like all the others." He laughed. "Just like you. The difference is it took litres of booze to loosen her frigidity. But when it did she went all out. So, I thought, the next one's going to be looser. An uncompromising slut. That's where you came in. I realised the moment I first saw you, you were just what I was looking for. Wanting to be watched every day, so predictable. I love that about you – you know you're sexy. But you're nothing else, you hear? You're nothing more than a fucking whore."

He had a bag with him. Rachel couldn't see it yet, but when the time was right he moved from where he stood and returned to where he'd got his first full view of her – the wardrobe. Rachel's face, twisted in fear, was still reflected in the mirror. He put the bag on the bed – a large black bag with the Nike logo on the side, large enough to carry a tennis racket and more – and unzipped it. From inside he withdrew a saw, about eighty centimetres long.

In response, Rachel made a noise at the back of her throat; she could do no more, for her mouth was also covered with duct tape. He held on to both ends of the blade and flexed it. His eyes were fixed on the shiny metal, the gleam it gave off from the early-morning clean he'd given it, and Rachel thought she could detect pleasure in his outward appearance. "It's going to be so easy now," he said. "Sarah Elson showed me what I believed years ago was right. You women are showing me the way. Elson. Those two bitches. And now you."

The thought of this sicko smiling at the sight of the blade made the vomit well up in the back of her throat again, only this time her mouth wasn't open to release it. She started coughing and was left with no option but to swallow.

Her eyes were wide open, wider than she believed they could ever stretch apart, and, when he moved mere inches towards her, she tried to wrestle herself free. All she managed was to shake the bed and tire herself out. No matter how much she moved, or how hard she tried, there was no getting free.

He looked at the blade again. The smile on his face was so wide that his crooked teeth were revealed.

It was only a matter of seconds before he was on his knees on the end of the bed, bringing the saw down into the space he had freed when he'd separated her legs and taped them down. It was only a matter of seconds before she felt the worst pain she'd ever experienced – the pain of dying. And then it was only a matter of seconds before she could feel no more – the relief that death provided.

Chapter Nine

I'm sitting on the armchair in front of the fire. Outside it isn't cold, but inside I'm freezing. I hold a mug of tea in my hands, cupped between both palms, and I'm still in a daze – until Jennie's found I'll never fully come out of it – but my mind's clearing up step by step. Trying to think, think carefully, plan what to do next.

It's gone midnight and it's been almost ten hours since Jennie was taken. She *was* taken; I'm sure of it. As each waking moment passes, as I'm in a daze or out of one, I believe that single fact. She wouldn't torture me like this. No person would. Jennie loves me; I know she does. She was taken and God knows what's happening to her while I sit here.

So now it's time to decide how to get the police to believe me, how to get them to listen. Because that's exactly what I'm going to do: I will get their attention and make them listen and help me find Jennie, before – I almost can't say the words – it's too late.

I've read enough to know that the first forty-eight hours are crucial to a missing person investigation. It's the time when the clues are easiest to locate. It's the time when the victim is usually not too far away. It's the time when the police are meant to be out searching. For Jennie. That's what they should be doing. How long has she got left? How long before someone's going to help her?

Tomorrow I'll do it. I'll get the police to find her. If it means jumping in their faces, shouting and shoving, that's what I'll do – anything to get their attention.

And her work – Jennie works in the city centre: Brown's

Solicitors. That's my second stop.

*

I'm up on my feet at five. The truth is I didn't really sleep. I just sat in the armchair all night, nodded off for only a few minutes at a time, visions of Jennie in pain jolting me back to alertness every few minutes. Making an occasional cup of coffee was the only reason I had to move.

I know I can't go yet. I need to give the important officers a chance to get to work. It'll be no good bashing on their doors, demanding they find Jennie, if I bash before the right people are there to hear me. No, eight o'clock – that's when I'll make my way to the police station and force them to listen to me. And then Jennie's office – I'll be able to find out things about her there.

I'm prepared to get violent, that's how determined I am. I'll force people to listen and to talk. I've thought about it long and hard and I'm ready to put the officers I encounter into headlocks and threaten to break their necks, if that's what it takes for someone to tell me they're willing to listen and help.

I spend the next three hours unable to focus on even the most menial of tasks. I try to iron, take the rubbish out, watch some television. But the whole time, my mind is stuck on what's going to happen at the police station. It's a place I've never been before, so I can't picture it in my mind, which is what I'd like to do. I'd like to be able to plan everything out in the finest detail, create a mind map, before I get there: where I'm going to stand, how I'm going to stand, when and where I might move, the tone of voice I'm going to use. But my ignorance means that's not possible, so I end up doing the only thing I think will be helpful: research.

I focus on missing women. I've watched the news in

recent days. I've scanned some newspaper covers, nothing in depth, but I know it's happening, like a craze. Several women have been taken in the south-east over the past few weeks. Perhaps there's a link; no, not perhaps – there's got to be. It's just the police haven't said it officially yet.

I walk up the stairs and into the room directly at the top of the staircase. My office is nicely furnished – everything from Ikea. It's not very large, but I've filled it well. My desk sits opposite the door and, to the right of the desk where the wall is, I have a filing cabinet. Next to that are two small chests of drawers. On the walls are a few posters of films I admire. Posters of a couple of plays too.

I sit at my desk and log on to the computer. It seems to take far longer than usual to load up, but my mind's starting to wilt from lack of sleep, so the wait doesn't irritate me like it would have last night.

When the computer's ready, I click to open the internet. I type in: *London, south-east, missing women, abductions.*

The search count is massive. Of course, it goes back years. I select 'Most recent'. I click on one result, then another. And another. Single women, abducted from their homes. Just like I remember hearing on the news. It's like there are two or three a week, it's so common. Were they followed home, or did they know their attackers? Attackers, abductors, murderers... I don't even know what to call them. And that's when the thought strikes me: *murderers.*

Bodies have been found. Jennie, she couldn't be. No. I couldn't live if she were...

I couldn't forgive myself, for I'd be to blame. It would only be my fault. I had to stop.

I left her in the car.

Chapter Ten

He's got me and I'm helpless. I agreed to this. I've signed my death warrant all in the name of a job. He's supposed to be here. He's supposed to help me.

I've been hit in the face. The pain in my right cheekbone is unbearable. I can feel my eye starting to swell up. I'm lying on the ground and I can't move. The part of my brain that's supposed to tell my body to move, to get up, to resist, to do whatever the fuck it is I have to do to get out of here alive, is dormant, it's gone away, it's fucked off when I need it most. My body is paralysed – because of fear, or because I've banged my head on something, or because I no longer have control of my bodily functions, I don't know – and all I can do is look up at him, blurred though he is in my vision, and wait for the next thing he's going to do.

He's stroking his groin and smiling as he kneels down over me.

I manage to get out, "Please."

It's a plea that falls on deaf ears. He doesn't so much as pause, doesn't show any indication that he's heard me, as he unzips and readies himself for what he's been waiting for since the last one.

"Please," I repeat. My voice is hoarse and now I'm not even sure if he can hear me, so weak and soft is my attempt to speak.

He kicks his jeans off. His boxers remain around his ankles.

He lies on top of me. Tears at my stockings. Stuffs them in my mouth.

*

Kate Nielsen woke up at seven thirty-five this morning. As usual, she was late and would have to rush to get to work on time. Her eyes kept closing and she wanted more sleep. She groaned at the thought of having to get up when it felt like she'd just fallen asleep.

Sleep never came easy to her.

She'd spent most of the night lying on her back, staring up at the ceiling, the same as every night. Pretty quickly, her eyes had adjusted to the darkness and she could make out the paintwork. She'd given up trying to close her eyes years ago, given up trying to urge sleep on, knew that it would find her when it was good and ready, knew that if she closed her eyes too many pictures would crowd around her, and she wanted to steer clear of them. The pictures weren't holiday stills and they weren't of happy memories of times gone by; they were horrifying images of faces she desperately wanted to forget. So she stared and stared until at last sleep came. And before she knew it, every morning, it was morning.

After another five minutes of her eyes shutting involuntarily, she tore herself from bed. Her feet hit the ground heavily. She sat on the side of the bed for a moment – her kind of routine – with her head in her hands, mumbling the words, "All over again."

Another two minutes and she was up. Same as always. Even at the weekends. The routine, even though she didn't want it, couldn't be broken. She stumbled, still half asleep, into the kitchen and flicked on the kettle that she'd filled the night before. Always the night before because she didn't trust herself to be able to do it in the morning.

While the kettle boiled, she went to the bathroom and peed. A final moment with her head in her hands, then she wiped herself dry and rose, washed her hands and face, and stared into the mirror. She hated what she saw. Couldn't care less what anyone else thought either. A look of disgust at herself, her shoulder-length blonde hair, which had plenty of split ends, and moved back to the kitchen. Now awake, she poured herself a coffee and took it into the bedroom.

There she dressed. No fashion sense. No desire or need, the way she led her life; men weren't knocking on her door. She just picked up what was on top of the pile in her wardrobe. A green jumper and a pair of jeans.

Once dressed, she downed her coffee as fast as she could. It burned the back of her throat; she never learned. It would be minutes before she felt its kick. By that time, she'd be devouring another.

A glance out of the window told her it was a nippy morning. With the second coffee finished and the cup in the sink to clean up later on, she went into the hallway where she kept her shoes. A pair of black trainers went on, followed by her coat. She opened the door, exited and locked it behind her.

Outside the house, she moved with some pace to her car. Green, just like her jumper. Volkswagen Polo. She got inside and began the twenty-minute drive to work, already ten minutes late.

Traffic was bad this morning. It always was when she left late, and she frequently left late. She caught occasional glimpses of herself in the rear-view mirror and, just like in the bathroom mirror in her flat, gave a look of contempt. She didn't like herself. She didn't like her past. She didn't like her memories. And she didn't like her days.

Every few minutes she repeated, "Here we go again," as if the repetition would somehow make the impending day easier. And it was the knowledge of the work that was waiting for her that made the sense of disgust increase tenfold. She needed a rest. She needed a change.

But she doubted she'd ever take a step in that direction.

After thirty-five minutes of boredom – for her, driving was just that – Kate Nielsen arrived. She parked her car outside the building and began the short walk across the paved area. As she began her ascent up the stairs, she noticed a man standing at the top. When she approached him, he spoke to her. At first, she didn't hear him.

"Are you all right?" she asked. She still cared, even though that care sometimes needed encouragement to show itself.

"Please help me," he said.

Chapter Eleven

I fill two-and-a-half hours researching and it's time to get ready before I know it. It's only now that I notice I've spent all night in the clothes I had on yesterday and haven't washed. I hop into the shower, aware that I might be late to the police station, quickly scrub myself clean and wash my hair.

Once finished, I get dressed. I go downstairs and straight into the kitchen, take a slice of bread from the bread bin and butter it. Placing it between my teeth, I keep hold of it while I put my shoes on and tie the laces. It becomes soggy, so I stuff the rest of it into my mouth as I put on my coat and leave the house.

I arrive at the police station twenty minutes later, stopping en route at a petrol station to buy every newspaper they have. I leave with a pile of seven in my hands. Traffic is heavy this morning – something I'd not anticipated. I park in the station car park and make my way up the stairs, the newspapers cradled in my arms. I pass a lady talking to a man and pointing. She's giving him directions, I hear, and then I open the heavy glass door and head into the foyer. I stand in front of a plastic window, behind which stands a policeman. He's writing something and doesn't immediately look up. I notice that the sense of urgency I had earlier has dwindled. I must rekindle it. If I don't appear urgent, how are they going to be convinced to help me find Jennie? They've got to believe the things I tell them, so here's when I start to go over the past twenty hours in my mind. It's amazing how quickly the feeling of urgency returns; I don't have to encourage it.

I cough to get the officer's attention and he tells me, "Just a minute, please."

"Excuse me," I say, "this is incredibly important."

"And so," he says, filling in a final box, "is this." He dots the paper. "There," he says. "Finished. Now what can I do for you, sir?"

As he speaks, I hear the main doors open. A gust of wind hits me. Its chill whip is sharp. I don't look at the door.

"My name," I tell him, "is John Simmons. Yesterday I was with my girlfriend, Jennie Michaels, and she disappeared. I tried reporting it to the police, but they didn't believe me. Since then I've been to her home and she isn't there. The people there told me she doesn't live there. But, see," I laugh, for the first time hearing how ridiculous it all sounds, desperate for him to take me seriously, "I've picked her up from that house many times before. I picked her up there yesterday. So I know someone has taken her. You have got to help me find her."

I lift up my hand to plead with him, but I can't make contact with him as the window is in the way. Instead, my hand hangs precariously in the air and I only take it down when I see the officer stare at it.

"Please," I repeat.

A door opens and closes to my left. A figure moves past me.

The officer says, "Listen, take a seat over there." He points behind me. "Let me speak to someone. See if there's someone here who can help you."

So someone has finally believed me. I feel a weight taken off my shoulders. I feel lighter. I feel that I might be getting somewhere. And now my hope has been justified; maybe we can find Jennie.

*

Fifteen minutes later, having flicked through two of the newspapers, read disturbing details about two abductions and one body found, I'm still sitting here alone like a gullible idiot. Tell the rowdy one anything to shut him up, and leave him to think things will get better. Well, I've had enough of sitting here and waiting while they make a fool out of me. It's been too long.

I stand up, scoop up all the newspapers and go to the counter behind which the officer was working. He hasn't returned. Still off trying to find someone to help me, no doubt. Doubt, actually. They're wasting even more time. There's no way they're going to keep me waiting any longer.

A pane of plastic stands between me and the empty room that the officer was in fifteen minutes ago. I bang on it. Three times and I wait. And no one comes, so I bang on it again, so hard this time that I'm conscious of it vibrating under the force of my fist, that my hand could go through it. But I don't care. Someone has got to come out here and help me. See me, at least. Someone has got to get their arse into gear to help me locate Jennie.

I don't hear the main doors opening and feet running towards me, I'm so intent on making a racket. I don't hear a man shouting at me. I don't see that a policeman is right behind me. I only know he's there when he grabs hold of me. Grabbing me is going to stop me finding Jennie, so I shout too, shout at him as he shouts at me, struggle as he holds me by both arms, kick my feet in the air, desperate to free myself, the newspapers falling to the ground.

Now it's only seconds before the officer reappears behind the window, before he charges off again and almost instantly comes through a door into the foyer, before he too is restraining me. Then there's a third officer and they're all clutching hold of me. I want to be free. I want to find a way out – out to the place where I have a chance of finding

Jennie. But they're too strong, the three of them. I can't resist any longer. And almost as quickly as the impatience heated up in me, I am deflated and wish I hadn't come here, that I'd done everything to find Jennie by myself, that I hadn't had misguided faith in the police.

I'm on the ground now. I'm mouthing words, but nothing's coming out. One of the officers is sitting on my back; the other two are holding my arms so that they can be cuffed behind my back. I see a woman – the woman who was speaking to the man outside – standing above them, giving orders. I can barely breathe, so heavy is the officer whose weight is pressing down on my spine. I try to shout, but I can do nothing – only endure the humiliation. Finally I can take no more. My head falls to the ground, the cold of the concrete stinging my sweaty face, and I submit.

*

I've been locked in a cell for hours. I can't tell how long: my watch has been taken from me. And even if I had it I don't think it would tell me the time. I'm sure it was broken when I was knocked to the ground by the officers. They've even taken the newspapers.

I'm pacing up and down. I'm unable to keep still. I've tried knocking on the door – knocked until my arms ached. No one came; of course they wouldn't. I shouldn't have fooled myself into thinking they would. To them I'm just some nutcase who's ended up in here because he won't keep himself to himself.

What was I thinking out there? Why did I do it? Banging on the window like that, causing such a scene. I'm so annoyed with myself. I have to get out of here and figure out a way to search for Jennie, and there I ruined my chances of getting the police's support.

But I can't get out of here until they let me go. And before they do that they'll want to talk – give me a warning or something. At least I hope that's all they're going to do. Right now my mind starts to trouble me. I start to think about what will happen if they keep me locked up in here for much longer, if they charge me with something and don't bail me out. Can they do that?

Yes, they can: I was disturbing the peace. But I had good reason to; surely they'll see that.

I finally sit down on the hard mattress. I'm exhausted and place my head in my hands. Exhaustion, though, doesn't take away anger and there's still fury within me – so much that I want to scream. Realising it can do no harm, that in all likelihood no one is listening, I scream for all my worth. The sound bounces off the four walls, pierces my ears and, for a second, I feel somewhat better.

I lie on my back. I have to wait, it's that simple. There's nothing more I can do. I'm going to try to sleep. That way, maybe time will pass more quickly.

But as soon as I close my eyes, there's a rattling at the door.

I sit up too fast; I see blackness. When it fades and my normal sight returns, I see the door opening a few inches. It doesn't open all the way and I'm left wondering who's there. For two, three, four seconds, no one comes in. All I can see is the light from the hallway. Then a hand, but that's all. No person comes in. Just the hand holding the door. I stand up, ready to open the door myself, but before I do I notice it's a woman's hand. The skin looks so soft. It reminds me of Jennie's hand, the way it feels as I press it into the palm of my own hand. The awkward acceptance of the fact that yesterday afternoon could be the last time I'll ever see Jennie is at the forefront of my mind, but I can't let it become something I believe in. I have to stay positive.

The door squeaks open all the way. Footsteps echo and she enters: the woman from outside, the one who was helping the man, the one giving instructions to the officers as they bundled me to the ground. I put my guard up; she's not to be trusted.

"Mr Simmons," she begins, "I'm Detective Sergeant Kate Nielsen. I'm sorry you've been kept in here for so long. I've been familiarising myself with your situation."

"My situation?" I'm surprised; maybe she's not so bad after all. She almost sounds like she cares.

"First of all, let me say that you're not under arrest. You were placed in here for your own safety. It looked like you were going to do damage to something out there, to yourself even. Since the officers put you in here, I've been making some calls. The officer on duty filled me in on your predicament. I'm sorry."

With those two words I feel calmer. A release. She believes me.

"You know then?" I don't know what else to say.

"Jennie Michaels, your girlfriend," she says and nods her head. She doesn't elaborate. I can tell she's waiting for me to say more.

Now I feel re-energised. I tell her about Jennie, about how we met, about my plans for yesterday. I tell her at such a pace that I worry she won't be able to take it all in, but I can't slow myself down. She's listening to me – a police officer is finally giving a damn – so there's no way in hell I'm taking a breath and slowing down. I tell her about the toilet break, about leaving Jennie in the car, about stopping for coffee. And I tell her about stepping back out of the services, coming to a halt when I couldn't see Jennie in the Mazda. About how waiting calmly for Jennie eventually turned into panic. And then helplessness. "So I called the police. Surely they'd help me. I was certain I'd get somewhere with them.

And it all seemed to be going as I thought it would until those officers accused me of lying." I relay what they told me, what I told them, and DS Nielsen nods. She doesn't say anything, but I find the nods reassuring. I'm speaking with such intent that my throat is dry.

"How do you explain the mobile?" she asks when I finish. "Why is its number not recognised?"

I shake my head. "I don't know." A simple, useless answer, the only one I can give.

"When was the last time prior to her disappearance that you dialled it?"

"Yesterday morning," I say, not having to think. "I'd called Jennie to confirm what time I'd collect her." From her house. The Wongs' house.

She looks at me thoughtfully. "Who is Jennie Michaels, John?"

"What do you mean?" I ask.

"Describe her to me, as she is to you. Let's say you wanted me to know everything about her in a sentence or so. What would you say?"

I shrug my shoulders. "She's the... nicest person I've ever met. I've never been happier. Because of her." I look at the floor. "Until yesterday."

"What else can you tell me about her?"

I don't know where to start. I pause to think about it. There's so much I want to say and so much I think I need to say. I try to organise my thoughts logically, but the more I go through them the more confused things become. Detective Nielsen has a lot of questions and I have just as many. I want to ask too. I want the chance to find out the things I want to know.

In the end, I haven't made anything clearer for myself. So I tell Detective Nielsen everything I think is pertinent. I describe Jennie, speak about how we met, the things we've done. The more I speak, the longer my sentences become and the more panicked I sound. So I slow myself down intermittently and try to seem calm. I think I fail.

My confusion must reveal itself on my face because Detective Nielsen says, "Tell me what you're thinking."

"Her home. I've collected her from there, must be half a dozen times, but that man, he said they've lived there for two years. How can that be? I picked her up from there yesterday."

"Your second call to the police." She nods and tells me about the recording of both the emergency calls I made. She informs me she's listened to them, which also added to her delay in seeing me. She tells me all kinds of things, but she has no answers. Even though we're both perplexed and to everyone else I've sounded like a nut, there's something about her that makes me believe she has faith in what I'm telling her, or at least that she wants to have it.

The moment I understand this is when I really look at her for the first time. She has light blonde hair that reaches her shoulders and then curls up. It's tucked behind her ears, which are incredibly small. There are a few lines on her forehead, bags under her eyes. No make-up tries to cover up that she's obviously tired; it's there for everyone to see. A shame, as she could look attractive. She's not very tall and doesn't look like a cop. Doesn't speak like one either. She just seems so normal. And I can see it in her eyes: there's empathy, recognition of the pain I'm enduring, like she's been there herself.

"Why would someone take her?" I ask.

"That's presuming she's been taken. We'll know for certain within the hour."

"But all these women. The stories in the news."

"I know." She peers down. "I know." She doesn't say any more on the matter and looks like she's holding herself back.

"I'm going to head out to London Gateway and take a look at the CCTV footage. If she's been taken, I'll be able to see who took her, what they were driving, how they left the site. I'll be able to see everything."

"Good. Thank you. And Detective, I brought some papers with me. Newspapers."

"I'll have them sent in to you."

I smile. Now I know she believes me. If I were lying, there's no way I'd let her see the CCTV recordings. No way, as all she'd see is me arriving on my own, going to the toilet and buying two coffees. She'll see the truth and then a task force, or whatever it's called, will have to be set up. Within the hour there'll be a group of people searching for Jennie, not just solitary me, and maybe we'll start getting somewhere.

"Thank you," I say again.

"Not just yet. I haven't done anything yet and I haven't found out anything. If she's been taken, we'll know really soon and then we'll get to work on finding her. But I must tell you, Mr Simmons, that if the footage shows something altogether different and she's not been taken – if she wasn't with you at all – then you're going to be in an awful lot of trouble, and I'm not going to be able to help you in any way. I won't even want to."

"I'm not and I won't be." I speak firmly to show her she can believe in me.

"I thought not," she says and she smiles. It's a really pleasant smile, but it looks strained, like an action minus feeling. She has straight teeth and they're quite white, but creases appear beneath her eyes when she smiles. Lots of them. She's worked hard for a long time.

"I appreciate what you're doing," I say. I pause and she looks at me, expecting to hear more. Must be the look on my face. I shrug my shoulders and simply say, "Why?"

She raises both her hands. "Why indeed," she says. "People get taken for all kinds of reasons, Mr Simmons."

"John, please," I interrupt her, but I don't think she minds.

"There are all kinds of reasons, John. Money's often the first we consider. Basically for ransom. After that, revenge, debt, obsession. Even the desire to murder. Some people just have a devil inside them and release it by hurting other people. The reasons, John, they don't feel real until something like this has happened to you, but I'm sure you've thought about the reasons a lot over the past day. Sometimes," she looks as if she isn't going to finish the sentence, but after a sigh and a pause she does, "people are just sick."

"Can't get my mind on anything else."

"Well, now's the time for you to take a breather from it all. Rest and let me deal with it. I'll be back within two hours and we'll talk more. I'll have answers, that much I can promise. How can I get a photo of Jennie?"

"My mobile. There's one on there in the photo folder." I realise how stupid it sounds when I tell her it's the only one I've got: a picture of Jennie, a close-up as she sat opposite me in a restaurant.

"Okay, I'll get it printed. Someone will be in to bring you a cup of coffee," she says with a nod of the head. "And the papers, of course."

I want to smile at her, but she's gone before I can. The door closes and I feel a rush of air pass over me.

She's going to get answers. I can't help worrying, though, that the answers she gets won't be enough. Things haven't gone my way so far, so it's hard to believe we might be at a turning point. And no matter what answers she might come back with, the question will still remain: where is Jennie? CCTV recordings can show a lot, but they aren't going to reveal Jennie's whereabouts. Not only where is she, but, more important, what's happening to her? As I sit here, as I'm alive and all right, as I'm being helped, what is she feeling? What is she going through?

I've not been a religious person for a long time – not since I was a child and my parents took me to church every Sunday, forced me to believe, forced me to pray – but right now I sink to my knees. It's almost instinctive, despite my years of absence from its practice. There are far more questions than Detective Nielsen will ever be able to get answers to. So I turn to the place where, as a child, I was told all the answers are known, and I pray, I ask. I wait to hear.

Chapter Twelve

4 Sanders Road looked like a normal three-bedroom semi-detached house. The kind a family could live in happily. Kate Nielsen wanted to see it and decided a detour en route to London Gateway would be beneficial. She wanted to be able to visualise it when she thought about John Simmons and Jennie Michaels' final day together. Before their world supposedly turned into a nightmare.

She didn't knock on the door – had no cause to disturb the Wongs. Not at the moment. But if she could establish proof of Jennie Michaels' existence, the Wongs would be her first stop.

Instead, she spent a short while in the street. She walked from one end to the other and approached people as they passed by. She showed them the picture of Jennie Michaels that had been printed before she'd left the station. She wanted to gauge their responses and didn't want to dismiss the possibility of having some luck. She gave her card out and urged anyone who thought of anything that might be pertinent to call her.

No one recognised the image she showed them, but if she needed to return she'd at least be familiar with the area. While she was there, she rang ahead and made an appointment to see the security manager of London Gateway services.

She left Sanders Road after about twenty minutes and arrived at London Gateway half an hour later.

Rod Taylor was a diminutive man with a bald head and thick spectacles. He looked to be in his late forties.

He welcomed Nielsen with an outstretched hand after

making her wait a quarter of an hour. "DS Nielsen, a pleasure to meet you." The words sounded nonchalant.

She resisted the urge that had started to overwhelm her; she wouldn't point out that she was busy and he was taking the mick by making her wait so long. "Thank you for seeing me."

"You said you'd like to see some CCTV footage from yesterday?" "That's correct."

"This way."

He led Nielsen from the foyer of the main building – past, she noticed, the coffee stand – to the left and then through a door. They appeared in a corridor out of bounds for customers and Nielsen followed Rod along it until they came to the fourth door on the right. He punched in a code and opened the door. "After you," he said.

Nielsen made her way into the room. To the left there was a large desk on which sat four monitors. To the right were bookcases on which there were several A4 lever arch folders stuffed full of paper overhanging the edges. She sat down on a swivel chair when Rod, with a hand outstretched, offered it to her. He sat next to her on another.

"What I'm looking for," she began, "is footage of the car park. Have you got a camera that covers the part of the car park that is closest to the building and another that covers the building's entrance?"

"Sure," he nodded. "We have both. There's a camera that covers the cars coming in over the bridge, another that shows a panoramic view of the main car park – a long distance shot, so it's not very clear – and also one that covers the first few rows of cars that are parked before the main building. Then there's the one on the main door."

Nielsen was relieved that the answers to the questions she had – primarily, was John Simmons in genuine trouble or, rather, was he trouble? – would soon be uncovered.

"I need to see footage from yesterday."

"What's this about, Detective?" His eyebrows rose. "I really should know. You're asking for a lot."

"And I'm sure you know all I need is a warrant and this conversation is over."

"Of course, of course." He paused. "It's just a curiosity. I'm always here, on the end of these tapes. Watching people, and you see people being suspicious all the time." Another pause. "You know, I always thought I'd be a cop. When I was younger, I mean. Thought I could do some good. Catch some bad guys kind of thing. Bloody eyesight messed that up, didn't it?" It wasn't a question and Nielsen was running out of patience. "But the curiosity has always remained. I'll never forget, never forget at all."

Rod Taylor was talking to himself; Nielsen's presence was just a coincidence. He'd been boxed up for too long, a personality lost, a lump.

"So sometimes I watch closely. See if I can spot things. You never know when that kind of thing could be helpful. You never know – maybe I can help you." He stopped. "What is it I can help you with, Detective?"

"I need to see the tapes. Then if I have any questions, I'll ask you."

"The trouble is," Rod continued, "and I really shouldn't reveal to you how long, but the external cameras haven't been working for the past week or so. Some fault in the system. The internal ones are all fine, but of the ones I've just mentioned only the main door one will have recorded anything."

Nielsen's heart sank. She'd sat listening to this man ramble, but she'd hoped it would lead her somewhere – that enough would be revealed on the cameras. Maybe the internal cameras would help, but she knew the problem lay outside the building, not inside. Jennie Michaels allegedly disappeared from the car park and if she didn't enter the building Nielsen would have great difficulty in proving Jennie Michaels existed. Nielsen had to put all her hope on Michaels walking into the building, which meant putting to use the description and photo she'd obtained from John Simmons.

"Okay. Play me what you can."

Rod placed a cassette in a recorder. Out of date and old fashioned, not being digital.

Nielsen looked on, scanning the faces that passed through the glass doors. Men, women, children. Faces of happiness, sorrow, humour, anger. Casual, relaxed, in a rush, anxious. So many, including images of John Simmons twice running in and out, but no Jennie Michaels.

All the while, Rod Taylor talked about what he did, what he'd wanted to do for years, how maybe he could help, how he saw all kinds of things from his shoe-box room, how he was capable of more. Nielsen tuned him out.

Thirty minutes of skipping and scanning was enough to convince Nielsen that the answers she sought would not be found on the tapes. She relented and asked Rod, "Do you remember seeing anything unusual yesterday?"

"Well, it was a busy day. It always is on Saturdays."

Nielsen wasn't going to let the conversation continue in a vague way. She jumped straight in. "I'm not interested in generalisations, Mr Taylor. What I need to know is whether you saw anything unusual yesterday. About three o'clock in the afternoon. Anyone behaving strangely. Any suspicious activity."

"There's so often so much. I keep my eye on them all, see. The customers, I mean. Although so many of them aren't customers – just here to use the loo."

"Mr Taylor, I haven't much time–"

"Okay, there is one thing that comes to mind. Probably

nothing, of course. There was an odd guy running around. I got called out of here. A report that a male in his thirties had appeared in the ladies' loos. Some kind of perv, I assumed. That's what it normally is. You get all sorts here. Public toilets bring out the best scum in the world and we're separated from towns, so people try all kinds of voyeuristic stuff. At least that's what I assumed it was. Guy wanting to catch some girls with their knickers down, nothing more."

"Did you speak to this man?"

"No. By the time I got out there, he'd gone."

Nielsen looked up from her notepad and forced eye contact. "And can you describe him?"

"Better still," he said and reached towards the monitor. He fiddled with a dial and then the screen came to life. "I can show him to you." He waited a moment while the footage played. "There," he said, looking pleased with himself as he pointed at the figure running in.

Nielsen leaned towards the screen. "John Simmons," she whispered to herself.

"What's that?" asked Rod. He didn't get an answer.

Minutes later, the figure ran back out.

"That's very good, Mr Taylor. You say he went into the female toilets?"

"Yes, and he scared the hell out of some women in there."

"So you spoke to these women, these witnesses then?"

"No, what makes you say that?"

"Well, you said they were scared. He scared the hell out of them, weren't those your words?"

Rod Taylor looked uncomfortable. He sat back down, shuffled in the seat. "No, no. I mean, I assumed that's how they felt. Wouldn't anyone in such a situation?" He laughed.

"I don't think it's very funny."

He stopped.

"So why didn't you speak to them, get their names and

details? That's standard police procedure. You were called out to a disturbance, after all."

Rod Taylor wiped his brow. "Well, by the time I got there they'd gone. I didn't know who he'd upset, only that he'd upset the women in the loo. You've got to understand, Detective, I ran outside, missed him, came back in with the intention of getting the details and found them all to be gone. The toilet to be empty. There was nothing more I could do. Nothing at all."

"Of course," Nielsen added. "Of course." She thanked Rod Taylor and left her card with him. "Do get in touch if anything else comes to mind."

"Likewise." He also produced a card. "Do let me know if I can help any further." They rose and left the room. As he was leading Nielsen down the corridor, he said, "You know, this has almost given me a taste of what I've always wanted. A bit of excitement."

"I can assure you it's anything but, Mr Taylor. This is potentially a very sad situation. In fact, I wouldn't call it exciting at all."

"I understand," he said unconvincingly. "But from an outsider's viewpoint." He didn't finish his point.

"Thank you, Mr Taylor. I'll most likely be in touch."

"And when you are I'll do my utmost to be of further service," he said, with a slight bow of the head.

Just as you were of service to the women in the toilet, Nielsen thought. Just as you searched rigorously for John Simmons, the man you said was gone when you got outside, but a man I know was out there for at least half an hour longer, waiting for the police and then being dealt with by them.

There was something about Rod Taylor that didn't ring true. Nielsen wondered whether he was all mouth, whether he really lived in the fantasyland of wannabe cop, or whether he was another lazy security guard, one who couldn't even secure a public toilet. Or whether there was more to him than met the eye.

She'd keep him close under her radar, she decided.

After she watched Rod Taylor disappear back into his corridor, Nielsen left the building and walked to the end of the path. She came to a stop at the curb and looked out towards the car park. She looked at the rows of parked cars, the spaces between them, the bridge in the distance.

Transporting herself back to the day and with her eyes on the bridge, she could see it – the Mazda. She could see it come across the bridge and then, moments later, she could see it enter the car park. She could see it pull into a space. A man and woman sat in it. The soft top was down. The woman was beautiful – her hair hung elegantly and her skin glowed. The man kissed the woman on the cheek and got out of the car. He approached Nielsen. She could see him as clear as could be, but she couldn't read him: John Simmons, a man moving in a hurry, or a man relaxed? Happy or angry? Preoccupied? She followed him, through the double doors, a right turn, the coffee stand on the left, and straight to the toilets. She waited for a moment, looked in all directions. Not many places Jennie could have gone. Then she went into the toilet. Six cubicles on the right, a mirror and sinks on the left. Now, back out and straight ahead. On the right side, a shop. She walked from one end to the other. Magazines, books, CDs, DVDs, chocolates, crisps and sweets, drinks and sandwiches. Nowhere in here for anyone to hide. So she went back out of the shop, looked at the line forming at the burger bar and approached the coffee stand. A pause in her step. A thought.

"What can I get you?" the barista asked.

Let's make this as authentic as possible, she thought. "Mocha."

"What size?"

"Small." He got to work and she kept the conversation going. "Were you working yesterday afternoon?"

"No."

"Do you know who was?"

"I think it would have been Mark."

"Mark?"

"Listen, I don't mean to be rude, but why are you asking?"

"My name's DS Kate Nielsen." She showed her identification. "I'm investigating the disappearance of someone who may have been here yesterday. Do you know how I can get hold of this Mark? Got a surname?"

"Mark Sampson's his name. I can give you his number if you like."

"That'd be great."

With the number in hand, she turned around and left, her arm brushing against the person waiting patiently behind her.

With a mocha in one hand and Mark Sampson's phone number in the other, Nielsen stood outside on the path, drinking. She saw John Simmons running out of the building. Saw him running around, dialling numbers on his phone. Saw him panicking. Saw his empty car.

Was the way she pictured it the way it actually happened? Sipping the drink, Nielsen thought about the story, but the more she thought, the more distorted her vision became.

She moved towards her car, reached it and placed her drink on the roof. From her jacket pocket she extracted her mobile phone. Looking from the piece of paper she'd just acquired to the phone and back again, she dialled Mark Sampson's number. On the third ring, he answered with what sounded like a grunt.

"Mark Sampson?"

"Yep," a nasal voice answered. "What I win?"

"Mr Sampson, my name is DS Kate Nielsen. I got your number from your colleague at the coffee stand at London Gateway. I hope you don't mind me calling you."

"Na, go ahead." Each word seemed to blend seamlessly, though unintentionally, into the following one.

"I'm investigating a possible disappearance. I wanted to ask if yesterday at the services you noticed anything out of the ordinary. Did you serve anyone who appeared odd in any way? Someone who might have been shaky, sweaty, unable to concentrate, who seemed particularly agitated?"

There was silence on the other end for a moment. Then: "Well, there was one guy who kept shuffling and looking at the door. Only reason I remember him is that not long after he left he came charging back in. A lot of commotion in the toilets after he went back out again."

"What can you tell me about him?"

"He seemed in a rush. Didn't say much."

"And was anyone with him?"

"Nope."

"You didn't see if there was anyone waiting for him outside?"

"Nope."

"Nothing else you remember?"

"Nope."

"And what about any security guards? Did you see any security go after him?"

"Na, never do. Bit useless, they are. Could nick anything you want from that place. Plus the guy who's usually on is so pot-bellied he'd make a pig look fast." He snorted a laugh.

Nielsen waited for the laugh to subside, but it didn't, so she chose to speak over it. "Anything else, Mr Sampson?"

"Nope."

"That's really helpful then. Thanks. Can you describe the man, the one you served who was in a rush, just briefly to ensure we're talking about the same man?" "Yeah, sure." He sniffed in through his nose, loud enough so that Nielsen had to pull the phone away from her ear. Then when she put the phone back to her ear there was a loud cough that made her repeat the withdrawal. "Thirty, I'd say. Maybe a bit older. Brown hair, about my height."

Nielsen waited for more. None came.

"Your height?" she said.

"Yeah, that's right."

Again, she waited and nothing.

"And that would be?"

"About six foot. My mum always says I'm more, about six two, but I don't think I am." "That's fine, Mr Sampson. Anything else?"

"Yeah, he had a bit of a pointy nose. Kind of stuck upwards, you know. And he spoke in quite a posh voice. Pronounced all his letters from what I could tell."

Nielsen opened the car door, took the coffee cup into her hand and sat inside. She closed the door quietly.

"And you're sure you didn't see anyone with this man?"

"No, no one. No one at all. Why, should I have?"

"Just a line of enquiry. Thanks for your time, Mr Sampson. Before we end this conversation I'll need a few details."

As fast as possible, she jotted down Mark Sampson's full contact details. She doubted she'd need anything else from him, but he was able to provide Nielsen with one piece of confirmation: that when John Simmons had charged back inside and then out of London Gateway, Rod Taylor had done nothing whatsoever. And she already knew that Simmons had driven into the complex. So far what he'd said seemed to be true, but there were still so many holes to fill. She needed to speak to him, probe his memory of what could have been the worst day of his life.

Maybe the worst day of Jennie Michaels' life too. If she

existed.

*

He sat in a car, sheltered under a baseball cap. The collars of his coat were lifted high and he kept his neck sunk low. She'd been inside for almost half an hour. He listened to the radio, but his eyes never wavered and stayed fixed on the entrance doors.

When she emerged, he started the car engine. But she stopped and looked at the cars in the car park. She appeared to be daydreaming, except her head moved from object to object. She looked back at the building. Then she went inside again.

An unexpected opportunity, he realised, so he turned the engine off and got out of the car.

When he entered the building, she was at the coffee stand talking to the barista. He smiled and recognised his fortune. He walked up behind her, the next in line. He was so close, he could smell her perfume. He inhaled deeply and received the intoxicating scent he hoped would be satisfying.

Interesting, he thought. You could be more use to me than a hindrance. There may be more to this game than I ever thought possible.

She was asking the barista questions and didn't indicate once that she sensed his presence. If she did, she certainly didn't hurry to help keep the queue moving.

He heard every word of their conversation. He made a mental note of Mark Sampson's phone number. When she was done and turned to leave, he kept his head to the side, stepped forwards to approach the counter and brushed his arm against hers as she went past. She didn't notice, but he found the touch electric, a thrill. Maybe she could play a bigger part than planned, he thought. It was a touch that just might change the way he'd determined to work. After a few more hours of this, he might want her. And if he'd want her, he'd take her.

He bought a bottle of water and left the building quickly, but he paused as soon as he got outside. He found her dialling a number on her mobile. He leant against the wall, head down, drinking his water. He was only about three metres away, facing her back. He looked at her hair. Noticed that it could do with work, that she didn't take care of herself enough, nowhere near as much as Sarah Elson, Rachel Price, Susannah Field, Stef Richardson and the others. She'd need to work on that. Perhaps he'd help her.

He smiled at the thought that he could practically reach out and touch her. He could grab her phone. Smash it. Pull her hair. Squeeze her neck.

He could kill her right here and he wouldn't even have to break a sweat.

But he wouldn't. He'd wait. He'd plan.

He listened to her voice. Liked how it sounded.

"Mark Sampson?" A pause. The wind was picking up. "Mr Sampson, my name is DS Kate Nielsen. I got your number from your colleague at the coffee stand at London Gateway. I hope you don't mind me calling you."

DS Kate Nielsen. No, he thought: Kate. You're Kate Nielsen. I like the sound of that. Good to meet you, Kate.

He heard most of what she said. The wind made some of it unintelligible, but the gist he got would be useful and helpful.

When she finished the conversation, she walked to her car. He waited for a moment, then walked to his car. All the while, he chuckled. You haven't a clue, he thought.

Chapter Thirteen

It must be two hours she's been gone now. Two more hours to add to the day that Jennie's already been missing. Two more hours for whoever's got her to get her even further from here, further away from us, from rescue.

I know the truth. I know they've wasted all this time and soon, when Detective Nielsen returns, everyone here will know it too. Everyone will finally believe me, will acknowledge they were wrong, will believe that Jennie is a living and breathing person.

I want to trust Detective Nielsen, but I can't, not just yet. Not after the way I've been treated by every police officer I've encountered so far. Nielsen, however, she seemed to take me seriously when we met, when she listened to what I had to say. And I appreciate that; I'll tell her so. I just want the opportunity to speak to her again, to find out what she's discovered, to share ideas about how we're going to locate Jennie.

The newspapers were sent in almost immediately after Detective Nielsen left me and I've been through every story in them carefully, circling with felt tip pen each story that's of interest; the officer who brought the papers in gave me a Sharpie. In the articles, what I saw was a world I didn't want to recognise. One body found yesterday and eight found in three weeks. One other still missing, now presumed dead. Their names meant nothing to me, but I couldn't help associating them with Jennie Michaels, even though it pained me. Sarah Elson, Rachel Price, Susannah Field, Stef Richardson, Annabelle Hoare, Becky Kitchener and Lucy Mitchell. Every line I read sent my heart racing as I learned of possible things that could be happening to Jennie.

After I'd reread each story, I realised there was little else I could do except wait and be ready to share the reports with Detective Nielsen. I've tried to sleep, but all I've managed is to sit here leaning against the cold wall; my eyes wouldn't close, no matter how much I willed them to.

I'm surrounded by four dull walls and I'm sitting on a mattress. There's no duvet, only one pillow that provides no comfort for my back. No windows in here either; just the grey door directly in front of the bed. To my left I've got about four feet to move around in. But I don't feel like moving.

My body feels numb. My neck is sore and I'm starting to get a headache, but I keep my thoughts resolutely on the conversation I'm going to have with Detective Nielsen. The conversation in which, I hope, she'll assure me that everything will be all right, that Jennie will be found, that I will finally have the police's full support.

Next to me on the mattress is an empty plastic cup – coffee that was brought to me over ninety minutes ago. In my hands, I nurse another. It's still warm and provides me with a modicum of comfort. Comfort from everything that's happened during these past twenty-four hours. The walls too, they provide some kind of comfort. But I can't think about my wellbeing; I should be out there looking for Jennie, doing everything I can to find her, so I only think of hers.

I replay what happened yesterday. Did I do everything right? Did I do everything I should have done? I picture the M1. The fields on both sides. The railway lines. The graffiti. The bridge in the distance.

Jennie by my side.

I ease off to the left, up the ramp. Twenty metres and

I'm turning to the right. I see the sign for the services. Lots of green on the right. A turn to the left, then the right, then we're edging towards London Gateway. The building appears. I park the car.

Before I go into the building, I take a look back, look behind Jennie. Try to see if I notice anything unusual, anyone suspicious hanging around, anyone paying too much attention to Jennie and the car.

I can't though; I can't see anything.

I fast forward the next part. Into the toilet and out again. To the coffee stand. Instead of giving the person serving me my attention, I turn around. I even walk to the door. I look out to check on Jennie. She's there, waiting for me, applying her make-up.

Or maybe she's not there. Maybe the seat is empty.

Or perhaps I see it as it happens: I see a man standing next to the car door, talking to her. There's a van parked behind my car. Another man gets out. Together they grab Jennie. She tries to fight them off, but they grab her hair and pull. A third man opens a side door on the van. Within five seconds Jennie's inside it. She might have screamed, but I'm inside and can't hear.

Or maybe I've gone outside. Maybe I'm running towards the van. Running towards them and they see me. See me and hurry to get in the van. But as they scamper I reach them. There's no hesitation in my actions: I grab the first man, hit him; get to the second, hit him; the third comes at me, but he's no match – I'm running on adrenaline, powered by the strongest drug in the world: my desire to save Jennie. Then I release Jennie: she's free and in my arms.

But none of that can happen because none of that did happen. I feel a mix of shame, anger and disappointment over my inability to have helped. I wasn't there; I didn't see anything. There was nothing, nothing I could do.

*

DCI Richard Morgan was the kind of man who never smiled. That's not to say he wasn't ever happy. On the contrary, he enjoyed a good joke – usually sexist, racist, egoist – and he was easily amused by the evening sitcoms he watched without fail. The lack of a smile came merely from the natural direction of his aged skin. Fifty-six years of life – twenty-five of those on the force – change a person physically. Or maybe that look was just his destiny. Either way, his face, his lips and his eyebrows pointed downwards.

"So what is it you want from me?" he snapped.

"Permission to launch a missing person's hunt for Jennie Michaels."

Morgan sniggered; his lips didn't move.

Nielsen persisted: "I just don't know how many more there are going to be. She could be his number eleven. We can't just wait and do nothing."

Nielsen sat opposite Morgan. She'd arrived back at the station and, before going to see John Simmons again, she needed to find out where she could move next case-wise. She knew her question was a stab in the dark and she'd predicted, accurately, Morgan's response. Knew she had no proof that Jennie Michaels had ever been at London Gateway. Knew she had no proof that John Simmons even knew someone called Jennie Michaels. Knew there was no Jennie Michaels living at 4 Sanders Road. Knew there was no proof that something had gone down.

But she asked nonetheless because there was something about John Simmons and his nature that appealed to her. Yes, she'd been fooled before – Morgan was the kind of superior who reminded her of this repeatedly and she'd felt foolish when it had happened, scarred and changed her – but this time something was different. Simmons' concern and

96

alarm seemed so genuine. There was something that came from within him, something base and instinctive, that she believed could never come from someone who was acting.

And she was desperate to prevent ten from becoming twenty, which at the current rate of the investigation could happen. Whoever he was – and they had no idea who – he was moving too fast for the police.

"But you've got nothing," Morgan said.

"I've got a hunch."

It was in Morgan's eyes that Nielsen could see he was, without interruption, laughing at her. She'd never see it on those downward lips. But his eyes, they gave his thoughts away. "A hunch?" His tone exuded sarcasm.

"Okay, more than a hunch then. Whatever it is I feel, I think he's telling the truth."

"Think and know are two totally separate things, Kate. You know that. And you know just how far our resources are already stretched. How could I ever justify sending officers out on a wild-goose chase, trying to find a woman we don't know is missing, a woman we don't even know is a human fucking being? Do you have any idea of the shit that would fly back up my arse if I said go ahead, get the media involved, let's start the chase, and then this guy turned out to be a fucking crackpot?"

"Just let me put her picture out there at least."

"This one's not like the others, Kate. Not yet anyway."

Nielsen left without another word and went down the corridor into her office, which was shared with three other DSs and two DCs. DC Sam Cook was the only person there. He looked up as she entered and said, "Hi."

She didn't respond.

*

They sat face to face. They weren't enemies; they weren't sizing one another up; they weren't trying to intimidate. They were trying to get information, extend the belief they had in one another, however surface-level and unclear its current state. They weren't trying to be anything other than equals, even though John Simmons was ready to rely upon Kate Nielsen more than a newborn baby relies upon its mother, even though they each vowed to themselves to make something of this meeting, to come out of it and feel like a course of action had been determined, to feel a degree of success, no matter how small.

Success for John, for someone was finally listening to him; success for Nielsen, for her belief in John Simmons would be justified.

*

She's got a pleasant face – worn but pleasant. Genuine, too. She comes across as someone who is easy to talk to, someone who wants to listen. The way her body leans forwards slightly, her right elbow leaning against the desk that separates us. Her voice, approachable. Occasional pauses separate her words. She's weary but trying hard. She cares, but she has to make an effort. Her smile, faded, but evidence of a once-joyful person still there, hidden beneath the defence system she's developed over the years. She's a police officer, after all; I know we're different. We have to be.

We're sitting in a room whose door has on it a sign that says Interview Room 3. It's quite cramped in here. Apart from the desk and two plastic chairs on which we sit, there's a bin in the corner opposite the door and a notice board. On it are signs about missing persons, wanted posters, helplines, drugs, drink and smoking warnings. On the desk there's a tape recorder, a pad of A4 lined paper and a pot of pens. They're on Detective Nielsen's side. To my right there's a plastic cup, the final remnants of someone else's coffee gathered in the bottom. Who knows how long it's been there.

*

"The really scary thing is," he said, "you see all this stuff on TV. You hear about all these stories – people disappearing, people murdered, knife crimes, guns, rape, torture. God, they make movies about this stuff. Like it's some kind of entertainment. But it's sick. When you watch it or read about it in a book, you feel removed from it all. Like it'll never happen to you. But when it does, it's like you're in the middle of a pile-up. You're helpless. And what makes it worse is the stuff in your mind. I haven't been able to clear my head since yesterday."

"It's perfectly understandable to have those kinds of thoughts," DS Nielsen said to John Simmons. She had questions to ask, lots of them. She had to get answers – but she wanted them to be succinct – and she wanted to feel she was getting somewhere. "Is there any other plausible explanation to all this?"

"Plausible?" John shook his head. "Is it plausible she's been taken? Is it plausible the woman I love is dead?" He put his head in his hands and paused. Then he looked up. "I've gone through all the possibilities. And I can't get away from these newspaper stories. Ten women, taken, raped, tortured, for God's sake. Tortured to death."

"And Jennie?"

"She could be number eleven."

"I'm all too aware of that." Nielsen shook her head and she blinked slowly.

John Simmons hadn't shown much of a reaction when

she had told him the CCTV footage didn't reveal anything at London Gateway, but he was close to trembling now. Nielsen studied him carefully. His body edged forwards slightly. His face didn't show much, but his bottom lip gave more away: it shook, just slightly – that she saw clearly.

"While the police have made me wait, all these thoughts – fuelled by the stuff in those newspaper articles – have jumped around my mind and they're stuck there. I can't get away from them."

Nielsen gave John a moment to compose himself. Then she said, "There's an epidemic of women being taken in the south-east, John. From their workplaces, their homes, nightclubs, shops, parks. Believe me, we're working tirelessly to find out who's doing it. We're going to stop them."

"I do believe you, I do. But I can't stop wondering if Jennie's his latest. Is taking Jennie from the services the most recent?"

"It's possible."

"Why? Why would someone do it?"

All Nielsen could answer was, "Like I said, everybody's got a devil inside them. Most people manage to keep it at bay. It's just there are some people who can't fight theirs off."

*

"With love to you, John. These two weeks have been the greatest."

I say the words aloud. They somehow make me feel better, like your presence is by my side. Hearing the sound of your words soothes me. Looking at your writing on my birthday card takes away a fragment of the pain that's inside me.

But only a fragment.

It seems like this nightmare has been going on for so

long, not just a day and a half. Jennie, why are only your words here and not you?

I went to the police station this morning, determined to put up a fight, determined to get them out there looking for Jennie. But I can't celebrate success because I only half succeeded. Yes, Detective Nielsen is looking for Jennie, but she's doing it alone. She's made me the greatest promise anyone could make right now, but she sees helping me as taking a gamble.

Having the birthday card in front of me again – the card I've displayed on my mantelpiece for a week – brings me one step closer to you, Jennie, because it means there's a piece of you here with me. It was the greatest time; you're right, it was bliss.

That is, until yesterday.

That's why I know we feel the same way and you haven't run away from me.

Detective Nielsen said wait: wait and let her do her job. She'll contact me. So I wait.

I'm waiting for you, Jennie.

Chapter Fourteen

Selecting victims had become easy for him. Things had progressed. He kept count of how many there'd been with a two-line cross on the dates of their engagements on a calendar in his kitchen. Each page of the calendar showed a different barren landscape of the world. This month's was of desert in Nevada.

After Sarah Elson, when all hope had faded, he came to the decision to settle on one requirement only: their look had to excite him, give him what he didn't get from what people saw as his normal life – it was as simple as that.

He'd developed a routine, had success with it. He researched each victim, followed them for as long was necessary, until he felt confident he couldn't get it wrong. Until, almost, he believed he could predict their next step before it was taken. Planned and waited with the eye and patience of a pro.

But tonight, which was supposed to be his time off, he found himself preoccupied. He was home alone, but he felt anxious. He wondered why and it didn't take long for him to realise the answer. His lack of patience was surprising. It was because he couldn't get Kate Nielsen off his mind. Not since he'd followed her home then back to the station. With all the others, it had been their looks that had attracted him, but not with her. He enjoyed the unusual feeling: the thrill of having power over someone whom society sees as powerful without them even knowing it.

The plans he'd spent the day conjuring for her had made him start to want. Now. The sensation was always tugging at him, day and night, but now it was at the strongest level he'd ever experienced and he was struggling to resist. It got so bad, he could barely keep still. The tension in his loins increased and he couldn't hold back any longer. So he decided to ride with it.

He left the house. He knew where Kate Nielsen lived. Maybe, just maybe, she'd become part of this now; maybe he'd forget the plans. It would, of course, be spontaneous, no planning involved, just execution. Not his way of working, he understood that, but something about her was driving him crazy. He might just kill her. Does she have to have a greater role in this? he asked internally.

He arrived at her house but couldn't see her car. He waited as patiently as he could, but he wanted too much. He started to think about what he'd do to her. The touch, the thrill. He could cut her throat. He could bathe in her blood.

But soon these thoughts turned to what he'd do if she didn't turn up. Wait for her inside and surprise her? Wait in the car? What would happen if she didn't return before dawn, if she was working on the case all night?

And with more time to wait, his mind travelled back to reality. He knew where he was. He knew what he wanted. But this, he recognised, would be an almighty risk. No planning and the detective hunting for him as his victim. "What kind of fool?" he said to himself. "Like some kind of spotty fucking teenager."

Plan, he told himself silently. Plan and wait for the right time. It might not be soon, but it will come eventually. She will have her day.

All this waiting and thinking didn't take him away from wanting gratification, however. He wanted satisfaction, only, he decided, with someone insignificant. For now.

So he ended up at a nightclub called Vision where, he believed, lots of insignificant people went. It was dismal to look at. Purple exterior, flashing neon lights, several bulbs missing. In his eyes, all nightclubs were hideous and loathsome. But they welcomed, entertained, then spat out women.

Clare Foxford was eighteen years old. An insignificant teenager. She loved the nightlife, she loved partying, she loved the guys who watched her, the ones who came up to her, the ones she brushed off, usually after they'd bought her a bottle of something, and especially the ones she let in. Under the flashing lights, surrounded by hundreds of sweaty bodies, with eardrum-pounding music filling the background, a drink in hand, a fag in the other, she loved getting close to older guys, smelling their aftershave, feeling their tongues down her throat. Older, incidentally, could mean nineteen or thirty; it didn't matter. She loved knowing that she turned older guys on, that her short skirts and tight tops didn't go unnoticed.

Tonight, she started on the Bacardi Breezers at home. Shouted down for her mum to open the front door when her friends, Nicole and Liz, arrived. Came to her home to knock back a few drinks before the night out began. Her place this time; could easily have been theirs.

Loud music playing on her stereo in her bedroom got them in the party mood and they spoke of the previous time they went out together – last week. They'd all ended up going home with guys, Clare with the oldest. He'd had his own car. They giggled, pleased with themselves, hopeful it would happen again tonight, confident they'd be successful. They'd had a lot of practice.

After an hour of drinking, applying lipstick and touching up mascara, they left the house, but not before they stumbled down the stairs and Clare struggled to put on her knee-high boots. They didn't bother to call farewell to Clare's mother who would, no doubt, have another sleepless night waiting for her only daughter to return home. It was likely that Clare would have a sleepless night too, but for a different reason altogether.

She thought it would be because of sex; she was wrong.

When the taxi pulled up outside Vision, they paid the driver, all too aware that he got a view of more than their legs from his vantage point, thanks to the lengths of their skirts. As soon as they stepped onto the pavement, they felt the alcohol hit them, their legs became unbalanced and they laughed. They loved this feeling.

Arm in arm they walked to the entrance, content, even pleased, that crowds of boys were staring at their legs as they passed. After all, they adored the attention. Some of the boys even got a wink for good measure. Clare wondered if it would be one of these guys who she'd go home with tonight. She even tried to spot the ones she fancied.

As Clare, Nicole and Liz stood in the queue – it was always long by eleven o'clock – they were unaware that he was sitting in his car on the opposite side of the road and watching them.

He'd never been to a nightclub as a teenager, never discovered how to feel young. And now, as he sat outside one, he caught sight of Clare, although he didn't know her name. He didn't notice the other two at all. He was desperate to feel her the moment he saw her and knew she would be the one; tonight it was that instant. It was her tight, sleeveless gold top, her short skirt that clung to her curves, black in colour and without stockings underneath, her brown hair, curled today, that caught his eye. And the long black leather boots with high heels, of course; her thighs looked so toned.

Within ten minutes Clare and her friends had paid and were inside. As soon as they stepped through the door into the foyer, the music was deafening. Conversation ended and all that followed would be loud, incomprehensible shouting.

As the second and final set of double doors opened and they stepped inside, they were surrounded by scores of people, many jumping up and down, many with beer bottles permanently attached to their mouths, many trying – and failing – to talk. Purple and blue dominated the lighting and flashed relentlessly.

The girls stepped through the first part of the crowd and went towards the bar. There were two bars – one on either side of the room. In the middle on a lower tier of flooring was the massive dance floor. It was already full of people. Hundreds of heads and bodies danced this way and that. On the dance floor there were also three podiums – large raised platforms on which about two dozen partygoers could dance. At the moment, the podiums were filled with girls, and groups of guys stood beneath them, looking up, eager.

While he waited outside, with no indication of how long – hours perhaps – he'd have to be there, alone, he could feel his sweat glands working overtime, anticipation, particularly without the benefit of his usual planning, causing it. He kept aftershave in the car, so he reached into the glove box and used it to freshen up.

He knew he had to have patience. With patience, he understood, came success.

Inside, unaware of what lay ahead, Clare was on a podium. More guys watched her than the other girls – lots of eyes trying to see what she had only partially concealed beneath her skirt.

Nicole and Liz were long gone.

One guy in particular caught Clare's attention. Dark hair, tanned skin and a tight white T-shirt covering what she could see was a toned chest and stomach. The view she gave him, her movements slower, more suggestive – he couldn't hold back his smile. When she grinded lower, her skirt rode up and he saw underwear, black and slinky.

She was on her second drink of the visit, not counting all those she'd had at home, when, with a stumble, she dropped down. As she landed, she continued dancing on the spot. She spun herself around, took the tanned guy by the wrist and started to dance with him. She placed her hands on his hips. He could see in her eyes that she was totally wasted. He knew he was going to get lucky; with his looks, he usually did.

It was a few minutes of dancing before one song blended into another and he said, "Drink?"

Throwing her arms around his neck and dropping all her weight onto him, she answered, "Vodka. Double."

He took her by the hand and led her to the bar. She couldn't keep steady. He couldn't wipe the grin off his face as the barman asked what he wanted. Clare was behind him. She didn't even know his name yet. He ordered her a triple vodka. For himself, only a single.

After paying, he turned to her and handed her the drink. "All in one," he shouted and made the sign of a toast with his glass. He downed his drink and she followed suit. She coughed and held her throat.

"Good, isn't it?" he asked.

"Fucking brilliant," she shouted.

"Another?"

She didn't answer, nodded her head. She was, in no uncertain terms, out of it.

He took his head close to her ear and said, "I can't wait to fuck you."

She giggled. It was what she wanted.

He turned to the barman and ordered, same again. Turned back to her. Same toast. Down the hatch, just the same.

Within minutes they were back on the dance floor, but they weren't dancing. She had her tongue down his throat.

After ten more minutes, they left. She'd whispered to him, told him it was time. As they emerged into the night's darkness, which was filled only by neon lights and flashes of headlights as the occasional car drove past, in the car across the road their observer came to life. He watched the couple walk to the left. She was in the guy's arms. As he saw this, his mind was cast back to the first time he put his arm around a woman. He was twenty-six when it happened. He'd spent his years since the factory watching and keeping his distance. He'd spent the years of isolation feeding his hate with plans: plans to hurt, to devastate. He'd wanted to take women by the hair, bite them, squeeze the air from their lungs. He'd decided to do it years ago, go for it, start and not stop until he was forced to. But each time he got closer to starting, it was their forms that prevented him from going through with it. Their curvaceous, smooth, supple forms. Could he really destroy what he craved so much? His eyes, once they saw, guided his hand the other way and fought against what his inner self demanded he do.

This battle continued inside him until on his twenty-sixth birthday, working in a firm's mailroom, surrounded by men and the talk of the relationships they were in, feelings given and in turn received, he made the choice to give normal life a try. He surrendered. "I'll try to be normal," he said. "I'll try."

One of the guys he worked with said he knew someone. A woman a few years younger. She wasn't much to look at, he said, but she was keen to find someone. Worth a try. "Very often," the co-worker said, "it's about the connection."

Foolishly, he listened. He met her, they went out several times, they got on well enough. After six months of attempting to lead a normal life, he believed he'd buried all previous plans in the deepest recesses of his mind. He *had* become normal, what he fooled himself into thinking would make him whole. So he proposed to her. She accepted.

How wrong he was.

He married her and, in one simple action, she sucked the normal out of his life, when she was supposed to be what brought normal to him.

In front of him, he observed the normality of youth as Clare Foxford and her beau continued walking away from him. They went around the side of the building.

He waited a few moments before switching the engine on. He didn't switch the headlights on as he gently pressed on the gas. The car pulled forwards, he turned to the left and then edged round the side of the building.

He saw them, the guy's arm around Clare's shoulder, her lips pressed against his as they stumbled awkwardly. They got to the end of the building, turned right and disappeared.

The car moved slowly as it approached the turning, but instead of going round the corner he parked in the space that was directly ahead. From there he could see where they were. The back of the building was part of the car park, but it wasn't used to park cars. There were several emergency exits, and wheelie bins were scattered around. Clare and the stud were stationed between two bins that were next to the building. They were on the floor, she underneath him, her toes pressed into the ground, jeans around his ankles. All he could see was their legs.

It was only a matter of minutes before it was over. The guy stood up, pulled up his jeans and backed away. He said a few things to Clare, shrugged when she didn't respond and moved off.

Their observer waited inside the car until the guy had gone round the corner, walked down the side of the building and turned left, no doubt returning to the party within, having had his fill. He pulled his baseball cap on. He restarted the car's engine, again no lights, reversed out of the spot and rolled the car to where she lay.

For a moment, he wondered if she was dead.

She wasn't. As soon as he rolled the window down, he could hear her heavy breathing. Her knickers were halfway down her thighs and her skirt was still lifted. Her top had also been raised, revealing the curve of her lower back.

He looked through each window of the car. No security cameras in view. He manoeuvred the car so that the back door was above where she lay, got out of the car and stood over her. Reaching down, prodding her as if she was a vagrant and he was concerned about her safety, he said, "Hey, are you okay?" Shaking her by the back of the shoulders, he added, "Do you hear me?"

He didn't see the mobile phone that lay on the ground near her body.

She stirred. A burp and she started to lift herself up.

"Here," he said in the likeness of a security man, "let me help you."

With his gloved right hand, he helped her up. With his left, he opened the back door.

"You're a silly girl," he said. She made no sign of recognition. "Letting him do that to you and now letting me do this."

Using both arms, he swung her round and deposited her on the backseat.

Then footsteps. He looked down at the ground, a moment to think, his heart pulsating now, and that was when he saw the mobile phone. Panic. He'd always planned so carefully; today was different and he sensed it going all wrong. He leant down and picked up the phone. He knew he had only seconds to decide how to act.

The footsteps were right behind him and stopped suddenly. "Hey," the voice said.

He heard the voice slur and knew he had the advantage.

The phone was in his hand. He didn't look back.

The guy behind him, the one who'd no more than ten minutes go had his way with Clare Foxford, turned and sighted what lay in the car. "What the fuck—"

He didn't get to finish. The man crouching down in front of him rose, spun around with lightning-like speed and brought the mobile phone crashing against the side of his head. His body was propelled into the wall and then tumbled to the ground.

The man was about to jump in his car when the young guy got up. Momentarily, their eyes met. Fear, for different reasons, flooded them both. But it couldn't consume one of them for long. The one who hadn't filled himself with alcohol had no choice.

As quickly as he'd first reacted, he reached out to the young guy, grabbed and repositioned him, and wrapped his arm around the thick neck. He used his other hand to push the head forwards and kept pushing, pushing, pushing, until at last he heard vertebrae snap.

The young guy was dead, his body left on the ground.

The man moved off. Things hadn't worked out as he'd hoped; he was angry and unsatisfied, and he determined that he wouldn't be spontaneous again. Although his swift actions and ultimate success increased his confidence, it was too risky. If he couldn't handle this, how could he handle a cop? He wanted to make his series last. He had years to make up for. And he'd waited too long before he'd started. So he knew there could be no more hasty choices, no more mistakes.

With his package in the vehicle, he fired up the engine, this time the lights shining brightly, and left.

*

Clare Foxford was still unconscious when he killed her. She was so drunk she couldn't be woken. He'd wanted to enjoy her, to fulfil the urge he'd had since leaving Kate Nielsen. He was furious with himself for messing things up so that he wasn't able to enjoy the nubile young body – he knew the male body at the club would be discovered soon, so he had to rid himself of this one. Despite the anger, he knew what had to be done, so he kept calm.

He strangled her. Looked at her the entire time, imagined her eyes wide open, that he could look into the whites of her eyes, that he could see the life inside her and watch it seep away. Imagined what she'd taste like.

It was almost half-past three and he drove the The Elms, a network of roads that surrounded a forest near his home. He struggled as he lifted her out of the car, but he didn't have to keep hold of her for long. He dropped her behind a tree.

It wasn't over in his mind. He knew he'd got away with it – he was too clever, had had too long to work out the ways of his work – but *someone* was clawing at the back of his mind.

He didn't know when, but Kate Nielsen would form the most satisfying part of this one day, the denouement.

Chapter Fifteen

Sleep evaded me again last night, so I dragged myself out of bed at four this morning. Computer, I thought to myself. More research, find out more, understand more and figure out something useful.

Detective Nielsen was honest with me – she told me about the ten women who have been abducted and killed so far, and confirmed what I'd learned from the papers. I double checked some of the facts I'd discovered from her – it was exactly as she said.

Three quarters of an hour ago, after reading another news page – another story, this one about a family coming to terms with their daughter having been followed from work and killed in her own home – I made my move, exactly as I'd planned yesterday before my day was taken from me and spent at the police station.

Jennie's office. Heavy traffic – not a surprise, all too common around here – meant the journey took me over half an hour. I pulled into the car park, which was behind and underneath the building, and parked in one of the dozen or so visitors' spaces. That's where I am now, preparing myself and trying to keep composed.

I know that Jennie works as a legal secretary for a solicitor named Dave Bryant. He works corporate.

I take a final glance in the mirror for a sign of encouragement. Something good has got to come as a result of the things I do today. I have to take a step forwards. Yes, Detective Nielsen is working on the case, but there's no reason why I can't help. I can't simply sit at home and do nothing.

I get out of the car and walk round the side of the building and onto the main road, which takes me to the entrance. To get in, I have to go up ten steps. I press a buzzer and the reception door is released.

I enter, hopeful that this will be the start of getting answers. The reception area is large, and to the left there's a set of stairs. The receptionist is seated facing the door. She's behind a unit that's spread from wall to wall. Behind her are several shelves filled with files. Another lady is sitting at a computer facing the wall on the right.

I walk towards the reception unit.

"Can I help you?" the receptionist asks as I come to a stop. She's wearing a smart navy-blue jacket, a white shirt and has her dark hair up in a bun.

"Yes. I don't have an appointment, but it's incredibly important that I speak to Dave Bryant, please?"

"Dave Bryant?"

"Yes."

"And he is?"

"One of your corporate solicitors."

She pauses for a moment and raises her eyebrows. The skin on her forehead creases.

I sense the words coming before I hear them.

"No, I'm afraid there's no one by that name who works here."

Not again. This can't be happening. "There must be some mistake." Even with the amount of surprises I've had in the past two days, it still takes a lot out of me. "David, maybe? Perhaps David Bryant?"

"No, I'm afraid not."

"Really–"

"Listen, sir, there are only six solicitors here and I know them all. I've worked here for eleven years."

It's starting all over again. "Look, there's got to be

someone who can help me. I'm looking for one of your employees. My girlfriend. She's gone missing. I need to speak to someone who works with her. Someone who might be able to help me." Maybe I've made a mistake and got Dave Bryant's name wrong. "Maybe not Dave Bryant, but then maybe someone else."

"And what's your girlfriend's name?"

"Jennie Michaels," I tell her.

She shakes her head.

No. No, no!

My breathing is heavy as I say, "I'm looking for Jennie Michaels. She's a legal secretary here. She's gone missing and I need your help."

"No one called Jennie Michaels works here either."

I step back and back and back. "The Wongs. Bryant. This isn't happening." I only know I've reached the door when my foot knocks into it.

I hear the receptionist say, "Are you okay?", but I don't answer. I turn around, open the door and step into the fresh air. Its chill pierces my lungs. I put my hand on my chest, try to inhale smoothly, keep still at the top of the stairs.

I picked Jennie up from her home many times. But she doesn't live there. I picked her up from here as well. But she doesn't work here. Why did she lie to me? She must have. I haven't got it wrong. She told me.

Now I only have one thought in my mind: who is Jennie? Do I know her at all?

*

I drove around St Albans for over an hour. After visiting Jennie's office, my mind went blank. I had no idea what to do, but I did know one thing: Jennie lied to me. For whatever reason or whatever gain, she got me to collect her

117

from two places to which she had no connections. Or at least connections I can't yet figure out.

I've never felt such confusion in my life. I'd give anything, my life even, for Jennie, and she deceived me. But despite the lies, I'm not willing to admit the love she showed me was false. There's no way. It was real. She loved me; you can't fake that kind of genuineness. So if she lied to me, she had reason to; and that's what I have to figure out. Right now, it's just too early to understand why.

After an hour of driving, I believed I had only one option left, which led me to where I am now. I'm in my car. I can see Jennie's house. It's still that to me; it'll always be Jennie's house, no matter how many police officers tell me she doesn't live here, no matter how many more Wongs appear. It'll be Jennie's house until she explains otherwise to me.

It's ten thirty and I've not seen any life within the house yet. I've managed to keep my breath steady, even though inside I'm quivering. If she's in there – if, as I now suspect, the Wongs are a part of some elaborate hoax or plan against Jennie and me – I will find out. They won't see me; I'm going to keep my distance.

A little after eleven, Mr and Mrs Wong emerge through Jennie's front door. They look like impostors, people who don't belong, people who have done something wrong; they keep glancing over their shoulders as if they're afraid they're going to get caught. They walk to the left of the house and round the corner to where their car is parked. I notice how different they are from one another, like two opposites: one, tall and slim, still with an air of youth; the other, short, fat and haggard. His hair is close-cropped and neat and hers is long and wild. Both black.

They get inside their car – a 2000 Vauxhall Astra, grey – and I see a plume of smoke shoot out of the exhaust when it starts up. They pull out into the road. I wait a few seconds before I start up my car and follow, careful to keep my distance. I keep so far back, in fact, that I almost lose them at a red light, but I plant my foot on the pedal and duck through at the last moment while the colours are changing.

In a matter of minutes, we're in the city centre. Mr Wong, who's driving, pulls into a space on the high street. He parallel parks with ease. I continue past them and struggle into a space about five cars ahead, all the while keeping an eye on them in my rear-view mirror. Only he gets out of the car. He walks into Lloyds Bank. I can't see her because of the tinted windscreen on their car, but I imagine her sitting in the passenger seat, lipstick in hand, looking into the vanity mirror. She's so unlike Jennie. Women like her, they must be so jealous of women like Jennie. As I compare them, the numbness that's weighed me down for the past two days hits me afresh. I won't let it win though.

I almost fail to spot Mr Wong as he leaves the bank. He jumps back into the Astra and pulls out of the space with as much ease as he entered it. I let a couple of cars pass by before I indicate to pull out and see where our journey will take us next.

We go out of the centre and onto a dual carriageway. The road is on an incline and he doesn't drive fast, so it's easy to catch up to a reasonable distance and keep up once I'm there. He's careful not to exceed forty as we pass a speed camera – he touches his brakes slightly – then he heads straight across a roundabout. A further mile and we go over another roundabout. Then straight over the next.

M1, southbound.

I was here only two days ago.

I realise that my connection with the Wongs was formed because of this very road.

He keeps to a steady seventy as we head south. Grass on both sides. Into the distance on the left, there are cows grazing in fields, and train lines make up the view on the right. Bridge after bridge, pedestrian and vehicular. Line after line, road markings, dizzying to stare at, separating the traffic that is fairly light today.

The sun is not out – not like the last time I drove along this road, when I was here with Jennie. I look to my left, see through the empty air in the space where she was sitting. The roof isn't down today, so there's no wind to blow in her hair to bring out her movie-star quality. There's just me and the silence that surrounds me.

In less than fifteen minutes, I break the silence with a gasp. My mouth widens. I don't say any words – nothing comprehensible comes out; it can't. It's like I'm being choked and I'm struggling for air. I grip the steering wheel tightly, fear that if I let go I'll veer off the road.

Wong's indicator light comes on to signal left as we pass the first of three countdown signs. Signs that tell travellers they are approaching the services. My hands are still gripping the wheel, so tightly that they might go through the material.

Automatically, without a single clear thought, I push down my indicator signal. It might be ten seconds later – but it feels like ten minutes – that I'm heading up that exit ramp. Everything has slowed down. I make the turnings. I bring the car into lane, the Astra out of sight now. My speed has slowed to the point of a stall; the car has started to shudder. Another driver behind me flashes his lights, but I don't react. It's not long before he goes round me and sounds his horn. My car has come to a stop, the engine dead, and I find myself sitting on the entrance road. The hotel is to my left, and to my right I can make out the top of the London Gateway building.

I don't know what to do. My body won't volunteer any ideas and I shudder at the thought of going back in there.

And at the thought of who has brought me here.

The Wongs.

Now I'm certain that something is up, something I don't understand, something the police wouldn't for a second believe. They're in on this – the Wongs. They've got Jennie, somehow, somewhere.

And they know I'm here.

As quickly as my senses disappeared, they return and a feeling of resolution comes over me. This is my moment. I have to act. I put the car back into neutral, restart it and press on the accelerator. It lurches forwards and I turn into the car park. I can see the Wongs' car sitting in one of the disabled spaces by the path that leads to the building's door. I still keep back, even though my instinct tells me to run inside and beat them to a pulp, make them tell me what they've done with Jennie.

I park to the right of the building, get out, lock the door and begin a slow walk towards the building. My legs pause by themselves as I come to the space in which I'd parked when Jennie was with me. Nearby sits a Volvo, its occupants nowhere to be seen. As I peer through its back window, a figure appears in the front seat and, for a moment, I can see the shining, flowing locks of Jennie's hair. She pulls down the visor and glances at herself in the mirror. I watch her for what feels like a lifetime. I even smile at her. She feels something herself – my presence – so she glances into the mirror. She sees me and smiles. My hand reaches out to touch the car boot and, for a split second, it's like I'm once again by her side.

The laughter of a child walking past pulls me out my daze, and Jennie's gone as quickly as she came into view. I realise where I am and understand what I have to do.

I retrace the walk I took the last time I experienced happiness in my life. When I reach the glass doors, I turn around. Jennie has returned; I see her inside the Volvo again. I raise my hand and wave. She laughs and waves back. While I'm still waving and when she's stopped, she disappears from the seat, a tease, a reminder of my past. My hand stays in the air but stops moving, my smile evaporating.

Jennie's gone. That's why I'm here.

And the answer lies within.

I walk into the building and immediately spot Mrs Wong. She's using one of the payphones on the far side of the foyer. She's talking animatedly. I look all around me: to the shop, to the coffee stand, to the fast food restaurant. No sign of Mr Wong, which means there's only one place he could be.

The toilets.

What the hell are they doing here?

Taking brisk strides, I make my way in. As I enter and walk round the corner, there's a line of urinals bolted to the wall. To the right of them is a wall that works like a divider. Behind that is a row of cubicles. Mr Wong isn't by the urinals, so I walk to the right and slowly pass each cubicle door. All of them are closed, the red mark on each indicating they're occupied. I stand at the far end of the room and lean against a tiled wall. To the other users of the facilities, I'm someone who's waiting for a cubicle to become available; but to me I'm doing something altogether different: I'm waiting, I'm preparing. I can be patient for this.

When he comes out, I'm going to confront him. And if he doesn't react in a way that will help me, I'll push him back into the cubicle and I will hurt him until he speaks; no, I will kill him if he doesn't tell me everything, and I mean everything. Fuck all the people who keep coming in and out of here. As far as I'm concerned, it's only me and him.

A toilet flushes and I prepare to strike. A door opens. A man steps out. Grey hair, grey suit. Not him.

The toilets absolutely stink, but I step inside the now-vacant cubicle. When locked inside, I get onto my knees to peer under the panel to see if Wong is on either side of me. I can't get my head low enough and the floor is wet – with urine for all I know – so I don't want my face to touch the ground. I stand up and get on top of the toilet seat. Holding on to the panels, I lean to the right side. I look over the top and see a young boy sitting on the loo. I move back and lean to the left. A flushing noise comes from further to the left and then a door opens. Footsteps move out. I drop down and open my cubicle door.

That's when I see him: Wong. He's standing by the sinks, which are beyond the cubicles on the left-hand side. He's looking at himself in the mirror as he scrubs his hands. He moves his lips, the top one higher, the bottom lower, so that he can see his teeth. When he finishes washing his hands, he prises at something in his teeth with the fingers of his right hand.

On the wall facing me, some ten feet away, are the hand dryers. He steps over to one and begins drying his hands. His back is to me. I step slowly towards him. Now I see an opportunity. All it would take is a grip of his hair. Then I could force his head into the wall. One sharp, quick movement and he'd be unconscious. I'm so close to him, I could do it. I want to do it. Want him to suffer as Jennie might be suffering, as I am suffering. Wouldn't take much at all. Then it would only be me and Mrs Wong. I'd be able to break her and find out the truth. She looks weak. She'd tell me everything, I have no doubt about it.

But as quickly as the idea enters my mind, the opportunity leaves me; he moves out of the toilets.

Frustrated at the lost chance, I follow him. When I come out of the toilets, I see them both queuing at the coffee stand. The same barista who served me is about to serve them. Expecting an equally long wait, I step into the shop. I stand behind the unit on which the newspapers are kept. A man tries to squeeze past me to get to where the sweets are kept but knocks into me, so I lose my balance. He grunts an apology, conveying the message that I should watch where I stand.

I glance down at the newspapers. Every front page is about a tragedy or a tragedy waiting to happen. Disappearances, murders, wars, gangs, political corruption. I can't understand why Jennie's disappearance isn't on the front of every national paper, and I'll never fathom why a celebrity's love life gets more coverage than everything else.

I pick up a copy of the two nearest papers. They'll likely hold stories of interest. If the police won't find Jennie, if it's left down to Detective Nielsen, who can only do her best on a solo mission, which I'm sure won't be good enough, then I'll find Jennie myself, and maybe there'll be some help in these. Not a word unnoticed, not an idea unturned, I'll study them and I'll find a way to get to Jennie.

By the time I've paid and bagged my purchases, I'm surprised to see the Wongs are leaving. The barista is much quicker today. I keep my distance behind them, follow them outside and watch them from the entrance. They get into their Astra and take off. As soon as they're turning out of the car park, I run over to my car, noticing the spot where I'd placed the coffees when Jennie disappeared, pass the place where she was sitting, and jump back into my car, the newspapers I've purchased falling to the floor on the passenger side. With the key in the ignition, I fire up the engine and accelerate out at speed, keen to get the Wongs back into view.

A minute or so later I'm on the M1 again, heading south, and I can see the Astra about fifty yards ahead. Once again, I follow at a steady distance.

"I'm looking for Dave Bryant," Nielsen said to the receptionist. "And an employee named Jennie Michaels."

The receptionist's eyes came alive, work no longer mundane. "You're the second person to say those names to me today."

"Really?" Nielsen leaned against the unit in front of her.

"Those people don't work here. They never have. At least for the past eleven years, which is as long as I've been here. That's what I told the guy earlier this morning."

"Guy?" She thought for a moment. "Short brown hair, medium build, about six foot, by any chance?"

"That's right."

"Damn it, John," Nielsen said under her breath, frustrated that John Simmons had failed, within a matter of hours, to comply with her stay-at-home request.

"What's this all about?"

"I'm investigating the disappearance of a young woman. How did this man seem this morning?"

"To be honest, I didn't get much out of him. He asked for Dave Bryant and then the girl, what was her name?"

"Jennie Michaels."

"That's right, Jennie Michaels. First, Dave Bryant, then Jennie Michaels, then he kind of looked shocked, went silent and then walked out. That was all."

"Prior to today, have you ever seen this man? Has he ever been here?"

"No, never."

Nielsen took a card from her pocket and handed it to the receptionist. "My card. If he comes back, call me immediately. What's your name?"

"Amanda Fisher."

"And a contact number? Mobile would be best."

Amanda Fisher told Nielsen the number. She wrote it down and put her notepad in the back pocket of her jeans.

"You know," Amanda said, cutting off Nielsen's departure, "he did say something as he was leaving. He said Dave Bryant and a name, sounded Chinese. I can't remember it."

"Wong?"

"Yeah, that's the one."

Nielsen nodded her head, thanked Amanda Fisher and left.

Wong again. Whether Jennie Michaels is real or not, whether she has disappeared or not, John Simmons believes what he's saying, Nielsen thought. I think.

Maybe it was time for that visit to Sanders Road.

*

I'm exhausted and frustrated. Today looks like nothing more than an overlong shopping trip. I sat for three hours in Brent Cross Shopping Centre. Three hours while the Wongs picked up a couple of books in WH Smith and plopped themselves down on a leather sofa in a coffee shop. Three hours sipping coffee after coffee, eating cake, while I waited for them to get off their backsides and move.

The only unexpected moment came when, mid-conversation, Wong turned to his wife and turned on her, scolding her for some reason I wasn't aware of; I was too far away to hear. He subdued her instantly.

After that came more journeying that ended in an hour-long stroll along Oxford Street, then Regent Street. Lots of window shopping and no actual shopping.

For the past hour and a half I've been sitting on a bench in Leicester Square, watching an Italian restaurant, waiting for them to come out. It's a cold day and the coat I'm wearing offers little protection from the elements while sitting still for so long.

So many people have passed me. It reminds me of the evening outside the Fortune Theatre: couples arm in arm; some walking separately, some walking far apart – too far apart; singles; dog walkers; people in a rush; people sipping coffee as they stroll; people – tourists presumably – looking lost and confused. So much life and so close to me, but the one life I want to see, to be with and to hold, is the one that evades me.

Jennie.

I daze in and out of focus as I think about her. The third day of nothing, not a word, not a sign. Three of the most miserable days of my life. Three of the most worry-filled days I've ever had the misfortune to endure.

I'm jealous of the lives I see around me. I'm jealous of all these people. In fact, I hate them – hate them for what they've got; it's what I want.

It's what I had.

The restaurant door opens and I see Mr Wong emerge, finally, followed by his wife. They pause only momentarily as he does his coat up. They move away from the building, Mr taking the lead, and then they walk to my right, around the square. I get up and watch them as they turn and pass nightclub and cinema and then cinema and nightclub.

I come out from the square and follow behind them onto Charing Cross Road. They cross the road when the traffic lights turn red. I'm so close to them, I run the risk of being detected. But I rely on the crowd around us to offer me protection from being detected.

A few minutes later we're walking up Long Acre and I spot – no, gaze longingly at and pause – the other side of the road as my eyes fall upon the place where I first met Jennie. Knocked into her, in fact.

But I have to keep moving. Have to keep up. So, reluctant,

I carry on. A right into Covent Garden. The Wongs pause as they gaze into a shoe shop window. I stand further back, partly in and partly out of the tube station's entrance. They move on, into the market. I trot to catch up – don't want to lose them in the crowds, which are en mass and everywhere. I push through a couple holding a map and hear what I presume are curse words in a foreign tongue.

I've lost view of the Wongs. My movements become sharp. I enter the roof-covered market and look down the path on my left. I can't see them here, so I look to the right. Nothing here either. I begin to move with pace, knocking into people on all sides. It's so noisy. My mind starts to become overwhelmed by the sounds and I can't focus. Children crying; children laughing; street performers asking people to gather round, keen to amass their own crowd; those with audiences already in place making them laugh, gasp, flinch; buskers, guitars playing, violins too. It's all too much. Dizzy, I hold out my hand and reach for the wall. My hand touches a middle-aged woman's shoulder. She jumps and makes a startled shriek. I let go. My head's spinning, so I don't see the child who walks in front of me. I tread on his foot, knock into his leg, and we both fall to the ground. Feet collide with me. People try to avoid me, but there are too many sets of feet. I don't pay any attention to the kid who's on the ground next to me. I don't even know if he's hurt. In only a few seconds, a young lady is pushed over me and lands on the floor by my side. A toddler goes down next.

I shout to myself, have to regain control. I can't let them get away. I have to find them.

Thinking of the Wongs makes me scramble to my feet, pull the toddler up and scramble through the crowd, some who are passers-by and some who have become onlookers. I must look like hell. My body is covered in sweat and I feel beads of it drip through my eyebrows and onto my cheeks. Some of it gets into my eyes and stings. I rub my eyes and push my way out of the market, emerging on its far side, near to the second and larger market. Here I look to the right and left. I run to the transport museum, hoping against hope that I'll somehow find the Wongs, discover their whereabouts.

And I see them. There they are. Ogling the chocolates in the window of an overly expensive chocolate shop, they stand leaning forwards, their noses almost touching the glass. With large steps I make my way towards them, wiping the sweat from my forehead. It's ok. It'll be ok now.

As I'm approaching, they resume walking. I look into the distance. My heart plunges. The sight before my eyes makes me double over. Whatever sweat I managed to get off is back in greater quantity.

Drury Lane. No, not here. Not now. No, they can't. They can't be doing this. How do they know?

The Fortune Theatre. The fucking Fortune Theatre. I can't move. Haven't moved a muscle. I hear voices as people, disgruntled, can't pass, have to steer round me, are frustrated. I feel them clipping my heels, but I don't move.

I can't see the Wongs any more, but I know where they are, know where they've gone, know why they've gone there. They've gone there to fuck with my mind, to push me over the edge. And it's working: right now, I'm losing it. With every tremble, I feel closer to the floor – I am closer to hell.

I crouch down on my knees. The first tear escapes and is swiftly followed by more. Silent tears. A man shouldn't be like this.

"Are you all right?" a voice asks. I look up. A parking attendant is standing above me. "Are you all right?" he repeats.

"No," is all I can say. "No."

He pats me on the shoulder. "Is there any way I can help?" he asks.

Again: "No."

"Are you sure?"

I stand up, look him in the eye. "No," I say, clueless.

Then the only words that I have in my head. "*The Woman in Black*," I say. "*The Woman in Black!*"

I run away from him, cross the road without looking, hear a car braking as it almost collides with me. Run on, further, faster. Just a few more steps, lunges really.

I stop. I look up. I look ahead. The signs tell me it's true, that I'm really here. All over again. I'm back at the beginning, the beginning of my journey, my journey into the abyss, into a fucking black hole. The Fortune Theatre. *The Woman in Black*.

They're inside.

*

DCI Morgan's feet were on his desk. He held a coffee mug in his hand. With the other he rubbed his temple. "Fucking headache," he said.

Kate Nielsen stood behind his visitor's chair. She shuffled on her feet.

"No," he said, "not enough. I'd be laughed at if I gave you permission and I'm not prepared to be made into a laughing stock ever again. Fuck!" He looked down at his lap where his coffee had just spilled.

"I only want to question them. If Simmons is convinced, maybe we should be taking him seriously."

"You know, sometimes people are just fucking nutters."

"Really, sir, I think it's worth taking a deeper look into them."

"Then look," he said, dabbing at his trousers with a tissue

he'd taken from a box on his desk. "But you look quietly and don't piss anyone off. I don't want any more complaints. Besides, what about this mobile phone? Have you got the records yet?"

"Still waiting. Should be with me by the afternoon."

"So that's what you need first. Get some proof that this Michaels woman is a fucking woman and not some chimpanzee at London Zoo. Poke your nose around. Find out what this Simmons guy is up to and find out everything about her. You've got no home address and no work address. So answer the question: is she fucking real?" He threw the tissue and it landed in a nearby bin. "And get me some fucking painkillers, will you?"

*

From a corner shop, down the road from the theatre, I bought a bottle of Evian and a packet of tissues. I poured the first part of the water over my face, dried it off with a couple of tissues, blew my nose and drank the rest to quench the indefinable thirst I felt.

Now I'm back at the theatre and walking inside. I've decided to go right in there, walk up to them and confront them. I'm going to stand in front of them and refuse to move until they explain how they knew I was following them, why they took me to London Gateway and how they knew about *The Woman in Black*. Do they know even more? Do they know what was in my mind when I was driving with Jennie down the M1? Did they know about my plans to propose? While I admit this all sounds ridiculous, nothing would surprise me any more.

I walk into the foyer, the vibrant red interior a stark contrast to the dullness outside. To my left are the stairs that lead to the stalls. I go straight to them, unsure of what I'm going to say to the Wongs when I reach them but confident that initiating a confrontation is the only way forwards.

As I'm about to move down the stairs, I hear a voice. "Can I see your ticket please, sir?"

I turn around. An usher is coming towards me. I try to speak, but words don't come out; he's caught me off guard.

"Ticket?" he repeats.

"I, em, I need to get one."

"The box office is there," he says, in a tone that implies I'm not going to get away with that old trick, and points to my right.

I take a couple of large strides to the box office counter. A stalls seat would take me downstairs, but I suddenly realise that the Wongs may have seats in the circle; they could be upstairs. Unsure, I gamble for the stalls – the best seats, especially for *The Woman in Black* and the woman's entrance – hoping that's where they'll be sitting, pay by credit card, grab my ticket and dash down the stairs, an announcement on the pager system informing me that the show will start in two minutes.

Hoping they're in the bar, I take a sharp right when I get to the bottom of the stairs. My feet involuntarily stick to the floor and I'm stopped when I see the table I was sitting at only days ago. And now I've been brought back here again. Why? I can't begin to comprehend a reason.

"Excuse me, sir," a voice calls, snapping me out of the memory.

I look to the side. The barman – the same barman who poured me some water the last time I was here – is drying a glass with a tea towel.

"Yes," I say, thinking I see a hint of recollection in his eyes. Perhaps he remembers me. His mouth moves, but I can't take in the meaning of what he says. I just nod my head, his words sounding like static. He raises his eyebrows.

"Okay?" I see him say.

"Sorry?"

"The show's about to start. You've had your final call. You really must take your seat if you don't want to miss the start of the show. Do you want anything?"

I can't tell him about the Wongs, much as I want to. "No," I say, "I've got a bottle of water." The words come out like a mumble as I take steps backwards and end up at the stalls entrance. An usher, a pretty young girl of about eighteen, sees me dithering and steps towards me.

"Can I take your ticket?" she asks.

I begin to pat my pockets and find the ticket in my back trouser pocket.

"Thank you. This way," she says and the lights begin to fade. She points. "Just in there. The third seat along."

I nod my head and smile my thanks. As I sit, I look around, trying to spot them. There are a lot of people in here. A rough estimation makes me think about two hundred. There are many empty seats, but they're scattered around. I can see that the Wongs are definitely not near me. I'm only able to see the backs of heads of the people at the front – I'm in the fifteenth row – so I'm unable to make out any faces. I can't see up to the balcony from where I am either, so I pray they're somewhere down here.

A man stands on the stage. He tries reading from a book.

I remove my coat and use the angle I have to put myself into in order to put the coat on the floor to scan the entire row to my right. No sign of them. To my left there are only two people. Not them.

The man on the stage isn't doing a good job; he's struggling to read. I'm vaguely aware of the voice that calls out from the back of the auditorium and tells the man on stage that he's doing it all wrong. When I realise what part of the play it is, I turn back to take the chance to see the back five or so rows of people. I keep looking behind me long after the point when the actor runs up to the stage and joins his partner. But the Wongs are not there. My only chance is that they're sitting up front, or that I can catch them at the end of the show as they come down from upstairs. For now, anyway, I have no choice: I have to sit through what Jennie and I were supposed to enjoy on Saturday. I have to sit through the fear, the emotions, that we were meant to share. And another pang of sorrow and guilt hits me when I realise that soon, very soon, if Jennie were by my side, I'd be comforting her from the forces that are about the consume the stage and theatre. The sheer thrill, the sheer horror.

If this were Saturday, I'd be only two hours away from proposing to her. Life would be perfect.

*

Nielsen decided to half listen to Morgan. She'd press the Wongs gently; make an impression without creating a nuisance of herself and risk a complaint. Respectfully and mindfully.

She parked outside the Wongs' house. There were just as few people around today as yesterday. She walked up the path and arrived at the front door. She pressed the doorbell.

When no one answered, she pressed the bell ringer again. Still no luck, so she knocked on the door with her hand.

She waited for a moment longer and, when no one answered, removed her mobile phone from her pocket. She rang the station. As she spoke, she moved to the side gate. She pressed her face close to its wooden structure and peered through a small gap. She could see a tidy garden, a shed at the bottom, nothing more.

"I need a number," she said. She gave the Wongs' address. "Patch me through."

The line came to life. She could hear it down the mobile but also from the phone inside. No answerphone. It cut off when no one answered.

The Wongs weren't home. She'd have to come back.

Before she left, Nielsen reached up and ran her hand across the top of the gate. Its surface was rough, sharp.

*

The play is a lot scarier than I remember. I've already jumped three times, which means that Jennie would definitely have wanted me to hold her. Everything would have been exactly as I'd planned.

The interval arrives in no time and I scan each of the rows in the stalls. That's when I spot them. They're there, near the front. I wait for the right moment to approach them, to grab them, to do something, anything. But they don't move; they stay in their bloody seats for the entire fifteen minutes and, before I can figure out what I should do, as if time has travelled on an express train, the lights are dimming and the show's resuming.

*

Nielsen sat at her desk, the phone in her hand. She'd received the list of all the Jennie Michaelses within a fifty-mile radius and spent the past hour working her way through it, making a phone call to each Jennie Michaels on the list. She'd just made her twelfth call and was none the wiser.

Sam Cook and DS Owen Hewitt were at their desks. Sam had offered to help Nielsen with the calls, but she'd refused.

The first Jennie Michaels was a teacher, the second a nurse, the third ran her own business, the fourth had three

135

kids and was living on benefits, the fifth worked in a shop. The sixth was actually a school girl – only sixteen years old, her mother had said, the girl at school for the day. And the same was true of next six – just normal women living normal lives. Nothing extraordinary, nothing unusual, nothing about the actual Jennie Michaels she was searching for.

Nothing more than a blank.

*

I know when the play is getting close to the end, so I ready myself to act fast. I plan what I'm going to do as soon as the curtain call happens. I'm going to stand, that much I know. A standing ovation, people around me will think, but I'll actually be looking to see when the Wongs move. And when they do, I will step in their way and cut them off. I have to approach them here, where the number of people around us will be fewer than outside the theatre and they'll have fewer options of escape. Approach them, confront them, then they won't be able to deny what they're doing here and trying to do to me.

In little more than ten minutes, the lights fade for the final time. The audience's applause begins. I'm up on my feet. Fortunately, only a few people join me in the standing ovation and they're over to the sides. I fix my eyes on where the Wongs are sitting.

The actors take their second bows and, if tradition is followed, there'll be one more. The Wongs are sitting.

The actors are bowing for a third time, they make their way off the stage and the house lights come up.

People start to stand, put their coats on and leave their rows. My view quickly becomes blocked, so I'm unable to see beyond the people only a few rows ahead of me. I decide to walk to the centre of my row. I squeeze past two ladies and three men who are either putting their coats on or standing around chatting. So many of the faces I pass look relieved that it's over. So many of them look pale. Believe me, I think, I know exactly how you all feel; the difference is a play has done this to you, whereas real life has done it to me.

I'm on my tiptoes trying to see through the crowds. The dizziness returns to my head and I really need to hold on to something, but I have to keep moving. And that's when they come back into view. Coming out of the third or fourth row, Mr Wong moves slowly, with his wife shuffling behind him. They look like they don't belong together: the more I see them, the more oddities I recognise.

I start to move towards the end of my row to head them off in the aisle. I tread on a man's foot as I try to pass him. He doesn't look pleased and I apologise without stopping. Three more people are standing in my way, so I squeeze past them. "Excuse me," I say with no politeness in my tone. I'm too rushed to bother what they'll think of me.

As I near the end of the row, I see they're not far away from me, down the aisle. Only one more person to pass. My foot catches hers and I stumble forwards into the aisle. I manage to catch hold of the chair on the opposite side of the aisle. As I regain my footing and straighten my posture, my eyes meet theirs.

They recognise me; I see it in their faces. But they look surprised. Shocked. Could seeing me have done it, or is it the effect of the play?

They take a step back. A final few people go around us. The words – I've lost my words. I know I have to speak, but I'm silent and just staring at them.

Mr Wong breaks the silence. "What," he says, "what are you doing here?"

I don't answer him. I can't focus.

"What do you want?" he says. Now there's irritation in his voice.

I clutch hold of my stomach, desperate to get the words out. All I manage is "Why?", fighting against the pain in my head. "Why?" again. "Why are you doing this to me?"

Wong takes hold of his wife with an arm around her shoulders. He looks concerned.

He's hiding it.

"What do you mean?" he asks.

"What do I mean?" I shout. "Me? What the fuck can I mean? What part of why don't you understand, you Chinese prick?" Footsteps are coming towards us from the back of the theatre. I don't turn around. "Why?" I repeat. Now even louder: "Why?"

"Is everything all right here?" an out-of-breath voice asks. I look to my side. The theatre manager – the same man as the other day.

"You," I say.

He recognises me. His eyes widen. "You," he says. "What's going on here?"

"This man," Wong says, "he's bothering us. Really, we must go."

He tries to step past us. I block his path. "No way," I say. "You're not getting away from me now. Not until you tell me why you brought me here!"

Mrs Wong is almost out of sight, behind her husband's back, her head bowed. The theatre manager is trying his best to step between us, block me off and give Wong and Mrs the space to leave. But there's no way that's happening.

"What have you done with Jennie?"

"Not this again," the manager says with a groan.

"They have her! They've done something to her! I know!"

I'm shouting all the time now. I'm getting louder and louder. I'm pushing towards Wong, and the manager has his

138

hands on my chest, trying to calm me down. I won't take it. I can't take it. I need to have answers.

"No more!" Now even Wong has started to shout. "Enough!" I can't believe he has the nerve. This is no coincidence; he's led me here. London Gateway and now here. I'm not letting it go.

"Tell me where she is! Tell me or I swear to God–"

I'm cut off. Wong tries to push through, his left arm securely around his wife.

I won't let him go though. "No!" I shout, grabbing him round the neck as he passes me. "I want to know!"

From behind, the manager grabs me round the waist. Two ushers join him and hold onto me. One of them takes me by my arms; the other by my neck. I kick at Wong and manage to connect with his hip. He falls to his knees and his wife jumps away from us. I continue kicking and shouting. One of my kicks is too wild and I end up falling back. One of the ushers goes down with me and we hit the floor hard. His knee ends up in my spine as we collide and I'm winded. I can't breathe. Sweat and spit cover my face and I shout Jennie's name repeatedly, even though I can barely take a breath.

I shout her name so intently that I don't see the police officers as they arrive and stand above me while the ushers and manager hold me down. I only realise they're here when they roll me over, as I gasp for air, as they handcuff me.

Chapter Sixteen

"What the fuck did he do?"

DCI Morgan was standing behind his desk. The volume of his words was louder than Kate Nielsen had ever heard from him – and she'd listened to him scream many times before. His hands were on his hips and his face looked like he was recovering from being punched.

"You're telling me that fucking prick is stalking people now?"

Nielsen had been interrupted from finishing the Jennie Michaelses phone calls by a call from officers in London revealing that John Simmons had been picked up at the Fortune Theatre. "Not stalking, he was following them. You understand he believes they've somehow taken over the house where she lived."

"Well, fuck him and what he believes. And fuck you if you believe his ramblings. The man is obviously insane. He follows a couple to London – that's almost thirty miles from where he lives – then he goes into the theatre they've paid to be in to see a show, causes a scene, then attacks this Wong fellow. You have got to be kidding me he's not insane. He's a fucking fruitcake."

Nielsen knew there was no point in trying to convince Morgan otherwise when he was like this; best to ride out the storm and wait for the squall to die down.

"You put your faith in what he told you. You're helping him out and then he goes and acts like this. Impatient little bastard. What I suggest you do is go and see him and tell him to fuck right off!"

As he sat down and pasted his legs atop the table, he said,

"Prick." Then, for good effect, he repeated himself three more times.

Nielsen waited to see if the silence was going to last. After a number of seconds, it appeared as though it would. Seizing the opportunity, she spoke up. "Sir, I will go to see him and I will tell him, in very strong words, that we're handling this."

"We're not handling anything. Not for that crazy prick."

"That I'm handling things, excuse me. And that if he wants my help, this kind of thing can never happen again."

"And what about the mobile records?"

"Got them. Pay as you go. Unused for calling out. Calls received were only from John Simmons' number and one other unidentified mobile number. Not registered, also pay as you go."

"So that proves it. She doesn't exist. He's nuts! Probably bought the phone himself."

"No, sir, not quite. I don't believe it does. That second mobile number came from somewhere. Who called it? And he had tickets for that show. Then the Wongs did. You can't honestly think they went there coincidentally. There's more to this, I just know it."

"You tell him," Morgan jumped in, "that if there's any more crazy shit he'll be answering to me. I'll have him in here and I'll fuck him up. And you better watch out too. You'll be answering to that side of me as well. Now fuck off and sort him out."

She couldn't have waited for a better time to leave. DS Nielsen was out of there.

*

It wasn't long ago that I was sitting in one of these holes and here I am again. This cell is cramped and cold and the echo of my breathing makes me even more nervous. I was literally thrown into here more than an hour ago and I've not heard a word from anyone since.

I had to take on the Wongs like that; I know I did. I had to challenge them, had to show them I'm not going to be messed with any more, that someone is on to them.

They led me to the Fortune Theatre – that much is clear – but I have no idea why, why they were toying with me, what their purpose was, what they hoped to achieve. Well, I achieved what I wanted to; I got their attention and made them realise they're not going to get away with it.

But now stuck I'm here. And the strength I felt when I went after Wong has subsided; loss has crept in – because I'm confined and not out there looking for Jennie, pursuing the Wongs and getting answers from them. Where is Jennie? What have they done to her? Why are they playing games with me? And who's behind all this? Is it them – are the Wongs the masterminds behind all this – or is there someone else? And what the fuck has happened to them? They could be escaping, now that they know I know.

The thought that there could be an unidentified person – or persons – behind the scenes, watching, making life-and-death decisions, lifts my concern to an even higher level. I can't leave Jennie out there for much longer. I have to get out of here, but I don't know what I should do when I'm free. I don't know what my next step is. It seems like I've exhausted all possibilities. I can go back to the Wongs and hassle them until they reveal what they know, follow them, threaten them. But what if that leads to nothing? What if I can't learn what I desperately want to know? What if Jennie forever remains a memory?

I'm getting sick of being helpless and I'm trying, believe me, I'm trying to make a difference and do the job of a police force. But if it is more than one person, do I really have the power alone to stop them?

I raise my head and all I see is grey walls. I'm sitting on a flat mattress – deflated, that's if it ever was inflated – through which the springs are poking. My skin takes an abrasive rub every time I shuffle, and I shuffle frequently because I can't get comfortable. There's no window in here; just the steel door, as colourless as the walls and covered in scratches.

Less than a week ago I'd never seen the inside of a prison cell – and I never imagined I would. I was a model citizen, and now look at me. In a prison cell twice in two days, and my behaviour in public was dangerous. But I'm desperate, desperate for the truth, and prepared to act.

As I'm about to close my eyes – hoping that sleep will take hold of me – I hear locks rattling. The door opens outwards and the uniformed officer who put me in here enters. He tells me to follow him.

I feel like protesting, telling him that I need to be released or at least spoken to and listened to, that I need to be allowed to get on with my life, or the life that I've recently been thrust into, but I don't. I've said so many things, protested till I was blue in the face, and where has it got me? Now it's down to me and me alone. Bide your time and you'll soon be out of here. Then act and act alone.

All this surely means I've got to follow through with what I saw before as my only option: get to the Wongs, get in front of them and get some answers – and don't take no for an answer. Don't back down. Don't surrender. Make sure they're the ones who give in.

We walk down a corridor and through a large door that locks automatically as soon as we pass. We turn right and walk up a set of stairs. At the top, it's a left turn, the area carpeted now, and we stop outside a well-kept door. Everything at this point is looked after. The walls are cream and the notice boards, which are full of information, are blue.

The officer knocks on the door. He opens it and steps aside so that I can enter.

I recognise her even though all I can see is the back of her head. She's seated facing the wall, a desk in front of her, another chair, empty, behind it.

"Take a seat," she says.

I walk round the desk and do as she tells me. She doesn't offer me a drink this time. And I'm thirsty as hell.

Detective Nielsen looks calm but serious. Her eyes are telling me that she's going to speak and wants to be heard. She waits until she sees I'm settled. "Mr Simmons," she begins, "you've caused a lot of trouble. For yourself and for me. If you think that going after these people is going to get anyone on your side, you're completely wrong."

"Listen," I blurt out, "I had no choice. Someone has to be looking for Jennie."

"Mr Simmons, I –" with the emphasis on the *I* – "am looking for Jennie Michaels. I've issued her description and details to over twenty forces. Her description is on our website and on three missing persons' websites. I've even pressed for a media appeal. Do you really think I could be doing any more?"

"Those people, the Wongs, they led me there. Don't you see? That was where I was taking Jennie the day she disappeared."

"Coincidences do happen, you know," she says nonchalantly. She's lost the concern she showed me before. And it's my fault. I've made her concern dissolve into nothingness, into a routine state. I have to persuade her – my cause is not lost, it's still worth the fight. I'd do this alone, but she's able to cover so much more ground than me.

"But really–"

"No," she snaps, not letting me try. "You'll do the listening now. I've worked on a lot of cases and you haven't, so listen. I'm working on ten others just like this one. I *think* they're connected. They seem the same in that it's always a young woman, twenties to thirties, and they happen in close proximity to one another. But the way it happens is always different. We've got a serial abductor and I thought Jennie Michaels was his latest victim. Everything seems to fit into the whole, except one thing. You, which is why I say *thought*. You're not behaving in a normal way. Attacking that man in the middle of a busy theatre at the same time as I'm asking my DCI to allow me to go on television to appeal about Jennie Michaels specifically, something that he doesn't feel is right but something I can work on with him, well, what you did fucked up every chance I had of getting his support and authorisation."

"But I'm desperate!"

"Don't you see – it's not all up to me. I have to answer to people too. And so do you. You have to answer to *me*. And right now there's little you can say to make the way you've crapped on this situation acceptable."

Her cheeks are flushed; she's annoyed with me and now I'm frustrated with myself for making things tricky for her. I didn't realise she was doing so much; I just thought she'd talk the talk and not act.

I punch the desk in frustration. "I wish that were my face," I tell her when I see her twitch in her seat, although she covers her surprise quite well. "Sorry," I add, now calmly, "I should have known better."

"Yes," she confirms, "you should have." A long pause follows. "So where are we now?"

It's rhetorical, I know, so I don't answer.

She leans back in her chair and looks around the room. I hear the strain in her voice as she yawns and says, "You know, I can only try so hard. I will keep on trying, but for now we'll have to wait and see if any of the contact I've made bears any fruit. We're going to have to be patient – you particularly. You can't go round being a vigilante. You just can't."

"I understand," I tell her, but something inside me still disagrees; it always will. "Hear me out though. This couple, who have somehow ended up at Jennie's house, from where I've picked her up time after time in the past three weeks, were my only hope. I sat at home and tried to get on with normal things, tried to feel normal, but I couldn't just sit around and do nothing. So I went to Jennie's workplace, Brown's Solicitors, and her boss, Dave Bryant, well he doesn't work there. And then they told me no one called Jennie Michaels works there either."

"I know. I went there too."

"But I've picked her up from that office a few times in the past three weeks. So then all I could think of after that was the Wongs. I didn't believe them when they said Jennie didn't live there."

"So are Brown's Solicitors lying as well?"

"Look, I've been there; I've seen her stepping out of that house. I'm not going mad. They must have been lying, or they must have something to do with this. I don't know about her work. There are too many holes." I clear my throat. "So I went to Sanders Road this morning and waited and watched. When the Wongs came out, I admit it, I followed them. Maybe that was wrong." Here she tries to interject. "Okay," I say, "I know it was wrong, but what happened made it right. They got onto the M1. I kept my distance. I was sure they couldn't spot me. What happened next, though, shows I was wrong. They knew I was there; they must have. There's simply no other explanation." I lean forwards so that our faces are close. "They turned off at London Gateway services, just as I did with Jennie on Saturday. Why would they do that? Yes, maybe a coincidence, so I went in after them and followed them back out, again thinking they hadn't seen me. They got back into the car. I was startled. Their move had shaken me up. But I kept my level head on as best I could, followed them to Brent Cross, then into town where they had lunch in Leicester Square. Not once did they give any indication that they knew I was there. Actually, I was quite confident about them not knowing I was there, even after the London Gateway turn of events. But then they led me into Covent Garden and I became a wreck. They went to the Fortune Theatre to see *The Woman in Black*. *The Woman in Black* is the play I was taking Jennie to when she disappeared. They couldn't have known that unless they are somehow involved. It's where I went after the police officers left me at London Gateway. Maybe they were watching me. Maybe they followed me or had me followed. I didn't know where to turn and thought maybe Jennie had played a trick on me and gone on ahead alone. When I got there, of course, she wasn't there. But I was there, at the Fortune Theatre. And today they led me there again. So they must have known. And how could they have known if they weren't somehow involved? That's no coincidence. They were fucking with my mind. Can't you see that?"

She leans back and takes a deep breath. "Maybe so," she says. She believes me. I smile in relief. Thankfully. "But that still doesn't give us grounds to accuse them of anything. Even if it sounds so coincidental."

"Much too coincidental," I agree. "So what now?"

"First I go and see if I can get you out of the trouble you're in. Disturbing the peace is what they said when I arrived and we'll hope the Wongs don't press charges of assault. Then you'll go home, if I'm allowed to let you go,

148

and I will speak to my DCI. I don't know what we can do, but something sounds off here."

Detective Nielsen leaves me with nothing more than a nod of the head. I sit in the room for almost half an hour; I know the time now because of the clock that sits on the wall above the door. And all the while I think there's no way I can do as she's asked me, despite everything she's said, even though maybe I should listen. There's no way I can go home, sit around as though nothing's happened and wait. I will act, I will find out the truth and I will not give up. I can only be sorry if that's too much.

Or, at the same time, not enough.

Chapter Seventeen

"Just give me permission to do that much."

"You mean, say it's fine for you to go after two people who have been assaulted in public by your wacko. I already told you. And now because of him I tell you doubly, no fucking chance."

Nielsen had felt obliged to try, despite DCI Morgan being the last person she wanted to face.

"You know, Kate, I really think you should have your head examined. Has it screwed your brain up that much? Are you really so lonely that you take to the first sad arsehole that comes along?"

She understood what the it was he was referring to. And it hurt. But she wouldn't show him how much. Yes, she was lonely and felt the need to help others, even though, on the whole, she couldn't sum up the desire to help herself. But she cared, even though the job drove her mad, the loneliness made her sick and the world depressed her. Even though sometimes she could see nothing in it worth fighting for. Even though the memories of one night plagued her on a daily basis, every sleeping hour, every waking moment. Helping others, even though it was hard as hell, was what kept her going.

They were standing in the area that was known as the detectives' corridor – a corridor off which several offices were located. Nielsen hadn't waited for Morgan to get comfy behind his desk; she'd leapt at him the second she saw him after returning from her visit with John Simmons.

"They could be coincidences, I get it," she said. "But really, we all know that coincidence after coincidence is just too coincidental. They must have known something. Surely they wouldn't have gone to the two places in London – out of everywhere they could have gone – where he'd gone when all this trouble began."

"That's if there was any genuine trouble in the first place," Morgan countered. "We still don't even know if this Jennie Michaels is real or part of that crazy bastard's imagination. So how about starting there?"

"I'm trying."

"Get your proof that she *is* real and I'll consider letting you bring the Wing Wangs in. Okay?"

He didn't wait for an answer. He took the two steps that were necessary to get into his office and closed the door behind him, leaving Nielsen standing alone, which she saw as a conversation-over indicator.

She walked to the end of the corridor and entered the open-plan office she shared. Space for the DSs and DCs. No office of your own until you moved up.

*

I'm home and have spent the early part of the evening doing more online research. I will not sit still.

The more I read about these cases, the more helpless I feel. It happens so randomly. These women, they're all different and taken from seemingly unrelated places. The only similarity between them is their ages: twenties to thirties, with the exception of the youngest who was eighteen. The police still hadn't officially announced that the disappearances were connected.

I've poured myself a scotch and tonic water. Normally I save a drink like this for special occasions, but I need it to help myself remain calm. In fact, the glass is almost empty and it'll soon be time to refill it.

I spent a couple of hours after being at the police station driving around the city. As many small roads and main roads as I could hit before it got dark. I'm thinking of everywhere Jennie could be – if only it would be as easy as pulling into a street and discovering her, but I won't give up hope. Anything is worth trying.

I can't help but think about the puzzles I've encountered so far and I try to make sense of them. Jennie disappears from the services, the Wongs live at her house, women are going missing, there's one police officer, at least, who's willing to give me the time of day and she's still unsure, Dave Bryant doesn't exist, I follow the Wongs and they lead me around London. Then we end up at the Fortune Theatre.

None of it makes sense.

Take Dave Bryant, for instance. Jennie spoke about him; she described him and, it was so clear, she knew him. He has to be her boss. He has to be as real as she is.

I sit closer to the computer desk. It's worth a try. I go to the Google homepage and type in 'Dave Bryant, solicitor, St Albans'. There's no direct hit, but there are mentions of a Dave Bryant, solicitor, and some cases he's worked on. Some newspaper articles. Some quotes. My eyes scan the screen. I'm not patient enough to read the text closely.

And there it is: Hertfordshire. Dave Bryant, Hertfordshire lawyer. Then: Harpenden. That's not far from here. Could it be that for some reason Jennie didn't tell me the full truth? Could it be that in every deception there's an element of truth?

I Google: 'Dave Bryant, solicitor, Harpenden, Herts'.

It's the first result. *Dave Bryant, solicitor at law.* I grab a pen and write down his office address. Could he be *the* Dave Bryant? It's the only lead I have, so I'm going to pursue it to my fullest capacity.

The doorbell rings. I check the time: almost ten o'clock.

Strange. Perhaps it's some news from the police. Perhaps it's Detective Nielsen.

I heave myself out of my desk chair and go down the stairs. I unlock the door and open it.

Nobody's there. I step out and look around.

Must be kids.

I look left and right again and see nothing. Kids are always so quick. It's not the first time this has happened.

I relock the door and go back upstairs. As soon as I sit in the chair, there it goes again: another knock at the door. Now I know it's kids, so I ignore it.

Then silence.

After two minutes, there's another knock. This time it's repeated consistently, a pounding.

Annoyed and unable to concentrate, I get up and return to the front door. It might be fun for kids, but they have no idea what I'm going through and they're not helping.

I unlock and open the door.

Nobody again. I step out, further this time. I reach the pavement and look left and right. Nothing. "For fuck's sake," I say to myself.

I turn around and go back inside, locking the door behind me. I take the stairs two at a time and grab my glass off the desk. Then I go back downstairs and into the kitchen. I take the scotch bottle from the cupboard, pour a large double into the glass, leave it on the counter and take the tonic water out of the fridge. Once the glass is filled I put the tonic back in.

The drink's smell is soothing. As I taste it, there's another knock at the front door. This time I'm close by, so I move at pace towards it. I unlock it and yank it open. As it moves inwards, I catch sight of someone dressed in dark clothing.

That's all I see. Something collides with my forehead and I fall down. The glass smashes and its contents covers me.

I see nothing else, just black.

*

How it went down:

Held down by handcuffs. Tied to a chair. The room in darkness. Noises. Breathing. Occasional sniggers.

Tears. Sweat. Fear.

Agony.

A broken nose. A black eye. A dislocated jaw. Swollen wrists. The taste of blood.

Death approaching. Heart racing. Sick inducing.

Awareness, despite blackness. Despite deliriousness. Despite death approaching.

Then unaware. Too much.

A hand on hair. A finger on neck. Then teeth.

Mouth open. Unable to scream. All internal.

Eyes open. Eyes closed. Aware. Then not.

Hand on breast. Squeezing. Unable to see. Able to feel. Hand between legs. One hand pressing, one pushing.

Naked. Woozy. Head spinning.

Agony.

A broken nose. Like mush. Face pushing against it.

Aware, then not.

On the floor. Weight on top. Unable to see. Tears. Lifeless.

Void.

No more movement.

Hands on neck. Squeezing.

Tears.

Unaware.

Over.

*

155

A female paramedic is patching up my forehead and Detective Nielsen is standing in front of me. I'm sitting on the bottom step of the staircase.

"And you don't know who it was?"

"I told you, he hit me and I went down. That's it. I don't know who it was and I didn't see anything other than dark clothing. It was black – that's all I can tell you."

"Okay." She nods. She's thinking about something – whether to believe me, I think. "And has anything been taken?"

"Not that I can see, no. But I haven't been able to look around properly. I don't know if whoever it was came in." She makes a note of something on a notepad. I can't see what – she's too high up for me to catch a glimpse. "Look, I know how this looks, but I'm telling you someone attacked me."

"And the alcohol?"

I realise what Detective Nielsen actually means is, why do you smell so badly of booze?

"When he hit me, I fell. I had a glass of scotch in my hand. It landed on me. I am not intoxicated."

"Sure."

"I am allowed a drink, aren't I?"

"So why did they only hit you?"

"Sorry?"

"They didn't want you dead then? Why did they only hit you, not more?"

"You're the police, you tell me."

She crouches down and takes a close look at my forehead. "Doesn't look too bad," she says. "Lucky they didn't kill you. Incapacitated like that, I mean, it wouldn't have been difficult. Easier to end an unconscious life than a conscious one. You don't have to look the person in the eye." She stands back up again. "Look, you clearly need to rest. Make sure you do that. Sit tight and I'll be in touch."

"I know, you told me that already."

"I mean don't go out tomorrow, John. Stay put and let me do my job."

"Somebody just attacked me."

"Exactly. Even more reason to stay indoors, locked up and safe."

I can't stay at home. I feel like a broken record, but until Jennie's found I won't change. I have to find out what Dave Bryant knows, whether he knows anything. "Detective, Dave Bryant exists."

"What?"

"There's a Dave Bryant in Harpenden. A solicitor. I have to see him."

She shakes her head. "No you don't, John," she says forcefully. "Leave the man alone. Jennie told you where she worked and she didn't work there. She lied to you, John. Understand that. Jennie Michaels as you knew her is not the Jennie Michaels other people knew. Get over it and spare innocent people who have nothing to do with this. I'm not going to get you out of trouble again."

I don't answer her. I want to listen, but something inside me won't accept that Jennie lied about her work. About her home too. About her life, in fact.

Nielsen takes a step forwards. "I mean it, stay here and wait for me to call you."

I don't make eye contact – just shake my head. I don't say anything either.

"All done here," the paramedic says, standing upright.

I smile at her – it's fake and redundant, but she doesn't seem to mind.

"You'll be fine," and she moves away.

No, I think, I won't. You don't know the half of it.

Nielsen turns away from me and walks with the

paramedic, talking all the while. The paramedic nods, then shakes her head. Nielsen writes things down.

When they're done, she comes back to me. I'm still sitting on the step, even though my backside has gone numb.

"I meant what I said, John. Do not leave. And do not bother anyone else."

Our conversation is over. There's nothing more I can say.

"Give me the space to do my job."

Before I look up, she's gone.

*

He had been thinking about her since the last time. The commotion after he'd hurt John Simmons had given him the chance to watch her. He'd been thinking about when would be the right time. When to make Kate Nielsen an even bigger part of this.

Not yet.

He was waiting for her to come out of the house. When she did, she jumped straight into her car and moved off. He followed. This time of night he didn't have to keep too much distance between them.

He'd always be nearby watching, until he decided when to end it for her. She wouldn't know, not until it was too late, but he'd be there.

First, though, he had an idea. It would bring a whole new meaning to this game of theirs.

He'd expected her to go home, get some rest, but she went back to the station. He decided not to hang around for her. He couldn't risk staying out so late too often. He had to remain undetected.

And Kate Nielsen always seemed to work late. She'd be easy to find.

He returned home.

Chapter Eighteen

I spent a sleepless night at home. I read a little, couldn't focus, couldn't eat, couldn't get close to resuming a normal life. Two things kept me unfocused: Dave Bryant and a hand coming towards me. If I can be hurt so easily, I can only imagine what Jennie is going through.

At eight o'clock sharp, I leave the house for Dave Bryant's office in Harpenden. Every road I turn into is filled with cars, rush-hour traffic out in full force. Traffic is particularly slow as I pass a school and have to wait behind rows of parents dropping their children off.

I arrive at the office, which is in the high street, at a little before quarter past nine. I park the car around the corner and walk to the building. As I enter, I immediately recognise how different this place is from Brown's Solicitors. This is clearly a one-man operation. There's a small waiting area, a desk and a sofa. Behind the desk is a door that leads to an office. The name Dave Bryant is printed on it. Behind the desk sits a woman. She looks up from reading a magazine and smiles at me. "Can I help?" she asks.

"I need to see Mr Bryant."

She pulls a diary towards her. "Mr Bryant has some time available this morning. His rate is a hundred and fifty pounds per hour."

"No, I don't want–" I stop myself. I don't want to explain again and risk her telling me to leave. She must think I'm normal. "That'll be fine." I take my wallet out and hand her my credit card. She swipes it through a machine and stares at it patiently. It responds slowly.

She says, "Takes a little time. It'll be done in a moment."

I smile at her, perhaps to reassure her that I do have the funds, perhaps to reassure myself that I have to do this. I don't know what I'm going to say to Dave Bryant, but however I tackle things I will find out whether he knows anything. When I smile at her, it's the first time I really look at her. She's maybe forty years old with curly blonde hair and a large nose.

The card machine comes to life and a receipt comes out of it. "Here you go," she says as she tears it off and hands it to me. "Take a seat. He'll be about ten minutes."

I thank her and sit down. There are magazines on a small coffee table, so I open one, but I'm unable to focus on reading, so I end up glaring at the pages. I pretend to read because I don't want to attract any attention from the receptionist.

In only a couple of minutes, she summons me into the office. It's a tiny space filled with a desk, a chair on either side of it, and a bookcase. Dave Bryant sits behind it. He has brown hair and a full beard. He's wearing a tweed jacket and rises as soon as he sees me. He reaches for my hand as he introduces himself. I tell him my name. He sits down and doesn't say anything else. He leans back in his chair and looks me in the eye. He's thinking.

As soon as I realise he isn't going to say anything else, I decide to lay all the information in front of him. I tell him about Jennie, but I don't say her name. I study him, look deep into the whites of his eyes to detect any kind of reaction that indicates he knows her, and say, finally, "Her name is Jennie Michaels."

As good an actor as any lawyer might be, he isn't good enough to hide it. I see it. His eyes change. He tries to conceal it, but it's there. I can't explain how, but I see a change clearly. And there's something in his demeanour, something slight.

160

His response surprises me: "Well, she's certainly never worked for me. It's a terribly tragic story, but I'm afraid, Mr Simmons, that I'm not going to be able to help you." He rises. "I'm not an investigator and it's clear to me that's what you need. You've met my receptionist and you can see it's not her. Now if you'll excuse me I really must be getting on." He pauses. "I have another meeting shortly."

I don't give him my hand. "But I've paid for the hour," I tell him.

"Not to worry," he says as he puts his hand to my back and ushers me out. "You certainly don't need a solicitor, so I'll make sure your payment is refunded."

He doesn't stop at the office door; he continues to move towards the main door and before I know it I'm outside on the high street. "But if I need to contact you?" I ask as he closes the door on me. I hear him lock the door from the inside.

He doesn't look back at me as I watch him through the window. He picks up the phone.

He's calling somebody.

I take several steps back and then move to the side so that I'm out of view. Something's wrong. He recognised Jennie's name. He got rid of me as quickly as he could. Then the phone call. To whom?

There are definitely more answers in there; he knows something.

I want to call Detective Nielsen, but something is stopping me from dialling. She won't be able to act immediately. I'm not even sure how much she believes me any more. Clues in there, clues we need to find urgently, might be lost if she takes her usual time. And I know she's being held back by her superiors, which won't improve in a day. So I quickly come to an unfortunate realisation: I'm going to have to find a way in there myself. I need to look around.

161

Tonight.

I walk back to my car and, as soon as I'm in it, I start to feel determined. This is necessary.

After a few minutes, I ring Detective Nielsen, knowing I won't tell her. I'll ask her for an update instead. Perhaps hearing how things are stale her end will make me feel better about committing a crime. I'll wait until I have evidence before I reveal the full truth to her.

Even though I'm not expecting any major news, I'm hopeful to hear that things are in motion the police's end and that they're making some progress, even slowly, on closing in on Jennie's captors. "Tell me," I say, "are you getting closer to finding Jennie?"

Wherever she is, the signal is weak. I can just about make out her words: "You've got to give me space. Be patient, John."

She sounds like a broken record. Plus I can tell she's still suspicious; too distanced. "You do believe me, don't you, about last night?" I decide to say.

She makes a noise.

"Really, Detective, I'm telling you. I was attacked."

She makes several noises and says little else. My story doesn't make sense, I can see that – why was I only hit and not killed? – but it happened. Just like Jennie's disappearance happened. It's as real as that. She doesn't believe me – so be it.

How do I know that she's even working on the case?

By being non-responsive, she convinces me that what I've planned is right: I have no option. Tonight I'll get into Dave Bryant's office and find evidence that he knows Jennie. Something, anything I can take to Detective Nielsen, and then she'll trust me and everything I've been saying all along.

*

162

Nielsen handed thirty pounds to the cashier and then took her change and travelcard from the counter. She walked to the left, put her ticket into the machine, and a green light informed her that she could proceed through the barrier. She walked down the corridor, picking up a free daily newspaper on her way, and went up the stairs. At the top, she came to the platform. She squeezed through the mass of people who were standing near the top of the staircase and found a space near the coffee shop window. Her choices were limited; it was the middle of rush hour. No way could I do this every day, she thought. No way I'd do it.

She checked out the monitor, which was high on the wall, and was notified that the train would arrive in three minutes.

It had been months since she'd taken the train to London and even longer since she'd been to London on a weekday. She rarely had time off work. Still had holiday entitlement remaining from last year.

She didn't see him enter the station behind her. He'd been thinking about her all night. Again. He was aching to take her; he didn't know how much longer he could hold out. But the next phase of their game would be soon, so he'd have to wait. His instinct told him she should be his last and it took all the force of his body to resist common sense and do her. He'd learned that being spontaneous didn't work in this game, he acknowledged that. Hers would be the most carefully planned.

Before Nielsen finished reading the two stories on the newspaper's front page, she heard the rumble of the train approaching.

When its doors opened, she stepped on board, along with dozens of other people. There were no seats free – she couldn't even see them. She stood in a gap, squashed between twelve strangers. No way she'd be able to read the paper.

He stepped aboard too. Into the next carriage along. He had to keep his distance. Until he decided otherwise.

During the whole journey, Nielsen's view was the back of a man's coat. That he was about six-five and that there were people either side of her and right behind her, pinning her in, prevented her from seeing anything else.

From the next carriage, he couldn't see her. He wanted to see her. He wanted to watch her every move.

Nielsen felt her phone vibrate in her pocket and somehow managed to get hold of it. "Kate Nielsen."

It was John Simmons. "Tell me," he said, "are you getting closer to finding Jennie?"

"You've got to give me space. Be patient, John."

"You do believe me, don't you, about last night?"

Nielsen cleared her throat and sighed.

"Really, Detective, I'm telling you. I was attacked."

Another sigh. "Let me call you later. I've got some things to check out and I'll call you with an update this evening." She didn't wait for John to answer. Hung up.

The train stopped five times en route and the journey to London was bumpy. Nielsen had nothing on which to grab, so she was relieved when the train reached Euston. She quickly got onto the platform and walked towards the exit barriers. When through them, she took the stairs on the right and entered the underground.

There was a crowd when he stepped off the train and most of it appeared to be moving in the same direction as Nielsen. He could easily go undetected. The baseball cap and the quantity of people around them would be enough.

If the train was busy, that was nothing compared to the number of people Nielsen encountered when she reached the Northern Line platform.

By the time the train arrived, it felt like an evacuee line

was gathered and desperate to board, desperate to evade an impending attack. As soon as the final passenger leaving the train stepped off, Nielsen was lifted and carried forwards by a wave of people behind her. She was taken into the carriage and clutched onto a metal pole, hoping she wouldn't be pushed out of the other side.

She hung on for the journey as more people got on. Somehow they fitted inside.

Again, he entered the next carriage. Again, he couldn't see her. He'd have to keep his wits about him; he didn't want to miss seeing when she got off the train.

Not much longer, Nielsen thought. Almost there. She was being hopeful more than anything.

She changed at Charing Cross, then did battle with the crowds again until she got off the train at Covent Garden. Up a steep and winding staircase and she found herself in sight of daylight. As she emerged into it, a sense of relief overwhelmed her. She felt better. She hated crowds that big, had been away from them for a long time.

Map in hand, she stood still as she searched for her direction.

As she looked at the map, surrounded by scores of people, he stood behind her. He decided to take a risk – he put his hand on her back. The touch made him want to take her there and then. He had to fight the desire.

He turned away quickly and didn't give her time to react, not that she did. She was still consumed by the map. The thrill remained with him. He wanted to turn around and go in for another feel, longer this time. But as he was about to make his move, she located what she was looking for and started walking to the right. A sharp right and she saw Covent Garden in front of her. When she entered it, she walked to the left and around part of the square. She took the road on the left and moved straight ahead.

It came into view within seconds. The Fortune Theatre. And the sign up high: *The Woman in Black*.

*

I'm in my car. I've moved it so that I'm across the road from Dave Bryant's office. My mobile is in my lap and I keep staring at it. I should call Detective Nielsen back and say more. I know that. But she doesn't trust me fully and I've got to be tactical. What good has her help done me – done Jennie – so far?

Something still urges me to rely on myself.

I guess sitting here is my version of a stakeout. I'm here, so I'll make use of my time. When I look away from the phone, I watch the office door. Want to see if I notice anyone or anything suspicious. If I can catch sight of Dave Bryant. If I can spot some kind of clue.

The longer I sit here, the more certain I become: I'm not going to call Detective Nielsen. I can't do anything that might give Bryant the chance to get rid of clues, that might put the momentum I've gained in jeopardy. Even though I hear Detective Nielsen shouting at me, asking me what the hell I think I'm doing, I'm ready.

I wait.

*

Nielsen showed her ID to the man behind the box office window.

"I'm looking for whoever dealt with a disturbance yesterday. When the police took away a man after a problem in the auditorium."

"That would be Larry Graham, the theatre manager."

"Can I see him?"

166

"He's just popped to the shop over the road to buy his lunch. Shouldn't be long."

"I'll wait."

In only a few minutes, a man entered and the box office worker nodded to Nielsen. She understood and moved towards Larry Graham, hand outstretched. "Mr Graham, Detective Sergeant Kate Nielsen. Can I have a few minutes of your time? Won't take long."

"Yesterday?" he asked blank-faced.

Nielsen nodded her head. "Not surprised then?"

"Hardly." Graham looked down the stairs. "This way," he said, making his way down them.

They settled in the bar, at the table John Simmons rested at a few days before. Graham pointed that out as he poured Nielsen a glass of water. He took it to her and sat opposite her.

"The man who was here yesterday," she said. "What do you make of his behaviour? How was he acting?"

"Completely bloody irrationally, if you ask me," the reply. "He was shouting and sweating and agitated much more than the time before–"

"The time before?"

"Yes. He was here on Saturday. That was the first time I heard about this bloody mess. Said his girlfriend had disappeared and that he was bringing her here. That maybe it was a joke and she was hiding somewhere in here."

That confirmed it: John Simmons had been here on Saturday. "And what did you do?"

"Let him in. Let him look around. Tried to help him. I put a PA call out for her. Nothing. She wasn't here."

"Did he have a ticket or did you just let him in to look around?"

"He had a ticket."

"Did he have two tickets?" Nielsen hoped Graham would

167

have a definite answer; in this one answer, he could provide evidence about whether Jennie Michaels existed.

"He spoke of them having tickets for the show, but I didn't see a second ticket. Why would I have asked? She wasn't with him."

Nielsen nodded. "Of course. I understand." She took a sip of water. "Did he do anything that concerned you?"

"Not on Saturday. Yesterday, yes. You know, attacking someone in a theatre isn't an everyday occurrence. We're not a bloody nightclub after all. He just went berserk. Had a ticket, watched the show and then went after them. He was shouting about Jennie and what have they done and where is she, that sort of thing."

"Yes," Nielsen said, "I've read the report. Local police faxed me a copy last night. His behaviour was certainly extreme." Another sip of water. "And what about the couple? How did they come across to you?"

"Bloody shocked. I mean, how would you feel if you're enjoying a show and some nut comes after you? Not your idea of a relaxing day at the theatre. So, shocked at first. Then the guy got a bit pissed off, shouted back. Don't blame him, to be honest with you."

"Why 'nut'?"

"Come on, got to have a fruit loose to behave the way he did. The couple, they didn't have a clue what he was going on about. Even I could tell that. Anyone would get frustrated in their shoes. Eventually, at least." Graham looked at his watch. "Look, I really must start preparing for today's performance. Takes a lot more work than you'd imagine."

"Yes," Nielsen said, "I'm sure it does." She took a final mouthful of water. "That's all for now anyway. Thank you for your time." She handed him a card. "In case you think of anything else." And she took his contact details.

The wait at Dave Bryant's office bore no fruit. I didn't see anything. I didn't want to return home, so I came to the police station. I'm outside. Detective Nielsen won't even know I'm here. I just need to see that she's working on the case and being proactive, that she hasn't given up on me.

I parked the car within sight of the station, sat in it with only the radio to fill the silence, and started waiting.

It was almost two o'clock before Detective Nielsen appeared, but she was heading into the station, not out of it. She parked in a space outside the main door and clearly wasn't in a rush.

It's now an hour and a half later and she's still inside. I think about calling her to try to prompt movement, but I don't. I think more about Dave Bryant. Tonight I'll be in his office and then tomorrow I'll tell her about him.

It starts to drizzle and I put the windscreen wipers on intermittent. As I do, Detective Nielsen appears. She comes down the steps and walks over to her car. As she pulls out, I turn my engine on. The lights come on automatically because of the declining weather, and I indicate to re-join the road.

We drive across town and I'm careful to keep well back. If the detective sees me, she's sure to have issue with what I'm doing, but the truth is I'm doing it out of frustration: I need to know the police are trying to help me. I need to know I'm not the only one pursuing the truth.

I become aware of where we're going long before we arrive. Sanders Road. As I watch Detective Nielsen park in front of Jennie's house, or the Wongs' house as it has become known, I keep driving. I'll park further down the road and watch what happens in my wing mirror.

Nielsen has switched off the engine as I pass and, by the

time I park, she is out of her car. She locks the door and crosses the road. I have a clear view in the mirror. I'm about twenty metres away.

She walks along the short path – instantly, I remember standing there just days ago – and knocks on the front door. She stands with her hands in her pockets. She looks at the ground. After waiting, she knocks on the door again. This time she looks up at the windows. Then she walks to the front window and peers in. She makes a third attempt at knocking and, when there's no answer, she removes her phone from her pockets and dials a number.

She speaks into the phone and nods her head. As she returns it to her pocket, she leaves the path. She steps onto the road. Because I'm concentrating on her, I haven't noticed the car that has slowly pulled up next to me. I only notice it when it suddenly accelerates. Its tyres make a noise that pieces the ear. Nielsen reacts to it, looking up. What she sees is the dark blue car ploughing towards her. She tries to run back to the pavement, but the car catches her hip and sends her careering out of the road. She lands on Jennie's garden bush and then sinks to the concrete.

I spin around and see the car taking off round the corner. I redirect my gaze to Nielsen. She isn't moving. I don't know what to do: get out and help her, or pursue the car.

I open the car door and am about to jump out when I realise how strange it will appear for me to be here. There's no evidence of anyone else here except me. So I close the door and start the engine. I slam the gearstick into first and then come out of the space. I lurch into a driveway and turn the car around. I'm in third before I get to the end of the road.

As I pass Nielsen, I pull my mobile out of my pocket. I dial for an ambulance and, as I turn into the main road, a right-hand turn, I ask for an ambulance and then give the address. I hope I've made the best choice and pray that Detective Nielsen will be all right.

I reach the roundabout at the end of the next road, slamming on the brakes. I ignore all the cars around me and stop. I don't know which way to go. The car was dark blue, a saloon, but I didn't see what make or model. I try to rescan it in my mind, but the visual has gone. I look straight ahead, to the left and then to the right, craning my neck to see round the corner, edging the car forwards. I make out a dark blue colour in the distance, so I ram my foot on the accelerator. The car howls.

I'm at almost sixty in seconds, gaining on the car, unsure of how I'll stop it and what I'll say. We're on a normal village road and occasional cars are coming opposite me. I overtake a couple of cars when the road ahead is clear.

I come up behind the car. It's a Passat. It's moving quickly but not as fast as me. I have to brake so that I don't hit it. Seeing that the road is clear, I decide to go for it. I pull onto the other side of the road and hit the gas. The car jolts forwards and I hold it steady by the side of the blue car. I can see through the window but can't make out the person's features. I can see the tip of a baseball cap.

The other car's not stopping. I keep switching my glances between the car and the road. Then I see a bus coming towards me. I hit the brakes hard and swerve the car back behind the Passat.

My head shifts round and follows the bus as it skims by me. I breathe a sigh of relief. It was only inches away from impact. As I bring my eyes back onto the road, the driver of the Passat brakes, suddenly and hard. I'm travelling at about forty. My instinct is to slam on the brakes and angle the wheel towards the pavement. I go into a skid. The left front wheel scrapes against the curb as the front driver's side of my Mazda collides with the back of the other vehicle. My head slams forwards and my air bag deploys.

As I hit it, the Passat must accelerate because I lose complete control of the car. I spin and the back of the car clips a lamppost. It only comes to a halt after it completes its fourth or fifth turn.

I hear a horn and another set of wheels skidding. Then I feel the force of a car from the other side of the road as it collides with the front of the Mazda, sending me spinning the other way. My head hits the side window and I lose sight of the things in front of me.

More cars braking sharply. Doors opening and closing. People's voices. But I don't see them.

*

Kate Nielsen was conscious from the moment the police and ambulance arrived at Sanders Road until the time she arrived at the hospital. Detective Constable Sam Cook sat by her side. Nielsen hadn't responded when he'd asked her, "How are you feeling?"

She knew why he was here and she wasn't happy about it. Detectives don't normally answer emergency calls.

It was Morgan. It had to be him.

Sam had been with the force for thirteen years, four of which in his current rank. He was respected and liked by his colleagues, but right now Nielsen couldn't have hated him more. It wasn't his fault, but under the circumstances she didn't care. Each time their eyes met, Sam showed Nielsen a wide smile and she didn't return it.

She looked at him suspiciously. "So," she said then paused. "He doesn't think I can handle this on my own any longer?" She lowered her eyes, picked up some papers from the side table, then added as if speaking to herself, "He thinks I need you to hold my fucking hand, to be my fucking babysitter."

172

"You know what he's like. Impatient without fail."

Nielsen was infuriated that Morgan had arranged this surprise for her and hadn't had the courtesy of telling her himself. Sam was to work with her on the case from now on. Morgan thought she couldn't look after things by herself any more.

When she didn't respond, Sam added, "Look Kate, I'm just doing as I've been asked. Don't be angry. I'll be here to observe. I won't step in unless you ask me to. You have my word."

"Too fucking right I do." She flung the pages onto the bed. A couple of leaves fell onto the floor. Sam got up, moved to them and started to pick them up. "Leave them," she said.

"It's no bother," he said, putting those he'd collected back on the table.

Sam was thirty-six years old, sporty, ambitious and more handsome than the other men Nielsen saw and worked with every day. He was also very modest, not a ladies' man, not at all, sensitive and always trying to do his best by other people. Especially when planted in difficult situations like this.

"I work alone. Got it?"

"Like I said, I'll be an observer. I'll only move if you give the word. I promise."

"Make sure that's exactly how it plays out."

He nodded and sat back down.

"When the fuck are they going to let me out of here anyway?"

"Soon as the doctor's been. Not long now."

"Is anyone checking out the scene?"

"Uniforms are questioning neighbours to find any witnesses and the car's already been found. But that's not for you to worry about at the moment. You need to rest."

"I need to get out of here is what I need." And away from

you, she thought.

*

I don't remember the journey to the hospital. One of the nurses told me I was cut out of the car, that I'm lucky. There's pain around my ribs and the side of my head hurts, but beyond that I don't think there's anything wrong with me.

I remember opening my eyes and seeing the hospital ceiling. I remember nurses reading from charts and I remember a doctor saying a few words to me. Since then, though, nothing's happened.

I don't want to stay here. I want to get out and find whoever was driving that car. I press the call button that's above my head. A nurse appears in seconds.

"When do you think I'll be discharged?"

"Ooh, not today, I'm afraid. The doctor will want to see you again, we'll monitor you overnight and then the police will want to speak to you in the morning."

I thank her and she leaves. I'm careful not to make her suspicious by reacting strangely. But there's no way I'm staying here. I have to get to Dave Bryant's office after sunset and I have no idea what I'd say if the police walked through the door.

The ward is quiet. There are three other men in here. Two elderly gentlemen, both asleep, and another in his late teens. He's surrounded by family members and his leg is in a cast, strung up. They won't see me slip out.

I wait until I'm certain the nurse's station is clear and grab my things from the wardrobe. I unplug the intravenous drip from my arm, tear off the tape and pull out the insert plug. I quickly move through the foyer and then down the corridor. I come to a door and heave it open. I move swiftly down three sets of stairs and out of the main door. When I emerge, I walk but with pace. I exit the hospital grounds and go onto the main road. A few buildings down, I come to a petrol station. I go inside and straight into the restroom. There, I change and put my clothes back on. The hospital nightgown goes into the waste bin.

I buy a bottle of water and a flapjack and leave. I need to find shelter – until nightfall.

*

He sat at home. He was shaking. He had his eyes closed and was trying to calm down.

Things had changed. He'd seen the opportunity and taken it. Even though the touch was electric and he wanted her so badly, Kate Nielsen's role in this had changed today. John Simmons' arrival on the scene had shown him that maybe there was a way out – maybe the end didn't have to come with his identity being revealed.

Simmons was clearly following Nielsen, not something that would endear him to the police. And with a dead police officer and John Simmons on the scene, as well as the supposed attack at his house and the girlfriend who might or might not have disappeared, the police wouldn't need any convincing to consider John Simmons a suspect. So Kate Nielsen had to be sacrificed early, he had decided.

But now all that had been messed up. She wasn't dead and he didn't know what had happened to Simmons; he hadn't hung around to wait for the ambulance and police to arrive at the accident scene.

So he was angry: angry at Simmons for turning up again and angry at himself for allowing spontaneity to show its ugly head.

He needed to calm down before heading back out. With

Nielsen alive, the game would resume as planned.

*

Nielsen had been checked over by the doctor, had been given an injection and painkillers to take for the next three days, and had been discharged. She and Sam were walking down the stairs, slowly. Her leg and side were sore. She hated feeling physical discomfort – it reminded her of suffering from years past, suffering she battled to forget every day.

"What now?" Sam asked.

"Back to the office. See if anything's come up."

Sam held the door open for Nielsen as they left the hospital, then did the same when they reached the car. She didn't offer thanks.

She put the radio on while Sam started the engine – didn't want to talk, and silence, she thought, would be uncomfortable. Sam backed out of the parking space, then turned right onto the main road. They passed a petrol station. Nielsen was gazing out of the window. Then they approached a man. He was holding a bottle of water. He made eye contact with Nielsen and started running.

Nielsen recognised him. "Stop," she said, spinning round in her seat.

"What?"

"Stop the fucking car! John Simmons."

"Where?" Sam asked as he braked.

"Right behind us. Why the fuck's he running away from us? Turn around."

Sam turned round sharply and accelerated. The engine revved fiercely. The man in the distance looked over his shoulder and ran across the road. A car coming from the other direction swerved to avoid him.

A horn sounded as Sam pulled the car over. John

Simmons was running down an alley. Trees hung over the fences that were on both sides. Nielsen thrust the door open and started to run around the car towards the alley. Pain in her leg made her stop.

"Are you all right?" Sam said, getting out of the car.

"Yes," she shrieked, unable to cover the pain that she was trying in vain not to feel. "Get him!" Nielsen leaned against the car's bonnet.

Sam charged into alley. He couldn't see the man he was pursuing. He had no idea why he was chasing John Simmons, but he didn't doubt Nielsen's instincts. He knew she was a good cop.

John was panicking; he didn't know whether to stop or whether to move, but he chose to run because he feared he was the suspect in the hit and run. Plus he thought Dave Bryant would be ignored if he didn't have the chance to investigate himself later tonight. No, now he'd run and he'd explain and apologise later, when he had proof of Bryant's involvement.

John came out of the alley and ran to the right. He didn't know where he was going, but after only a few metres he had another choice: left or right. He chose left and then he ran into a road on the right-hand side twenty yards ahead. He weaved in and out of roads as much as he could, never looking back. He didn't see that Sam Cook had lost him. He only stopped running when he was out of steam and came across a row of village shops. Then, finally, he dared to look back.

Behind the shops was a park. He entered it and exited the other side through another alley.

Shelter. Have to find shelter. Now's the time, he decided.

Chapter Nineteen

More officers arrived on the scene within ten minutes. Once Nielsen had been told that John Simmons was a suspect in the hit and run that involved her, and once she had been informed that he'd fled the hospital, she ordered the area to be sealed off and put four units of officers on the hunt for John Simmons.

Looking for shelter, John Simmons kept moving. He knew he had to get as much distance between himself and the police as possible and he wanted to find the kind of shelter that would prove impenetrable to those seeking him.

Nielsen had frustrated her hip injury and the pain throughout her body was relentless. She'd stayed leaning on the bonnet while she spoke to the officers and sent them on the search. Right now she was staring at a map of the local area, trying to identify a place where she thought John Simmons might end up going, but she was drawing a blank. Sam stood at her side.

John arrived at a supermarket and went inside. He searched up and down the aisles while thinking of his best next step. He couldn't think of one. He had to remain free for the next six hours, at least. It would be dark in about four hours and, he suspected, he'd be able to move quite freely to Dave Bryant's office after that time. He'd go by taxi, get dropped off down the road from it. So he just needed to fill the time between now and then.

DCI Morgan had been on the phone almost as soon as the back-up officers had arrived. He'd barked orders at Nielsen and told her not to return to the station without Simmons in cuffs.

As John was moving towards the exit, his eyes fell upon a sign for the toilets. He stopped. Who would think of looking in there? he thought.

So he settled on it: he'd lock himself in the toilets until it was time to move. He purchased another bottle of water, a sandwich and a handful of today's newspapers. It would give him time to search for any new items about the disappearances.

Nielsen snapped at Sam every time he tried to speak to her. She kept in regular radio contact with the officers who were searching for John Simmons – too regular for their liking. She told Sam they would join in the search. They got into the car and started circling the area.

John locked himself in one of the three cubicles. It didn't smell like most other toilets. He wolfed down his sandwich, his stomach growling in hunger as he did so. He opened the first of the papers. He had time.

*

Nielsen had given up on the search an hour ago. She'd deputed an officer to sit and wait outside John Simmons' house, all night if necessary.

Now she was at her desk, trawling through paperwork, trying to identify her next action. She'd decided to brave Morgan's wrath by returning to the station, but by the time she'd arrived he'd called it a day and was probably on the golf course.

Her body was still in pain and she felt shattered. She'd been told to go home and rest, but she couldn't.

Her level of frustration was increasing. She had to make progress and felt like she was failing. Progress with Jennie Michaels, whoever the hell she was, if she existed at all; with John Simmons, wherever the hell he was; with the missing women and who had killed the ones found, with finding the bodies of those who hadn't been discovered; with satisfying Morgan. With discovering the truth.

Sam Cook sat at his desk watching her. He saw how tired she looked. He thought she was pretty in an unusual way but knew she'd never take a compliment. He focused on some papers in front of him. "You okay?" he asked, aware that looking at her for a prolonged time would only anger her more.

"Tired like never before," she answered.

Nielsen didn't look at him when he said, "When are you going to get over this?"

She didn't respond straightaway. "This what?" She pretended not to understand.

"You can't always rely on yourself, you know that. You have to let others back in. You have to start trusting us again. We can help you, you know?"

"Trust?" She shot him a look of disdain. "Don't talk to me about trust. I trusted before, remember? I trusted that Weldon prick. He sat where you're sitting right now. And I trusted him and you know where that fucking got me. So no fucking thanks."

"It was a long time ago, Kate. What, four years? I won't let you down, not like him."

"Let me down? Look... I don't want to get angry." She could feel tears welling up in her eyes. She'd hate to show them. "Look, I don't want to talk. I've got work to do."

Four years. Had it been that long already? Nielsen thought, Seems like yesterday, as she kept her head down.

The last day of November. Detective Constable Kate Nielsen, only in post for six months, and Detective Sergeant Ray Weldon – the one who had her trust, the one who made her no longer trust DSs and anyone else – were out to bust a serial rapist. Nielsen, who at that time cared about her

181

appearance perhaps too much, was to be the bait; she fitted the role perfectly. Weldon was to wait and watch. Then, at the right moment, he was to strike. The arrest would be made; the crimes would come to an end. The man – Mike Butcher – would be brought to trial and punished. That simple.

Only it didn't work out like that.

Mike Butcher had raped seven women in the space of seven months. He always picked the last day of the month. He found his victims through an internet dating site. Computer examination, analysis and comparison meant that Weldon and his team were able to identify two potential suspects – two men with whom all the victims had had contact.

Nielsen, keen to impress her superiors, ambitious, adventurous, volunteered her details to be registered on the site, volunteered to hope to become Mike Butcher's latest victim.

The first meeting that was set – with one Dave Mortimer – led nowhere, except to Nielsen putting her guard down. Mortimer was actually quite good natured and, as soon as she realised he was not the man she was looking for, she began to enjoy his company. She was single; there was no harm in it.

So it was Mike Butcher; it was a meeting at La Rouge, a nightclub; it was the last day of the month. And they would get him. Weldon was on following duty and, in the car park as backup, two cars filled with officers waited for the signal to move.

Mike Butcher arrived twenty minutes late, to the point where Nielsen almost believed he wouldn't show, that he'd somehow found out about the trap, or that he'd thought better of what he'd planned to do.

He was a tall, disarming man. He had closely shaved

black hair and a goatee beard. His eyes were narrow and his Adam's apple stuck out as if he'd swallowed a small box. He didn't bring with him the pleasantries – no flowers like Dave Mortimer was kind enough to give her, no friendly chat, no smiles. He talked about sex a lot: what he liked, guessed what she liked, what he'd tried, what he wanted to try. He didn't ask her any questions, just made statements, and didn't seem to care whether she was happy with him or not. In fact, she found the whole experience boring and frustrating.

He talked for over an hour. An hour while DS Ray Weldon was supposed to be looking on, waiting for his opportunity to strike. But like Nielsen, Weldon had become bored. A cute blonde had caught his eye and it was to her that he'd turned his attentions. Although only twenty feet away from Nielsen and a crazed rapist, DS Weldon didn't see them stand up, didn't see them walk towards the toilets, didn't see them leave through the back exit. And Kate Nielsen, inexperienced and full of trust for her older and wiser colleague – misguided trust that would alter her life forever – didn't know that Weldon hadn't seen them leave.

The cute blonde's tongue had been in Weldon's throat for a full five minutes before he was kick-started back into the present, before he remembered his purpose here, before he looked over to where Kate Nielsen and Mike Butcher were. Only they weren't there, and he started to panic.

The couple had emerged into a yard that housed the waste area and doubled for a delivery zone. It was about ten metres by ten with a gate on the far side, and beyond that and the road that turned sharply off to the left were lots of trees. The moon hovered over them, the towering trees a painted waving silhouette in the fierce breeze against the dark blue of the sky.

Mike Butcher led his latest prize to the other side of the

yard, over the fence and onto the grass. It was only metres until they'd reach the woods. Nielsen's nerves, which started as a form of excitement, became full of dread. She wanted to glance over her shoulder, wanted to see that she was being followed, that this façade would soon be stopped and that she'd have help, but she knew she couldn't; knew that would give the game away.

They were only the distance of two trees into the woods when he grabbed her round the neck, kicked the back of her knees and quickly had her on the ground. It was only a matter of seconds before he fumbled around with something he'd pulled out of his pocket, before the cloth was pressed over her mouth and nose, before she felt herself starting to lose consciousness.

She awoke fifteen minutes later, confused. Scared. Beaten.

Weldon had found them, but not before Mike Butcher had started to have his way with Nielsen. He'd torn her skirt off, pulled her blouse open, forced her stockings into her mouth, made his way inside her. For how long, nobody could be sure. But only a second would have been a lifetime too long.

After she'd been checked out, taped up and sent home, Nielsen was kept off work for eleven months. And there was only one dream that stayed with her all the time: the stockings and the helplessness. She'd not had a relationship with a man since. She'd not had much faith in life itself, just a vague hope that she might be able to help someone other than herself. And she'd not placed her trust in a colleague, especially a man, since then. She'd managed, while wallowing in self-pity and disgust for herself and her department, to destroy the sorrow that others felt for her, the pity they'd initially felt. So when she returned to work – even though Weldon had been relieved of duty and was nowhere to be seen – she couldn't connect with another soul. She couldn't rebuild the relationships she'd tried so hard, in her youthful zest, to start. And she couldn't forgive the place that had put her in the position of violation in the first place. The place that allowed her to be raped, however briefly.

Then Morgan and his regime of damn-the-helpers work ethics came into force, and his disdain for all his underlings, Nielsen and her feelings in particular, meant that she didn't have to walk around labelled any more, that she didn't have to hate everyone else for being different, because they were all the same – they were all treated like shit.

Was Sam Cook any different? Nielsen wasn't so sure.

"Like I said," she added, even though Sam had resumed working and followed her request not to talk, "I'll speak to you when I want to."

*

At just before nine o'clock, I leave the toilets. My body feels stiff, but I'm definitely motivated to start achieving. The newspapers didn't tell me anything I didn't already know – and there have been no more disappearances announced, which is a plus. But of course Jennie's not in the paper either and in all likelihood she's slipping further away from me.

That thought motivates me further. I purchase another bottle of water and a woollen hat before I leave the supermarket. A taxi is dropping a couple off at the pick-up point, so I ask the driver if he can take me to Harpenden. He looks pleased for the business.

With little traffic this time of the evening, we get there in less than twenty minutes. I have the driver drop me off at the far end of the high street. After putting on the hat, I walk towards Dave Bryant's office. It's connected as a terrace to four other buildings and it's the one on the far right. A road goes along its side. I follow it and reach the back of the buildings where I find a courtyard with a row of office car parking spaces. They are next to the back of the buildings. I recognise the window of Dave Bryant's personal office, but the blinds are drawn so I can't see in.

On the other side of the courtyard are a collection of bins. I head over to them and search for a heavy object. I find some kind of piping, which I take back to Dave Bryant's window. The hell with it, I think, and smash the piping against the window. It shatters.

An alarm immediately sounds. A high-pitched whizzing sound. Stupid – I didn't think there might be an alarm. I can't back off, though. If I do, all this will be for nothing.

I estimate that I have five minutes before the police arrive. I hit the window again, then I use the piping to clear the bits of glass that remain in the frame. I scramble in and land in front of the desk. My body hurts, but I dash over to the filing cabinet and pull the top drawer open. I remove a handful of paperwork and sift through it. I've already entered illegally, so I drop the papers on the floor as soon as I see they're worthless. I keep looking towards the door, hopeful that that will help me hear the arrival of anyone outside. I pull more papers out, but I work too quickly – I can't find anything.

I empty the next drawer and the third. My breathing is heavy. Time's running out, so I barely glance at what I hold. I go to his desk and try to open the drawer. It's locked. I look through the papers that are on the desk, but again, nothing.

I open the office door and enter the reception area. I go to the receptionist's desk and open a drawer. As I start to push my hands through its contents, I see a swirling blue light in the distance. It's getting stronger. My heart's pounding and I freeze. What happens if they go around the back? What should my escape route be?

I settle on the back window, run into Bryant's office and leap through the window. I clutch my ribs. A car's coming down the road to my right. A faint blue light.

I quickly look around the courtyard. Hide behind the bins perhaps. I run over to them.

The car is getting closer.

No, the bins are no good. If I go behind them and the police seal the window off, I'll be stuck here for hours.

My body's shaking. What am I doing here? What did I really expect to find? A picture of Jennie on his desk? He wouldn't be as stupid as that. No, I'm the stupid one. I'm the one now committing the crime. Why didn't I tell Detective Nielsen about this?

There's a wall in front of me. I pull one of the smaller bins towards it and climb on top of it. My legs tremble. I stand on the bin – the car's light is coming round the corner – and I jump. I fall through a bush and land hard on the ground. Something grazes my chin.

I get up, fighting the pain, and run as I hear the car coming to a stop and two doors opening and closing. I run so fast, too fast, and I trip. But as soon as I'm on the ground, I get up again.

I don't stop running until I reach a bus stop several roads away. I sit here for only a few minutes before a taxi approaches me, so I hail it, get in and take off.

Chapter Twenty

The following morning, needing fresh air and desperate for even more time to think, I took a taxi to the park, which is down the hill from the cathedral. I haven't been able to call Detective Nielsen yet – I don't know what to say. I'm wanted, for God's sake. I didn't go home yesterday, knew the police would be looking for me, most likely expecting me to go there. So I returned to the supermarket, aware it's open twenty-four hours, bought some fresh clothes and deodorant, and had some food in the cafe. When it got late, I returned to the toilets. I managed to nap for only minutes at a time, so right now I feel exhausted and my body's joints don't want to move.

My first stop was to a car rental office in the city centre. I've hired a Citroen Saxo for the next three days. As I've not been home, I've not had time to sort out the insurance matters regarding the Mazda. Those affairs are in a state. And because I left the hospital early, I didn't even have the chance to find out what I need to do about the car. I don't know where it is. Maybe someone from the insurance company wanted to see me.

When I arrived here, I spent time walking around the gravestones, nameless because age has worn away the details, thinking about how I could move things along, thinking about any connection I could make to Jennie, any line of inquiry to pursue next. I know I should call Detective Nielsen, but I don't know what to say. I didn't run you over? I broke into Dave Bryant's office and have nothing to show for it?

With no evidence from the solicitor's office, no idea

who tried to run her over and not a clue about Jennie's whereabouts, my mind spins. I can only think of questions and fail to find any answers.

There's little to do in the park apart from sit on the grass. It's still damp. As I rise, I'm sure I've forced grass stains onto my jeans. I walk along the path and downhill, round to the right and past the pub, over a small bridge, and I come to the lake. A rather odd shape, you can walk all the way around it. To its side, there's a smaller lake, and swans, geese and ducks are everywhere. They approach me in groups, hoping I'm there, another stranger, to feed them bread. I'm not. I have nothing with me. No bread, no plans.

I keep moving around, slowly. To make a circuit takes me almost fifteen minutes, and when I return to the bridge, the place from which I started, I begin the route again. This time, when I'm just over halfway round, I come to a stop and sit on a bench. I stare at the water, my mind still on Jennie. What to do and how to find her. Never before have I felt as hopeless and useless as I do now. Never. And I wouldn't wish it on anybody, not even my gravest enemy.

It could well be an hour before I move, before I stop staring at the birds chasing one another, hustling for food, shrieking either with joy or derision. I get up with the intention of making another round. I'm fewer than ten feet along before I have to step aside for a group of women. There are five, one leading and the others behind her, side by side in pairs. They're wearing tank tops and tight full-length exercise bottoms. Trainers too. They're jogging. The woman in front, dark hair, slim, is giving encouragement to the women following her.

She's their instructor.

And then it dawns upon me. Yes. An instructor. Exercise.

Jennie had talked about an exercise group she attended at the leisure centre. *Group* means lots of people, and lots of people mean I might be able to find someone who is close to Jennie, someone who might be able to guide me to something important, someone who might have the key to all this.

I start jogging. Jogging back to the car. Jogging becomes running. Despite the pain. Running now with some hope. Hope that I might get somewhere.

What I don't know is what exercise group Jennie went to, on what days and at what times. But I do know her group is a spinning class, so I bank on the fact that there's only one spinning group.

How wrong I am.

"I need to speak to the instructor of the spinning class," I tell the receptionist when I arrive at the leisure centre, out of breath from the run I've had from the car, ashamed of my lack of fitness, clutching the area around my ribs. She's nothing more than a teenager, a spotty girl with greasy brown hair, a ponytail and glasses.

"And which class would that be?" she asks.

I deflate as quickly as I'd become pumped up. "Well, how many are there?" I ask.

"Three."

"When do they run?"

"There's a morning class, an afternoon one and one that runs in the evenings. They all on three times a week. Not at the weekend though."

Jennie works. Or, at least, I thought she did. "Evenings," I say eagerly. "Evenings. Can you ask the instructor to come down for a word?"

"No can do," she says, shaking her head. "Doesn't come in until two."

"But that's almost a two-hour wait," I say, disappointed. "Is there any way I can speak to her? A phone number perhaps?"

191

"Him," she corrects me. "And no, I don't have a number or anything."

I turn away from her and swear. No fucking luck on my side.

"Can I ask what this is about?" she says, regaining my attention.

"Membership," I say, springing back to her.

"Sorry?"

"Membership. Does everyone in a class have to become a member of the sports centre first?"

"No, but most people do. You can pay per visit. Some people do that. But it's cheaper if you pay an annual membership fee."

"Great," I say, thinking quickly about how I should broach the subject, how to get her to help me. "Look, I need your help. I'm in a terrible jam. I desperately, more than anything in the world, need to find someone. My fiancée, she's gone missing. I need to know if she's got membership here. If she left any contact details other than the one that's no longer working."

She tries to speak up, already shaking her head, but I interrupt her. "This could be life and death. Please. I'm not exaggerating. The police are involved and I'm desperate with worry. I need to do something to help. Imagine if the person most dear to you in your life just vanished without explanation. You'd feel… helpless. So if you could just look up a name for me, I only need to know if she's got membership. That's all for now. I don't need you to tell me anything else at the moment," I lie. Of course it's totally untrue: the second she says Jennie's a member I'm going to leap at the computer and see all the information on there. I'll be able to see what I need before anyone can pull me away. It'll only take seconds. I've learned these past few days that asking gets you nowhere. Take advantage of a situation and then take what you can before that advantage is taken away from you. "Just a yes or a no. That's all, I swear. Just is Jennie Michaels a member or not? Yes or no, that's it." Then I repeat, "I swear."

She looks at the computer screen, biting her lip.

One more time, softly: "I swear."

She looks behind her. No one there. Relenting, she types the name. A sigh of relief from me. I hold my gaze on each key as she presses them down. Then she taps the enter key.

I see it in her eyes. Jennie's on the screen.

Jennie.

I grab the screen and spin it around. The receptionist shrieks. Ignoring her, I inch forwards.

Jennie. Her name, I see it at the top of the screen.

I lean over the counter, the receptionist edging back, and I grab the mouse. I scroll the page down.

The receptionist is cowering away from me.

But the screen. An address I don't recognise, a mobile number I've never seen before, and a picture. A picture of a woman. A woman I've seen before.

No!

Not Jennie. Not *my* Jennie.

The woman in the picture, Jennie Michaels... the secretary from Dave Bryant's office.

I'm frozen still and cold. Chills run the length of my spine. How the hell? What the hell? How is it her? What has Dave Bryant done?

I'm unaware of what's going on around me. All I can see is the woman in the picture, maybe forty years old, curly blonde hair, a large nose. Nothing else enters my consciousness. Not the receptionist who has come close to me and picked up the phone. Not the footsteps behind me. It's like the police station all over again.

There's a hand on my shoulder, a man's voice, and I nod

my head. At what, I don't know. Just a voice.

The man leads me over to the seats opposite the reception desk. We sit down, but I still can't see him. I just see Jennie Michaels. But not Jennie Michaels. I see a face, a stranger.

Then another stranger – the man in front of me – starts to come into focus as he leans closer and closer to me.

"What?" I say to him.

"Sir, what do you want?"

"Jennie," I say, making no sense to him: the confusion's in his eyes.

"What do you want, sir?"

"It isn't her," I say. Inside, I know I have to snap out of it. I try; I shake my head. But I fail.

I don't think about what I say next. I don't think of the consequences. I'm just desperate. I fix my eyes on his. "Detective Sergeant Kate Nielsen. I need DS Kate Nielsen." He doesn't move. "Now, please." She might arrest me. But now I don't care. All I know is I need her.

When he still doesn't move, I say it louder. "Please!" And then again, this time shouting: "Please!"

Chapter Twenty-One

She's standing no more than ten metres away from me, her hands on her hips, talking to the manager. There's a man I've not seen before standing behind her. He's keeping silent.

She's pissed off. I put my hands in my head, realise there's a line of sweat on my brow, wipe it.

I have managed to calm down, but I can't handle this alone. I need Detective Nielsen. I felt like I was going crazy when I whipped that monitor around.

What's happening to me? Jennie's gone. But Jennie's not Jennie. Jennie is Dave Bryant's secretary.

Jennie told me she was Dave Bryant's secretary. A different Dave Bryant, one at Brown's Solicitors in St Albans. But Dave Bryant works in Harpenden.

And the car. Someone rammed me off the road after trying to kill Detective Nielsen. Probably the same person who attacked me. But didn't kill me.

Detective Nielsen doesn't believe me. She likely thinks I tried to run her over. It's agonising, all this. It's incomprehensible.

She keeps glancing over at me but hasn't acknowledged me yet. The man behind her hasn't looked at me yet. He keeps his eyes to the ground, his hands in his pockets.

I don't know how I'm going to explain things to Detective Nielsen, but I know how I have to find a way to be convincing. Now there's no proof that the Jennie I know and love exists, so I'm going to have to work twice as hard to encourage Detective Nielsen to keep the case alive. Yes, what I've discovered here makes Jennie seem even less real than before. Yes, I'm an idiot for the choices I've made these past few days. Yes, I don't know what I'm going to do now. But the woman I love is real.

If not as Jennie Michaels, that means she was lying to me. If she was lying to me and I have no idea what the truth is, how can I convince someone else – Detective Nielsen – of a truth I can't prove? And why would Jennie have lied to me? I don't understand.

I'm tempted to sneak out and hope she doesn't see me. Work out what I should do, how I can convince her that I haven't dug myself an even bigger hole. But I've done too much of that lately and before I can move she's walking over to me. Alone – the manager has backed off and is now speaking to the receptionist, who's being comforted by another member of staff and is nursing a steaming mug of something. The other man has stayed where he was.

Detective Nielsen stands above me. She signals for the man to come over. He stands by her side. I don't get up. She doesn't immediately speak up. I hear her breathing. She sniffs. Then she says, "John, John, John," and she sits next to me. The man remains standing. She puts her hands in her lap, cups them and remains silent. Then she leans back and crosses one leg over the other. "You're a bloody nuisance, you know that?"

I nod my head; I don't answer.

"So, Jennie Michaels," she says. Whether it's the start of a question, I'm not entirely sure. She doesn't continue.

After ten, maybe fifteen seconds, I say, simply, "Is real."

"She is, is she?" Nielsen asks, monotone.

"I know it." I don't have a clue what to say; I wasn't expecting her to approach me like this. I was expecting my rights to be read and cuffs to be pulled out. I want to involve her, so I add, "And you know it. You have to."

"I know nothing, John. All I know is this situation keeps getting more confusing and more out of hand and, for some reason, you're always at the centre of it. You couldn't blame anyone for believing you're behind all this. If you could've just done what I told you from the beginning–"

"I care too much," I tell her. "I won't ever stop. But whatever I've done, you've got to know I didn't try to hurt you yesterday."

She sees me looking at the man, so she adds, "This is Detective Constable Sam Cook. He's here to observe."

DC Cook nods at me. I try to smile.

"What were you doing in Sanders Road then, John?" Detective Nielsen asks.

"I was checking to see if you were on the case."

"You were following me?"

I don't answer quickly enough. "Yes, I was. But I was just checking on you, that's all."

"Is that so?"

"Yes, you have my word."

"Not sure your word's worth much any more."

"But–"

"I know what car you drive, John. Calm down. And I do remember the car that knocked me over and I know it wasn't yours. And as soon as some of the neighbours, who were interviewed as witnessed, said they saw your car take off right after the car that came at me, they proved it wasn't you." She pauses. "Anyway, the Passat was found abandoned about a mile away from where you had your accident."

"Accident?" I say. "I was chasing him. He rammed me off the road."

She looks like she's piecing it together. I think she believes me.

"What brought you here, John?" she asks.

"I didn't think I should go home because I thought I'd be arrested. I thought I'd be accused of running you over." I hesitate but decide it's not worth holding back. "And… and

197

last night I broke into Dave Bryant's office."

"That was you?"

"How do you know about it?"

"Oh, John. Why the hell did you do that?" She looks frustrated with me again.

"I found his details in the Yellow Pages. I didn't tell you I met him because I wanted to have some kind of evidence for you, something that you could take to your superiors. When I went to see him and told him about Jennie, he threw me out." I tell her he knew something. I tell her I had no choice. I tell her I had to find out what he was hiding.

She glares into my eyes. "So what did you find out?"

"Nothing," I submit.

Detective Nielsen clears her throat. She stretches her neck. She looks as exhausted as I feel. "Dave Bryant phoned the station the moment he put you out of his office yesterday morning. He thought you were some kind of nut, someone threatening him or his secretary. To him, you're someone who walked into his office and told him the woman who worked for him and was sitting outside his office was missing. He felt threatened. So Jennie Michaels does indeed work for Dave Bryant. Just not the Jennie Michaels you're talking about."

More confusion. "This is ludicrous."

"You could say that. Now, what made you come here?"

"I'd forgotten that Jennie told me she came to a spinning class. I thought someone might know more about her. An instructor, someone in the group, I don't know. And then that picture." It's not her.

"You know, you're making this all a whole lot more difficult than it needs to be. I should be your first port of call."

"Tell me you believe me."

"I don't know what I believe. You'd be the same in my

198

position. But I'm still talking to you, so that must count for something." She looks away. "So tell me," she continues, "if the Jennie Michaels in the picture is Dave Bryant's secretary, who is your Jennie?"

I have no idea. "She's Jennie," I say. "Just Jennie."

"You, me and DC Cook are going to stay here for another hour. Then people will start arriving for the spinning class. It's the afternoon session and Jennie Michaels, the one in the picture, comes to it."

I don't know what that will prove. "So we'll find out..."

"We'll find out something for sure, you're right there. What exactly, I'm not sure. But maybe this will start to make some sense."

"I've been nothing but honest with you."

"For your sake, I hope so. For Jennie Michaels' sake, I'm not so sure."

*

I haven't kept my eyes off the entrance since Detective Nielsen told me Jennie Michaels will be arriving for her class. She and DC Cook haven't spoken very much.

The hour dragged. When she finally stepped into the building, I thought my heart might burst. She hasn't changed since yesterday. And she looks exactly like she does in the picture. She milled around for a bit, like she was waiting to meet someone. Detective Nielsen told me to stay put, approached the woman – I don't want to call her Jennie; it wouldn't be right – and she's been over there talking to her since. DC Cook stayed by my side. We didn't speak, even though I wanted to ask him questions, probe him to find out what was really being said about me behind my back by Detective Nielsen and the police.

The woman recognised me as soon as Detective Nielsen

pointed me out to her. She didn't seem surprised.

I'm watching them now. DC Cook is watching them too. I'm making the woman uncomfortable, but I don't care. I want to know what they're saying and even though my lip-reading skills are non-existent I'm trying.

It's perhaps another five minutes before Detective Nielsen comes back towards me. She's followed by the woman, the secretary. I stand up, clear my voice. Get ready. DC Cook also rises.

"John," Detective Nielsen says, "I want you to meet, again and formally this time, Jennie Michaels. As you know, she works for Dave Bryant. She comes here every Wednesday. I've explained the situation to her. She's willing to help."

The woman – I still don't want to use her name – speaks up. "Anything I can do to help," she says, full of concern.

"And this is Detective Cook. John, I want you to describe Jennie… the person we're looking for… to Ms Michaels."

I do. I go into minute detail. Although I haven't seen Jennie for days now – and it seems like weeks – she's as clear in my mind as if she's directly in front of me.

"Okay," the woman says, breathing deeply. "Before you came up to me," she says to Detective Nielsen, "I was waiting for a friend. Someone I've become friendly with, just someone to exercise with. We've been meeting here for the past month. A really nice girl." Now she turns, giving her attention to me. "Really nice. Her name's Michelle Keating."

Michelle, the 'friend' Jennie told me she had. So that would mean she was talking about herself. Why?

Nielsen speaks slowly: "Are you certain?"

"Like I said, without a doubt. You are looking for Michelle Keating. She moved here just over a month ago."

"A month ago?" I interrupt.

Nielsen doesn't let my interruption stop her. "Did she

say where from?"

"Up north, Detective. That's as much as she wanted to say. Something had happened there. Friendly as she was, that was all she told me. And who was I to pry? We were getting to know one another. We'd meet half an hour before the session and have coffee. Have another after the session. That was the extent of things. I thought, when we got to know each other better she might say more, but I certainly wasn't going to push her. Anyway, the lady you describe is definitely Michelle Keating."

"Is she a member?" Nielsen asks.

"I don't know," Jennie Michaels – I'll say it – answers. She thinks for a moment. "Well, no. No, I don't believe she was, come to think of it. When we paid, she paid seven pounds. I only pay five – that's the members' rate. So, no, she couldn't have been."

Detective Nielsen asks DC Cook to take Jennie Michaels' full details, says she'll be in contact soon, and Jennie Michaels wishes me well.

"Thank you," I say, derailed more than before, "and I'm sorry if I concerned you in any way yesterday."

"Don't worry about it. I think Dave was taken aback more than me. He's not very brave. I just hope you find Michelle. She's a nice girl."

Yes, I think, she is.

Days ago I knew and fell in love with Jennie Michaels. Now to discover, without any doubt whatsoever, that she was not who she said she was, despite the time I've had to prepare for this, I don't know how to feel... If Jennie Michaels is Michelle Keating, then why did she tell me she was Jennie Michaels? Why deceive me? I thought we were in love.

None of this makes sense.

Detective Nielsen goes behind the reception counter,

speaks to the receptionist and leans on a desk as the receptionist does something on the computer. In no time, she looks up at Nielsen and shakes her head, saying something I can't hear.

DC Cook finally speaks to me. He says, "Don't worry, if what you say is how it is, we'll be able to help you. Patience, that's all it takes."

I don't answer but find his words strangely comforting.

Nielsen returns. She admits, "Nothing of use on the computer system. No Michelle Keating listed. She isn't a member."

"This is bullshit," I say to myself, the discomfort returning.

"It's okay, John. We've taken a step forward. We're getting somewhere."

Even if that means I don't know the woman I love. I think it, can't bring myself to say it.

"You're free to go," she adds. "So, this time, go home. You've seen that I'm working on things. I *will* call you." When she sees I'm about to speak – not that I know the words I want to say – she takes me by the shoulder. "I mean it, John. Do as I say. I'm going back to the station and I'm going to search the databases for all the Michelle Keatings on it. I might find something."

"What about Dave Bryant?"

"What about him?"

"He might still be involved." I'm clutching at straws. Detective Nielsen rolls her eyes. "This might not be just another coincidence," I add, unconvincingly.

"I think this is one time we can be sure. Dave Bryant was brought into this by a person called Michelle Keating. He called us, remember. And Jennie Michaels knew Michelle Keating. A simple case of name swapping. Either way, his bearing on this case is down to me to decide. And I've decided. You need to be patient and wait, then maybe, without your interference, I'll get somewhere."

I have no words. I can only breathe. I start to walk away. I'm of no use now. There's nothing more I can do. I want Jennie; that's all I know.

I stop. If Jennie Michaels *is* Michelle Keating, then how is finding Michelle Keating's name on databases, finding if she's real, going to help? Hasn't this proven that she's real? Jennie Michaels just said so.

I speak up. "Detective," I say, stepping back towards her, "what does it matter what her name is and if it's on a database? That doesn't take away from the fact that someone needs to be looking for her, not looking for proof that she's this person or that. Jennie Michaels just told us."

"John, I have to do this. I have superiors. You have not endeared yourself to them."

"This shouldn't be about me!" I'm starting to raise my voice. "This should be about Jennie." I can see she's about to speak up, so I say what I know she's going to say. "Or it should be about Michelle. Whoever the fuck she is. What's important is where she is and who's taken her. You should be looking for them."

"Cut this out, John," she says, taking hold of my arm.

"It's not good enough. All I'm doing is waiting and being told to wait even longer."

"You're not waiting. That's the problem. But that's what you're going to do right now. Get home and stay put!"

She's past me and out of the door before I can say another word.

"Do as she says," DC Cook adds as he leaves as well.

An image of Jennie tied to a chair enters my mind. How can they tell me to wait? What kind of fiancé would I be if I ignored what must be pleas for help?

I can't.

Chapter Twenty-Two

He'd caught up with her in the supermarket the evening before it happened. She was carrying a basket and walking slowly. Her hair – it swayed so slowly, as if it was dancing with the non-existent wind.

He'd known she would be his next the first time his eyes fell upon her.

She had on a pair of jeans, a cream jumper and a black jacket. Nothing too fancy. He liked that about her. Despite dressing modestly, she still looked amazing. He walked up and down the aisles, keeping enough distance so that he remained invisible, pretending to take an interest in what was on the shelves, occasionally in the labels on items he picked up. He saw, time and again, men and teenagers passing her, taking a look and then a second much longer look. The idea that she was the object of fantasy of others as well as of himself was a source of excitement. He'd get to do what so many others wanted to do. The only difference between him and them was that he had the nerve to do it – to want and take – whereas they'd merely stand back and watch, thinking about it and never actually achieving. But he believed that deep inside all male psyches, the same thoughts lurked. Use and discard, take and throw away. And if there's a little pain added to the situation then all the better.

She browsed for almost an hour, filling her basket with only a few items. He didn't mind though; the wait would give him time to think about what she would be like before he felt what she was actually like. He wasn't going to rush; he was going to feel out his territory-to-be. The wait made the game more exciting, the result at the end more rewarding, the woman more satisfying.

And with an added element to consider, he'd have to plan in more detail than usual.

She paid using cash, packed her purchases into a carrier bag and left. The evening's air was crisp and he watched as she pulled the lapels of her jacket together. He stood still, next to the trolley return area, as she took a seat on a nearby bench and got her mobile phone out. She laughed as she spoke, then ended the call.

She sat there for five minutes, made another call, and then a car, sporty, pulled up into the pick-up point. The added element – her boyfriend.

The boyfriend's arrival was his cue to move. He got into his car and followed them out of the car park. They got caught by a red light at the exit. He stopped his car, the one he'd borrowed for this evening's entertainment, just behind the couple, his eyes fixed on the top of her head.

They weaved in and out of light traffic, the engine of the sports car far more powerful than the one he was in, until they came to a residential area, one he knew well. She got out of the car, which sped off. As he drove past her, he caught her waving at the boyfriend's car as it disappeared from view and then she turned and went into the house. He pulled into a space several yards away and waited.

It wouldn't happen tonight; he knew that morning would bring with it the opportunity he'd been waiting for. He'd retire and be back out in the morning.

*

She and her gentleman made a start before lunchtime the next day, Saturday. The sports car arrived a little before twelve. He'd been waiting, ready to follow them when they left. She did indeed look radiant this bright, sunny day and the boyfriend had clearly made an effort.

Traffic was heavier than last night but, even so, keeping up with them wasn't difficult. On two occasions, at red lights, he brought his car to a stop in parallel with the passenger door of the car she was in. She was only three metres from him on these occasions, three metres, so close that he could almost reach out and touch her, and he knew that today's wait would bear the most sumptuous fruit. She didn't see him – he kept his baseball cap low and head pressed well into the headrest and the car angled slightly behind the sports car. The red lights lasted only a minute between them, but it was a minute that lasted hours for him and the thrill was intense.

Eventually they ended up on the motorway. He didn't bother keeping a great distance between them. The top was down on the sports car and he enjoyed watching as her hair played in the breeze. He could see their heads turning towards each other, mindless conversation no doubt, and for a moment he envied the other man. It was only for a moment, though, before his mind was back on track.

The sports car came off the motorway and went up the exit ramp. He followed at a greater distance now and brought the car to a halt some way away from them. He watched the guy, through the car windows that separated them. The guy left the car and went inside the building.

That was when the moment presented itself. Despite the planning, this was too perfect to miss out on. He wouldn't wait any longer.

She was looking at her fingernails. She'd painted them only this morning and she was happy with the result. Her mind was filled with thoughts of what was to come. Things were still so new, so fresh, that there was much excitement, euphoria – that feeling you get in the pit of your stomach when looking at the latest special person in your life, when holding their hand, when feeling their touch upon your skin.

Her eyes rose up – it was a sense, that was all, a sense that someone was watching her.

Their eyes met. She smiled when she saw who it was, his car parked right behind the one she was in. She got out of the sports car, walked over to him, and he said something to her, something she didn't quite hear.

"What was that?" she asked.

He was standing in front of his car, the rear passenger door open behind him. He didn't answer her. Instead, he looked to the left, to the right, behind him.

He signalled to her with his hand to come closer. She did, for what did she have to fear? It was him, after all.

When she was close enough, close and comfortable, he punched her, busted the nose that made her look so pretty. Flung her into the backseat. Closed the door behind her.

It took only about three seconds for him to be in the driver's seat, pressing the button that locked the doors and speeding off. And in the backseat lay the woman John Simmons knew as Jennie Michaels, unconscious, unable even to call for help.

Chapter Twenty-Three

Nielsen had barely got started on her search for Michelle Keatings when her mobile phone sounded. She answered it. "Nielsen here."

"Detective Nielsen?"

"Yes. Who is this?"

"Detective Sergeant Kate Nielsen?"

The voice – nasal, raspy.

"I just said yes. Who am I speaking to?"

"It's Mark Sampson, Detective. Do you remember me?"

"It's not been that long, Mr Sampson, so, yes, I remember you."

"Oh, that's nice," he said. "I'm mostly forgettable, or so I'm told."

I'm not a fucking psychologist, Nielsen thought.

"You said to call," he said, "if anything comes up."

"Absolutely. Has something happened?"

"Indeed it has. This guy, the one from the other day – Mr Nervous." Mark Sampson laughed, a sharp laugh. "That's a good name for him." He didn't go on.

"What about him, Mark?"

"Mr Nervous?"

"Yes."

"He was back again two days ago. I didn't know whether to call. I saw him as soon as he came in. Still looked nervous, only this time not running about so much. He came in and hung around the newspaper shop. Thought he might come by for a coffee, but he didn't. He was definitely waiting for somebody. Then he went into the toilets."

When she realised he'd stopped, Nielsen spoke. "What

did he do then, Mark? What came next?"

"What came next is I got busy, so I don't know. Didn't see him again. But as soon as I'd served my queue, I saw... the thing is, I only noticed because you asked the other day and because it's so rare to see. Moved like lightning, he did."

"Who? Who moved like lightning, Mark?"

He cleared his throat. "This thing you're investigating. How bad is it?"

"Could be very bad, Mark." She wasn't going to lie to him, wasn't going to hold back. "Could be life and death. If you know anything, you've got to tell me. Anything that can help. Just say the words, Mark."

There was a pause. He was breathing more deeply, faster.

"Just say the words, Mark. Help me."

She waited. Still, nothing was forthcoming.

"Any little detail could mean so much. Just say the words."

"It's just... It's... If I tell you and if he's involved somehow, couldn't I get into trouble? Is my job safe?"

"Yes, Mark. I can personally guarantee that the police would help you. Just tell me what you know."

"It's probably nothing really, probably nothing at all. Probably just being silly."

"If it's nothing, then there's no reason not to tell me, isn't that right?"

After another pause: "Well, put it that way. But if it turns out to be something, promise me my name won't come into this."

"It won't," she lied. Means to an end.

"So I saw that guy, Mr Nervous." Another snort of laughter, shorter this time. "Then I served, what four, five people. Mr Nervous was gone when I finished. I kept an eye out for him, of course. And then, what, a couple of minutes later, he comes running out of the back offices and charges out the front door. I've never seen him move like that. And you mentioned him the other day. Got me thinking."

"Who, Mark? Who are you talking about?"

"The other guy you mentioned. The security guard. He's the manager, I think."

"Rod Taylor?"

"I don't know his name," Mark snapped. He was losing focus, too nervous. Nielsen could tell she'd lose him soon. Had to get something positive.

"Describe him for me."

"Short, fat, bald. Glasses, like fucking binoculars." No laugh this time. "Look, I don't want to say any more. If that means something to you, use it, but leave me out of this mess. Life and death you say – that's too much for me."

"You've been very helpful, Mark. Thank you. Listen, I'll be in touch–"

"No, don't call me. That's it. That's enough."

He hung up and Nielsen was left with the phone in her hand.

She searched in her pockets for Rod Taylor's number. She found it and dialled. What was Rod Taylor doing chasing after John Simmons and the Wongs? How did he even know they were there?

The phone was picked up by an office worker.

"Rod Taylor, please," Nielsen said.

"Moment."

Nielsen tapped her desk.

The voice came back on the line. "He's unavailable."

"Unavailable as in he's not there, or unavailable as in he doesn't want to be disturbed."

"Just unavailable. Wanna leave a message?"

"This is DS Kate Nielsen. I must speak to Rod Taylor immediately. If he's there, put me through. If he isn't, get me his mobile number now."

The line went dead. Cut off.

"Bitch," Nielsen said.

She grabbed her coat. "Sam." Sam lifted his head from the paperwork he was buried in. "Continue calling round these Michelle Keatings. See if you can find anything." She dropped the list on his desk and left before he could say anything.

As she drove towards London Gateway, she got on the radio. "Get me the details of all Rod Taylors in a twenty-mile radius of London Gateway services." The answer would be with her, she hoped, by the time she reached the Gateway. "And I need to know if there are any Michelle Keatings on the missing persons list. If not, then check if there are any Michelle Keatings listed up north."

"Up north, Sarge?"

"Just try your best. York and further up maybe. I can't be more precise than that at the moment."

It was no more than twenty minutes before she was crossing the bridge and pulling into the car park. She got out of the car, lifting her coat collar up in response to the blistery wind that had developed, and entered the building.

Mark Sampson, attending the coffee stand, saw her immediately. His eyes opened wide and he shook his head. She raised her hand to tell him to calm down, that it was all right. He lowered his gaze and turned around.

Nielsen moved towards the information desk. "I need to see Rod Taylor," she said, not even waiting for the woman, mid-twenties, perm, plump, to look up.

"Sorry?"

"Police. DS Nielsen. Get Rod Taylor out here now."

The woman swallowed a bit too audibly and looked away. She picked a phone up and spoke quietly.

When she'd replaced the receiver, Nielsen added, "You know, rudeness doesn't always pay off."

"What?"

"Hang up on me again and I'll have you for interfering with an investigation."

The woman said nothing in return, but her face burst into red spots.

"So where is he?" Nielsen asked.

The woman answered, voice inaudible.

"What?" Nielsen said, raising her voice.

"He's not here."

"Unavailable, eh?" The woman kept quiet. "What's your name?"

"My name?"

"Yes, name. Now."

"Jennifer Carson."

"Right. Now get me Rod Taylor's mobile number or get me his address. And be fast."

The volume got Jennifer Carson moving. The phone was in her hand in an instant and Nielsen was almost impressed by the effectiveness of her own assertiveness.

While she was standing there, her mobile rang. "Nielsen," as she answered.

"Three Rod Taylors, Detective. Harrow, Finchley and St Albans."

"St Albans," she said, not even thinking. "Give me the address. And keep the others on file for me. I might need them later." But I doubt it, she thought.

She pulled out her notepad and wrote the address down.

As soon as she finished on her mobile, Jennifer Carson spoke up. The red spots had disappeared. "I don't have a mobile number, but this is his home number. And this is his address." She handed Nielsen a piece of paper. Nielsen put the paper next to her notepad.

The addresses – a perfect match.

*

213

Rod Taylor lived in a flat. Nielsen stood at ground level by the communal entrance. She pressed the buzzer – number 29 – but there was no answer. She waited before pressing it again. She repeated this twice more before removing her mobile phone and dialling the number she'd received at London Gateway. An answerphone picked up and Rod Taylor's voice spoke to her. He wasn't there. Leave a message.

She didn't.

She started to think of John Simmons. Why did Rod Taylor follow him?

Taylor not being home concerned her. If he left the Gateway, as Mark Sampson had said, in pursuit of John Simmons and the Wongs, even though it was two days ago, and if his intent was in any way harmful, she should warn Simmons. Maybe she should warn the Wongs as well, although she and the police had troubled them enough over the past few days.

She decided to call Simmons. She dialled his number and waited while it rang. That's all it did: no answer.

"Shit, John," she said. He wasn't supposed to create any more problems and he should easily have made it home by now.

She tried his home number next. The same result, so she redialled his mobile. When she got the voicemail, she left a message – better than nothing. "John, Kate Nielsen here. I need to speak to you urgently. Call me on my mobile." She recited the number. "And stay at home. Potential danger – don't leave your house."

She hung up and hung around for a few minutes longer, walked around the building, then rang the flat buzzer once more. Still no answer. So she pressed the buzzer for another number. An elderly voice answered.

"Police, can you open the door?"

Duly the buzzer sounded and the door released itself. Nielsen pushed it forwards and entered. She took the first set of stairs two at a time. Then she came to his door. Number twenty-nine. The door to number thirty was open and an inquisitive small head was peering out. A perm, the second Nielsen had encountered today, was evident.

"DS Nielsen," she introduced herself, showing her warrant card. "Can I ask your name, Mrs…?"

"Mrs Brown, love. Mollie Brown."

"Have you seen anyone in this flat today?" she asked, pointing to number twenty-nine.

"No, leaves early, does he."

"Do you know Mr Taylor at all?"

"You mean Rod? Oh, a bit. We say hello sometimes. Bought me a bottle of wine last Christmas. Still got it in the cupboard – only don't tell him that. Don't have much company now that my husband's gone."

Nielsen smiled at the old lady. She wanted to make her feel better, even though she seemed just fine.

"Do you want to come in love? I can make a pot of tea if you like."

With no sign of Rod Taylor, Nielsen lost her sense of urgency. "You know what," she said, "I'd love a cuppa. Couldn't hurt." Searching the old lady's memory could prove useful.

Mollie Brown smiled and stepped back. The heat from within the flat blasted Nielsen as she entered, took off her shoes and left them on the mat by the door. A request by the lady of the house.

And she was a very house-proud lady of the house. Mollie Brown's flat, the home of an eighty-five-year-old, was the definition of cleanliness. A few pictures adorned the mantelpiece and the fire was on. Nielsen sat on a two-seater sofa, rugs in front of and behind it. A coffee table was before her and a bookshelf behind. *Countdown* was on the television, but the voices had been muted.

"Always thought he was a handsome one," Mollie Brown said as she came back into the room with a tray in both hands, a pot of tea and two mugs on top of it.

"Who's that?" Nielsen asked.

"Him," she said, nodding towards the television set and the presenter shown on it.

"Yes, he is rather dishy," Nielsen agreed, much to the old lady's amusement. "Here, let me." She rose to help with the tea.

"No, love. I haven't got this far on my own by letting others do for me. This one's on me."

Nielsen sat back down. "How long have you lived here?"

"Since they were built. All the blocks here, five of them, they were built at the same time. My late husband, Alf, Alfie, he built them. He was a builder. He was in the team that built them and we got this place. Special offer, it was. About five of the lads he worked with did the same. They all died years ago though. Some of them moved out first. But we stayed. And I'll stay here till the end. This is my Alfie's gift to me. I'm never going to leave it. Not until I'm ready to join him, anyway."

Nielsen was touched by the closeness she sensed between Mollie and Alf Brown, even though one of them was no longer here. She didn't know from personal experience that love, feeling so close to someone, could stay with a person for such a long time. She didn't desire closeness herself, still couldn't bring herself to, despite trying to forget, despite trying to change. Ultimately, she'd given up on the prospects of love.

"So," she said after trying the tea, giving compliments and allowing Mollie time to sip her tea and eat a biscuit, "as you've been here such a long time perhaps you can help me with some information."

"If it's about this place, love, I should be able to tell you. Of course, the memory's not what it used to be, but I try."

"Rod Taylor, how long has he lived here?"

"Oh, be about five years now. He moved in just after Alfie passed away. So five years next month."

"And you say you have little to do with him?"

"Hellos, as I said. There was the wine he gave me at Christmas – still in the cupboard. He waves from a distance, too, if he sees me."

"Does he live with anyone? A wife, family?"

"No, he's alone. Has been since he moved here. I've never seen him with anyone. Always thought that was a bit strange – a man should be with a woman. Husbands and wives, you know. Have a family. You can't make do on your own, love. You just can't."

"How long were you married?"

"Fifty-seven years. Alfie was my first and last love. A true gentleman. He built this place, you know."

"Yes."

"A special man. I miss him. Miss him terribly. Today as much as five years ago."

"And—"

"Do you have anyone special, love?"

"Me?" Nielsen gave an embarrassed laugh. "No."

"No? Attractive young lady like yourself and no boyfriend. Don't you want to get married, dear?"

"Get married? Don't you need a boyfriend first?" Nielsen mocked herself. "I always thought I would, you know, but thinking and doing are two totally separate things, I've come to learn."

"What's stopped you, love?"

Nielsen shrugged. "Life, I suppose. Work." She hadn't opened up in years, didn't want to now, but there was something about this little old lady, so innocent in her age, so wise in her years, that made Nielsen want to talk. She knew she'd only be able to say so much though. Couldn't do more than that.

"Being a police officer can get in the way of relationships."

"Of course, dear, but you must try. We're born to love."

"Yes."

"So try."

"I will." The old lady looked Nielsen in the eyes, finished off her tea and smiled. Nielsen felt she needed to say more. "You have my word," she added in a whisper.

They both giggled.

"I watch them, you know."

"Watch them?"

"Neighbours. It's no secret. I'm old, love. We old ladies need to find entertainment in one way or another. Can't always get it from TV. *Countdown*'s only on for so long each day."

"You watch and…"

"I see things. Five blocks around here. That's a lot of people. My dear friend Vera, she used to say, before she passed away last year, that there isn't a thing I don't know around here. A thing I don't see."

"And have you seen anything about Mr Taylor? Have you seen him do anything unusual?"

"Well, he goes out a lot, dear. Late at night, I mean. I always found that odd. Wakes me up in the middle of the night sometimes. Sometimes he's away for a whole day."

"Do you know anything else about him?"

"I don't know what he does or where he goes, if that's what you mean. He's a nice enough man. The wine at Christmas. Waving at me. But there's something odd about him. It's not normal, is it, coming and going at all hours?"

"And how long's this been going on, do you remember?"

"Oh, many years, dear. Many years. Since he moved in, I'd say."

Mollie Brown couldn't tell Kate Nielsen anything more of note. Nielsen finished her tea, said her thanks and made her way out, with a lot – both about Rod Taylor and also about herself – on her mind.

After Mollie had closed her front door, Nielsen knocked on number twenty-nine. No change – no answer.

She checked her mobile for messages. None. Why wasn't John Simmons calling her back?

She left. The office was her next stop.

Chapter Twenty-Four

It had been over an hour since Nielsen had returned from Rod Taylor's home. Uniform officers had been deputed to stakeout his address, a description of him given to them, and Nielsen was waiting to receive a progress report. She wasn't holding her breath for good news; she believed he was well and truly hidden. Why, though, she didn't know.

She was sitting at her desk, staring at the clock. Sam had so far drawn a blank on the Michelle Keatings front. She opened an email from Missing Persons. Pissed about how things were going, she said, "No luck here," pointing at the computer monitor.

"What about further afield?" Sam asked.

"Needle in a fucking haystack. Where am I looking? Manchester? Liverpool? Birmingham? Some small Scottish village? Bloody impossible."

"Got to remain positive."

"I don't need a pep talk." She turned away. "I'm out of ideas."

Sam walked over to her desk. "We've just got to wait, Kate. Sooner or later, whoever it is will make a mistake and we'll be ready to pick him up."

She made eye contact. "I certainly hope so. The moment can't come too soon. There can't be any more killing."

Bathroom, she thought. I need to be out of here.

She left Sam standing by her desk.

*

The mobile phone rang.

"Yep," said the nasal voice.

"Mark Sampson?"

"Yep."

"Police."

"Look, I told the officer earlier. I'm not interested in saying more."

"We just have a few more questions, Mr Sampson. It will all be hush hush. What time do you finish work today?"

"I said I don't want to." His voice had become hoarse.

"Two minutes, Mr Sampson. Just two questions, literally."

A long pause.

"Five o'clock."

*

Nielsen's phone rang. She picked up and listened. "Great. Hold tight. He'll turn up." She put it down.

"Taylor?" Sam asked.

"Officers are stationed at his place. They'll wait and we'll get him. If he doesn't turn up, he's due in at work at London Gateway at six tomorrow morning. I'll get him there myself if necessary."

"What makes you think he'll turn up?"

"He has no reason to think anything's wrong. He has no reason to think I want to see him."

"Unless someone speaks to him. The woman at the Gateway?"

"We'll see."

Nielsen had tried calling John Simmons again. Wanted to make him mindful of Rod Taylor. Wanted to know, finally, that he was doing as he was told. But he hadn't answered his home phone and his mobile had been switched off.

"Where the fuck is he?"

Sam didn't answer.

After she couldn't get through to John Simmons, she

requested his next of kin information. Marion Simmons was his mother. Her details were now written on a piece of paper that was on Nielsen's desk. She looked at it, thought for a moment. She surprised Sam by leaping up. She tossed her jacket over her shoulders and lifted her warrant card wallet from the desk. "Come on," she said, "I'm driving. I'm not waiting for him any longer. He can't play by his own rules." There was also the thought lingering in her mind that maybe something had happened to John Simmons.

"Wouldn't have it any other way," Sam responded with a smile in his eye, also getting up.

Despite the anger she felt and would feel from some time to come, Nielsen couldn't help but smile as she walked past Sam. She was careful not to show it to him though.

She didn't wait for Sam, even when she heard him say, "Don't suppose you want to fill me in on where?"

*

In the car. Nielsen driving.

The rain had started to fall. The windscreen wipers did their best to keep the onslaught of water at bay. The rain meant that drivers took more care, which resulted in the journey to Marion Simmons' house taking far more time. Taking more time meant Nielsen's frustration continued to grow.

Sam looked at Nielsen as she spoke and nodded at the responses she got. He liked the line of her neck, chin and nose. But she was withered beyond her years, that much was obvious. And he understood why; anyone who'd been through the hell she'd endured would have been no different.

"Just what do you expect to find here?" Sam asked as they got out of the car.

"Answers." She said nothing more. She didn't want Sam

Cook inside her head; he was too nice and she didn't want to be distracted.

"Answers?"

She stopped and turned sharply to him. "Back off. Got it?"

Sam held up his hands.

"And what about Taylor?"

"Why all the questions?"

"Just let me help, Kate."

She turned away and walked towards the door. He followed. Instead of knocking, she looked down and said, "Looks like he was lying to me, or maybe this Mark Sampson fellow got it wrong. All I know is there's no way Rod Taylor chased John Simmons when he left the Gateway the day Simmons says Jennie Michaels disappeared. Rather Michelle Keating."

"Maybe Taylor was just lazy."

"I thought about that." A pause. "Told me he'd always wanted to be a cop, so I guess he could've just said those things to sound more on the ball. Instead of being a lazy son of a bitch who chose to do nothing. But if that's the case and if he didn't run out the other day, why'd he run out after him two days ago? Why all the fuss now? So you want to help me, come up with a reason why because I'm stuck."

There was silence. Like her, Sam didn't have the answer.

"The tapes," she said, answering herself, clicking her fingers together. "He'd seen the tapes. Of course he knows what Simmons looks like. But what was the likelihood he'd spot Simmons there the second time? Hardly likely at all. So he runs out and he's not been seen since. And now Simmons won't answer his phone. He's involved, that's all I know."

She dialled John Simmons again. One more try.

Voicemail.

Marion Simmons lived alone. She was seventy-eight years old. Her perm looked immaculately kept and she touched it regularly as she spoke – with pride or nervously, Nielsen couldn't tell. She held a cup of coffee in her hands, which weren't steady, and the saucer perched precariously on her lap.

Maybe John Simmons had been here, maybe Marion knew something important, maybe she could help them find John, or Michelle Keating.

Marion Simmons had welcomed Nielsen and Sam with enthusiasm. Even when they said her son was suspected of a crime, her smile remained intact. It was as if she heard the words, but the meaning didn't filter through. Either that or she just welcomed the company.

"My John's a good boy," she said for the fourth time in as many minutes. "He's going to visit soon. He's busy, you see. He doesn't get much time to come all this way over to me, but he called me the other day and said he'd be coming soon."

"When was this?"

"Oh, less than a week ago. He said he wanted me to spend some time with his girlfriend. He said, 'Mum, you've met her before'. Oh, what's her name? Jane or something."

"Jennie," Nielsen said.

"That's right, dear. Jennie. 'She's beautiful,' he said. Told me I'd met her. But I said no, I hadn't."

"You've never met her then, this Jennie?"

"No, dear. He's a bit forgetful sometimes, is my John. Takes after me that way." She chuckled. "Doesn't know if he's coming or going, sometimes. But it's good if he's got a girlfriend. It'll do him good to have someone. He's been alone for such a long time."

Much as she wanted to, Nielsen couldn't bring herself to tell Marion Simmons that her son's girlfriend, the person who'd do him good, might be dead, or might be made up, the figment of her son's overactive, and incredibly dangerous, imagination. "How long has he been alone?"

"Oh, I don't remember, dear. His last girlfriend, why it must have been three years ago. Oh, what was her name?" She looked thoughtfully at the wall. "Fiona, that was it. Fiona Redding. Like the city, only spelt differently. He wanted to marry her."

"You don't by any chance have her number, do you?"

"No, dear. But I remember her address." Marion Simmons looked proud as she recalled the house number and street name. "Of course, I don't know if she still lives there."

"How can we find your son, Mrs Simmons? He's not home, he won't answer the phone and we're worried about him."

"Oh," she said, pushing her hand in front of her face, "there's no need to worry about my John. He always takes care of himself. He's always fine when he goes on his travels."

"Travels?"

"Yes, it's quite normal for him to go away for a while."

"And where does he normally go when he goes away for a while?"

"Oh, he never says. Secretive, that's what my John is. But it happens a lot – has done since he was a youngster."

"How do you get hold of him when he goes away?"

The old lady giggled. "Oh, I don't. John always calls me, whether he's home or away. That's just the way he likes it."

Just as Nielsen and Sam were about to rise and leave, Marion Simmons added, "Of course, when he goes away for longer he always stays with me for a few days afterwards. Caring, he cares. He doesn't want me to feel abandoned, so he stays to remind me that he loves me, to make up for his time away, I think. He hasn't told me so, but I'm sure that's why he does it." Marion Simmons was in a moment of deep thought. "This Jane, have you seen her? Is she pretty?"

"Jennie," Nielsen corrected. "Jennie Michaels. Yes, I have a picture. Would you like to see?"

"Oh, yes please." Marion Simmons' demeanour perked up. Nielsen pulled the picture from her pocket – the one that had been printed from John Simmons' phone before it had been returned to him. Marion Simmons took the picture and studied it carefully. "What a beautiful, beautiful girl. Oh, she and John will be so happy."

Nielsen realised, not for the first time, that Marion Simmons wasn't really paying attention to what she was being told. As a result, she inwardly questioned the reliability of what she was hearing from the old lady.

Sam thought nothing of the words and took a deep breath to indicate he was about to speak, but Nielsen's eyes indicated he should remain quiet. She interrupted Sam's movement with a hand on his arm and said, "John stays regularly, does he?"

"Oh, a few times a year." The old lady looked proud, but Nielsen couldn't tell whether that was because of the picture she was still looking at or because of her son's visits. "Yes. It's not happened for a while now, of course. He's been busy, you see." She lifted up her drink and took a slow sip, satisfied.

"And when he stays here," Nielsen continued, "where does he stay?"

"In the house."

"Yes, but where? Does he have a room?"

"This is as much John's house as it is mine. I always say that to him. All mothers should, don't you think?"

"Of course," Nielsen said. "So does that mean he has a

room of his own here in the house?"

"Absolutely," Marion said with a broad smile, broader than all she'd shown so far, and nodding her head. Her perm flicked up and down. "It's just upstairs."

"Can you show me?"

"Well, if you think it will help, of course." She stood up, a little too quickly, and a measure of her drink spilled onto the floor. "Oops," she said. "I must get that. It could stain."

"That's fine, Mrs Simmons—"

"Ms Simmons, please. I prefer Ms. John's father left me when John was only a child. I've always considered myself to be a single lady. Funny really. Must sound silly – I still use his surname, but I can't bear to be called Mrs." Her attention sprang back to the carpet. "Oh, the stain. The kitchen. I must dash to the kitchen."

"Ms Simmons," Nielsen said, "allow Detective Cook and me to go on up. Don't let us rush you. Which room is it?"

"I don't see why not. Turn left at the top of the stairs and it's at the end of the hall."

"Thank you."

Nielsen and Sam moved slowly out of the room but, as soon as they were in the hallway, they leapt up the stairs. The door at the left of the landing was open and revealed a bathroom. Even from outside, the enamel of the sink and toilet sparkled. A door on the left as they walked down the corridor and one on the right. They opened both, quietly and quickly, checking to see if John Simmons was hiding. Nielsen took the door on the left; Sam the one on the right. Each room contained a bed and wardrobe and nothing else. Minimalism to the extreme, similar to John's home. The rooms checked and cleared, their attention went to the door at the end of the landing. Closed.

"If he's hiding," she whispered, "there must be a reason."

Nielsen placed her hand on the door handle, nodded and

228

indicated three to Sam with her left hand. Using her fingers she counted down, three to one. Then, with the same speed and silence as before, she shot the door open. Sam entered, then she followed. Curtains closed, so the room was dark, but the light from the landing revealed the room was empty of people.

A bed against the far wall. A desk in front of the room's visitors.

She flicked on the light switch. A dim light.

A wardrobe. A chest of drawers with a television on top of it.

They went through the drawers, pulled out a handful of papers, but the room was all but bare.

"Is everything all right?" It was Marion Simmons, her head peering into the room before her body followed.

"Fine, thank you," Nielsen answered, the papers in her hand. "In fact, I think we're done here. May we take these?"

"You will bring them back – for when John comes home?"

"Absolutely."

"Very well. And if he comes back soon, I'll tell him you were asking after him."

"Yes, please do that. Thank you. My number is on here." She handed Marion Simmons her card.

"May I keep this?" the proud old lady asked, indicating the picture of Jennie Michaels that was still in her hands.

"Yes, of course," Nielsen told her. "I have copies."

*

Sam sat outside Marion Simmons' house. Nielsen had gone back to the station – home, he'd told her, go home, but he knew she'd return to the station, even when she said yes, she'd go home, get some sleep, rest. Sleep meant dream. Dream meant feel like death warmed up. No, she'd work instead.

Darkness had fallen. It was a little past nine-thirty. Sam was inside an unmarked police Volvo. He'd parked on the opposite side of the road, about three houses along. A single light illuminated the front room of Marion Simmons' house. John Simmons' presence in the house seemed too recent; he anticipated that the old lady might have been holding back on them, so, without telling Nielsen, he'd decided to stay.

A solitary shadow had moved across the room when Sam had passed by. Since then, no movement. Upstairs all was dark.

It was a peaceful street. Sam saw no sign of people as he sat there. Two hours, all told. But before he left he decided to get out of the car and take a closer look. He was fairly certain that no one except Marion Simmons was home, that John Simmons was not there, just as Marion had told them.

The back of the house was accessible through an alley, so that was where Sam headed. It was narrow and about twenty metres long. He took a right turn at the end of it, onto a path that drew a line along the back of the row of terraced houses, and came to the gate that led to Marion Simmons' back garden. By now the night's sky was pitch-black and Sam could easily enter undetected. He closed the gate behind him and stood with his back to its wood. No lights on this side of the house. He made his way across the grass and came to a paved area just in front of the house. Two windows, both with nets behind the glass. He cupped his hands around his eyes and leaned towards the window. He could make out a few shapes – furniture, that was all – but no signs of life. The same in both windows. The kitchen and a dining room. When he was standing in front of the dining room window, he could hear the faint sound of a television. Some kind of quiz show – lots of audience laughter and clapping. Certainly no sign of John Simmons;

just a lonely old lady watching television, doubtless the way she did every night.

Sam thought it was time to call it a night. But something still stopped him from going straight home.

*

Nielsen was also preparing to call it night, despite resisting for such a long time. She was sitting behind her desk, a pile of paperwork in front of her. None of the documents she'd taken from Marion Simmons' house had amounted to much, other than to demonstrate John Simmons was a workaholic. She'd spent the late evening reading through it, trying to get a clearer picture of what was going on, trying to find a clue of some sort, something that could help Sam and her find John Simmons.

She was currently engaged in deep conversation with several stations in the north of England to gather information about anyone by the name of Michelle Keating. It was a difficult task; the area was much larger than the fifty miles around St Albans.

Nielsen felt nothing but frustration as she waited, thought, and wasn't sure where to turn next.

She'd written Fiona Redding's address on a post-it note and stuck it on her computer monitor. She'd visit in the morning, perhaps learn more about John Simmons, his character and his past.

As she stood, her mobile phone rang. She pulled it out of her pocket and answered. "Yes, Sam."

"He's here."

"What? Where are you?"

"Marion Simmons' house."

"Why?" He was supposed to be the onlooker and keep out of the way; this was her case.

231

"Just felt I should."

"Good for you," she said, sarcastic. "And?"

"John Simmons. He's just walked up to the front door."

"Shit. Stay there, I'm on my way," she said, moving out of the office.

"Oh, fuck!" Then silence.

"Sam?" She stopped. "Sam, what is it?"

No answer.

"Sam."

Then: "Fuck!"

"Sam?"

*

Whatever feeling or intuition it was that had kept Sam in his car, it had been right.

He picked up his phone from the seat next to him. He dialled and as soon as he heard Nielsen's voice he told her, "He's here."

"What?" she asked. "Where are you?"

Sam kept his eyes fixed on the figure in the distance, the man walking in shadows, looking over his shoulder, approaching the front door. The man stood motionless in front of the door, didn't go in. It appeared as though Simmons was trying to force the door, pick the lock maybe, but Sam couldn't see for sure. Why not just use a key, he thought.

His phone was by his ear. "Marion Simmons' house," he answered Nielsen.

"Why?" She sounded angry with him.

"Just felt I should."

"Good for you," she said, sarcastic. "And?"

"John Simmons. He's just walked up to the front door."

Every few seconds Simmons glanced over his shoulder.

"Shit. Stay there, I'm on my way," she said.

John Simmons was still in front of the door. He wasn't looking behind him. He didn't see the other figure as it approached him.

"Oh, fuck!" Then silence.

"Sam?" She stopped. "Sam, what is it?" No answer. "Sam."

Sam didn't know what to do: get out of the car and go to them, and risk losing them both, or wait and watch.

It was when the second figure grabbed the first from behind, when John Simmons was dragged to the ground, that Sam moved, repeating, "Fuck!"

"Sam?"

*

As Nielsen pulled into the street, she could see Sam kneeling down beside a body, its hands tied behind its back. It was lifeless. Shadows surrounded them.

Killing the engine, she stopped the car and left it in the middle of the road. She ran to the path and stopped just short of Sam and, she quickly saw, Rod Taylor.

"What the..." Nielsen started but couldn't find the words to finish.

"Managed to apprehend him," said Sam, still out of breath.

"And where the fuck is Simmons?"

"Got away as I was cuffing this one."

"Shit."

"My words exactly."

"Word."

"What?"

"Nothing. So what the hell happened?" She looked straight at Taylor who now looked up. "What the fuck are you doing here? Why are you involved in all this?"

"You've got to hear this," Sam interjected.

"Laugh all you want," Taylor said, "but it's the truth."

"You shut up," Nielsen said. "Sam, what is he talking about?"

Sam stepped a few feet forwards and took Nielsen to the side. He kept his voice low. "He says he followed Simmons here, has been tracking him since Simmons left the Gateway two days ago. As I was talking to you, I saw him lunge on Simmons. Simmons was trying to get into the house."

"And Marion Simmons?"

"None the wiser. She's still in there. TV's still on."

"But why's he here?" she said, replacing her line of vision on Rod Taylor.

"Says he saw Simmons again yesterday. Saw him acting suspiciously. Followed him. So when I saw him grab Simmons, I ran out of the car. I leapt and took him down. Couldn't see faces clearly. As I held him down, Simmons took off. Didn't even see what way he went, sneaky bugger."

"Mr Taylor," Nielsen said, pushing past Sam. "Just what the hell do you think you're doing here?"

"There was something wrong at work," he said. "There was something wrong with him, so I've been following him since. He was following a Chinese man in and out of the Gateway. I saw him."

"Chinese?"

"Yes, Chinese."

"Wong," Nielsen said to Sam. "Just like he said." She walked to Taylor and helped him up. "So why the hero act today then?"

"Look, I haven't done anything wrong, okay?"

"Well, so far you've prevented us from apprehending a suspect, so I'd say that was something." That was it; she'd acknowledged it: John Simmons was, somehow, a suspect.

Not answering his mobile, he had to be. "That's obstruction, Mr Taylor, if that's what I want to make it."

"Okay, okay. Look, can you take these cuffs off me?"

"Depends on what you can tell me."

"I followed him, okay. I saw him, recognised him and followed him." A hesitation. "Okay, I admit it – when he first came to my work, I didn't do my job. I didn't react and didn't get to him. I saw him outside, but I didn't go after him. You know, I never wanted that bloody job. I told you, I wanted to be a copper. And every day I sit in that bloody room I hate it. So I don't bother. I've been lazy. For too long. Talking to you the other day, you made me want to bother. So when I saw him yesterday, it was my chance. I reacted. I followed him and, today, he came here. And I got him."

"Did you see him do anything wrong?"

"I saw him follow that Chinese man. Then the man was with a Chinese woman. I followed them into London. He followed them to a theatre. Stayed in there for two hours and was pulled out by police. I saw him being taken to the station."

He stopped.

"What did you do while he was in the station?"

"I stayed outside." Sam was now by Nielsen's side. "He left about four hours later. I followed him home but, the whole time I saw him, something wasn't right. I couldn't put my finger on it. So I stayed outside his house. A person appeared." This piqued Nielsen's interest. Maybe John Simmons was telling the truth. So why hide and run again? "There was some knocking and some hiding and then when the door was opened your guy was hit in the face. He went down like a tonne of bricks. The other person stood over him, then knelt down. He moved towards the body. I couldn't see what he was doing."

"Did you see this person's face? Anything distinguishing about him?" Nielsen sensed a breakthrough coming on. Or, at least, that was what she prayed for.

"I'm sure it was a man. His build was athletic maybe, from a distance, or maybe he was wearing a thick padded coat – and I thought for a moment maybe he was going to strangle him. But he didn't. He walked away. Not long after, you guys arrived.

"I've watched Simmons since. His behaviour's increasingly concerned me. He was rammed off the road, broke into an office in Harpenden, slept in a supermarket and went to a fitness club where you came along. When you both left him there, he looked totally dazed. I saw him stand next to his car, staring at his reflection. He didn't move – minutes, it must have been. Then he started shouting at himself."

"Then where did he go?"

"He headed back home and approached the turning into his street, but as he came to it he turned sharply the other way and sped back the way we'd come from. After that, he drove around some more and, in the end, he turned up here." He pointed to the end of the road. "He parked down there and then walked to this door. He looked like he was trying to break in, so that was when I decided to take him down. Make a citizen's arrest or something. But then I was taken down by you." He tilted his head towards Sam.

Nielsen stepped forwards and uncuffed Rod Taylor. "You're going to need to come with us. Answer more questions."

"Sure," he said.

"Will this night never end?" she asked Sam, rhetorical, as she led Rod Taylor to her car, not waiting for Sam to answer her. They got in and she accelerated away, with Sam following in the Volvo.

Who was that fucking guy? I didn't see his face. It's like nowhere's safe any more. I thought being at Mum's would give me time to think. I didn't expect to be jumped. Couldn't find my keys and then was on the ground. Maybe the guy who took me down – I couldn't see his face – is the one who's got Jennie. Maybe it was Wong. He came at me from behind and I didn't know what hit me. And then the police officer, the DC – what the hell was he doing there? Sam Cook, that's his name. I don't know what he thought he was doing, but I'm glad I managed to get away as they tussled. I can't get taken back to the station. I know now they'd not let me go if they manage to get their hands on me; they're obviously putting the blame on me. I'll be locked away and Jennie will be lost forever.

It's morning now, almost six, and I've stayed in the car, a public car park my place of solace, unable to sleep, unable to rest my mind, scared for myself and petrified for Jennie.

I open the contacts on my mobile. I need to know why that officer was outside Mum's house.

"Mum," I say, relieved to hear a familiar voice when she picks up. "It's John."

"Oh, John, how nice to hear from you." She sounds genuinely pleased, almost as if she's speaking through a smile.

"Mum, are you all right?"

"You know, the usual."

I choose to breeze over the chitchat. "Has anyone come to see you? About me, I mean?"

"The police were here," she says, as if she's just remembered and is surprised. "They came to see me yesterday, John. Oh, they were nice people. They asked to see your room."

"My room?" I ask. So that means they were snooping

around my things. That confirms it: Detective Nielsen doesn't trust me. She's after me. Me more than Jennie. I raise the phone in the air, ready to bring it down to the ground, but I know I can't. I need it. In case Jennie calls. I still have that naïve hope. Even though Nielsen and the police are fucking things up by coming after me, I clutch to it.

I still honestly believe the answer lies within that house. I truly believe that. And I'm not going to wait to be caught.

"Speak to you soon, Mum," I say, cutting the call short.

She sounds disappointed as she responds, "Oh, okay dear. You take care." Then she remembers: "Oh, John. If those officers call by again, shall I give them a message?"

"Yeah, tell them they're looking in the wrong place."

"What do you mean, dear?"

"Nothing, Mum. It's okay. Tell them nothing."

I click off and then get moving.

Before I know it I'm once again sitting outside the Wong residence – or Jennie's home, as I prefer to call it. I'm further back this time, parked down the road in between two cars and facing the opposite direction. I can see the end of the path that is in front of the house, so I'll be able to see when they come out. And as soon as the Wongs go out, I'm going in. Jennie was in there and I'll find proof of that; that way, Nielsen won't be able to be against me. Even if I have to search through every cupboard, every drawer, in every pocket, then so be it, that's what I'll do.

All through the night I couldn't think of what else to do. I thought about everything Jennie told me in the short time I've known her. Her home, the job that doesn't exist, the fitness group, just how little I actually know about her. Whether she's not Jennie but Michelle. Michelle Keating. I still can't say it, can't call her that; it's like the name of an imposter.

And yet I felt I knew her enough to want to marry her and spend the rest of our lives together. Being with her had that effect on me. She was so friendly, caring, warm to be around. But she was closed up – I see that now, but I was blind to the fact when we were together.

I'm drawn back to the present when Mrs Wong appears at the end of the path. She looks both ways down the street. I sink deeper into my seat so that she can't see me.

When I lift myself up a few minutes later – when I'm positive the coast will be clear – I can't see her. Within moments the Wong car exits the side road and leaves the street. I can't see inside it. I've no idea if both Wongs are in it, which worries me. I have to get inside, but I'm loath to the idea of finding someone in there when I break in.

To make sure that no one's home, I get out of the car and walk slowly to the house. I keep close to the fence and as close to the properties that I pass as I can, in the hope that I can't be spotted by anyone who might be inside the house. I knock on the door and quickly move off, dashing back past the fence. If anyone answers, I'll see them. Then I'll know whether I should step away and wait all over again, or whether I can make my move. I focus on the house, try not to even blink so that I don't miss a single detail: someone at the door, a flicker of a curtain, any sign of life.

I see nothing. So that means it's time to move in.

From the backseat of my car I collect a hammer. Without any hesitation, without even looking around – I don't want to arouse a neighbour's suspicion – I walk up to the side gate and swing at the pad lock with all my force. It gives way and falls to the ground. I pick it up and move inside, this time making it through, closing the gate behind me.

The path on which I've found myself takes me along the side of the house, and to the left of the building there is grass. Not much; just enough to host a swing and a bed of flowers. I walk along the path and come to its end, which is level with the back of the house. I stop. Here the garden opens up. It's the entire width of the house and travels to a back fence, which is about fifteen metres in the distance. At the back is a shed, no window. To my right I see a rabbit hutch and just beyond that is the back door. It's white and covered in cobwebs. Before the door, just to the right of where I'm standing, is a window. Again, its main feature is a pattern of cobwebs. I edge towards it and bring my head to it slowly so that I can see inside.

The kitchen. On the right there's a fridge freezer, a large one like you see on American television shows. The ones used by big families. On the left there are several cupboards, some hanging from the wall and others at ground level beneath sideboards.

I walk past the window and reach the door. Aside from the filthy white and cobwebs, there's a frosted window in the middle of it. I'm not sure whether to smash the glass and risk making a loud noise, or come up with another idea. I didn't get that far in my planning; I didn't plan beyond the gate door. I hope more than anything that this task will be just as easy, if not easier.

I notice a small window that's open above the main window of the kitchen. There's no way I could get in there by fitting through it, but it makes me pause and realise that perhaps there is a better option than blasting the window to gain access. On both sides of the main window pane are two large panes that, like the small one above, can open. Definitely a possibility. I need something to stand on. Looking around, I see the wheelie bins we get from local councils to encourage us to separate our waste and recycle our plastic, paper, glass. I go to the nearest one, open its lid and see that it's quite full. I pull it over so that it's underneath the window and try to climb on top of it. The memory of falling over when trying to climb over the gate a few days ago comes back to me. But I'm determined not to fall – I'm determined to make it in there – so I get to it. There's no way I'm being beaten this time.

With the bin pushed firmly up against the window and my hands pushing down on it, I jump as high as I can with the intention that I will land on top of the bin on my knees. I hit the top of the bin and my knees slide off. I land back on the ground and it takes that length of time before a shooting pain hits my legs. I reach down and rub them. Frustration wants to hit me with its fullest force, but I won't let it. I'm determined to get in there, so I take to the task again. The bin is against the wall, it feels secure and my hands press down. I jump up, jump high. My knees connect with the top and I angle my weight towards the window. I'm there. I've managed and I'm holding on.

I grab the gap under the open window and pull my body weight towards it. I manage to get up so that I'm crouching. My arm fits through the gap where the window is open and I reach down to release the larger window on the left. I have to push my body against the window and scrape my underarm, but it doesn't take long for me to get hold of the catch that releases the window. I push it from inside and pull it from outside and it's open.

I climb through and end up on the sink. As I'm trying to manoeuvre myself over the sink and down to the floor, my leg catches something and I fall. I slide down the sideboard and land arms-first on the floor. I manage to cushion the fall, but I'm startled and pins and needles travel the lengths of my arms.

I realise that I'm inside the Wongs' kitchen – in somebody else's house – and, even though I believe this is where Jennie lives or where she's being held against her will, a sharpness fills my stomach. There's no turning back now. Whatever crime has been committed against Jennie, I'm now joining the ranks of crime breaker. I've not listened to Detective Nielsen and I've broken into this house. Now the police have a genuine reason to come after me.

But if breaking in leads me back to Jennie, what does it matter? Does a crime really mean anything if I can rescue her? I'd do anything to find Jennie – I'd kill – and breaking and entering isn't anywhere near as high up the list. So I'm doing this. I'm finding her and there isn't anyone who can stop me.

Straight ahead is a door through which I walk. A left turn takes me into the lounge-cum-dining room. The dining table is on the right, and on the right of that there are several cupboards. I go over to them, open them up and start pulling out the contents. If I'm going to do this, they're going to know someone was here, so I might as well do this properly. And if that means making a mess then so be it.

Whatever I find in envelopes, I pull out and drop. Bills, letters, all dated, dated from months and years back even, and addressed to the Wongs. Stacks of paper that I let fall to the floor. There's so much my eyes can't keep up as I read, scan, try to spot. There are some photo albums. I open them up. Picture after picture show the Wongs on holiday in various places: New York, Italy, Las Vegas, Ireland, Rome, Florida.

Nothing of Jennie, though.

I take one of their pictures – a clear one of them standing in the centre of Times Square – and put it in my pocket. In it the billboards advertising plays and musicals are to the sides. Virgin Megastore, when it was still open, is to their left. And behind them neon signs advertise Coca Cola. NASDAQ figures are listed above a building's doors and windows. So many people are walking around them.

I walk away, leaving the mess on the floor. As I walk into

the main lounge area, I see a three-seater on the right side and a television, mantelpiece and unit on the left. On top of the unit is a stereo. Under the stereo is a cupboard. I open it, find nothing of note, and empty the contents. As a result, papers fall everywhere.

Opposite the entrance to the lounge is a door. Behind it is a cupboard under the stairs. I open it and look inside. The natural light from behind me is enough to illuminate what's there. Again, lots of paper. I've never seen so much. Too much of a puzzle to sift through. I'm getting exasperated, so I shred some of it in my hands, leaving it to drop at my feet. The rest I toss over my shoulder when my eyes can help me no longer, can't even fix on a word. Shoes, coats and boxes. I pull all the shoes out and fling them across the hallway. I feel my way through each coat pocket. Tissues – some used and others clean – fill them, along with receipts and keys. Everything finds its place on the floor when I release my hold.

I walk down the hallway, which takes me towards the front door. I pass pictures hanging on the wall. Pictures of *them*. My left hand brushes against them and they fall to the ground. In most cases the glass that acts as their protection smashes. Some of it crunches beneath my feet as I move along. To the left of the front door is a small unit on top of which sits the telephone. Much more space than the small phone takes up is left empty. I open the two doors and pull out the contents of the unit. All that emerges are phone books and a copy of the Yellow Pages. The frustration is starting to build now as I realise I may not find anything. I tear at the Yellow Pages and the small pieces that end up in my hands. Throw them all over.

Behind me and a little to the right is the staircase. More pictures hang on the wall to the left. I retrieve the hammer from the kitchen and make my way up the stairs. As I pass each picture, I smash the glass with the hammer. At the top of the stairs is a plant pot. I swing at it. It shatters, and I hear a scream. More like a gasp.

I spin round and try to work out where the sound came from. The landing doubles back on the direction I came up the stairs. There's a door to my immediate left. It's closed. Next to that is the bathroom. The door is open. The final two doors are shut and I'm pretty sure I can hear movement from within the first. I walk onto the landing and glance into the bathroom as I pass the door. Steam sits on the mirror that I see above a sink. Without pausing I step deliberately and push through the third door along. As the door slams against the bedside table and comes to a stop, there's another scream. Instinctively, I hold up the hammer. To my right and on the other side of the bed is Mrs Wong. She's standing with a towel wrapped around her body and another around her hair.

"Please," she gasps and she lifts up her hands. I notice they're trembling.

"Where is she?" I say, not moving.

"Please don't hurt. Please don't hurt."

She hasn't listened, so I repeat, "Where is she?" She still doesn't answer, so I pull the hammer up behind my head as if I'm going to bring it crashing down on something. On her? I don't know – I haven't thought my actions through. There wasn't supposed to be anybody here.

As I'm standing here and she starts to sob, I recognise the power I have. Whatever power she's had with Jennie and with leading me halfway around London the other day, right now it's reversed and I'm the strong one, in control, and anything that I want to happen will happen.

I surprise myself – I'm not scared. No. I didn't want her here, but maybe this is the best way. Maybe I can get to the bottom of this sooner than I thought. Maybe I can end it all now.

"Where –" I say each word slowly and deliberately so that she understands me clearly – "is Jennie Michaels?"

"Who? Who?" she says instantly. "I don't know."

"Tell me." I don't want to lose it with her.

"Who you speak about?"

"Just tell me," my tone rising. I don't know how much longer I can hold myself back. She knows something; there's no way she doesn't. "Tell me where she is!"

"Who you speak about? Who?"

"Jennie fucking Michaels, you stupid fucking cow!" The rage in me releases itself. "The woman I've picked up here a dozen times in the past three weeks. The woman I was with on Saturday. The woman who went missing when I stopped at London Gateway on the M1. The woman I was taking to see *The Woman in Black* at the Fortune Theatre in Covent Garden." Some kind of recognition emerges on her face. I see it. "Do you get it now? Do you see what you've done?" My breathing has risen to the highest level it can reach without bringing on a heart attack. I'm trying to keep still, but my body wants to run at her. "Where? Where is she?"

"I no understand."

"Yes, you do! And why did your husband attack me? He came to my house!" I lunge at her, reach the other side of the bed as she cowers against the window sill, and grab her by the towel that is around her head. I'm going to show her that she and that bastard husband of hers are over. She's going to crumble and tell me the truth about Jennie. I'm not going to back down. "You know her, you know why, you liar. You know everything. What have you done to her? My God, what have you done?" As each sentence passes through my lips, the volume of my voice increases. They might have killed her already.

She tries to shake free and the towel that's wrapped around her body comes off in my hand. She rushes past me, but I catch hold of her arm. She's completely naked and I spin her round.

"It didn't have to be this way," I tell her.

"No," she says.

"Just tell me!"

"No!" she shouts and she slaps me.

I hit her back. I've never hit a woman before – never hit anyone actually. She falls to the ground. Her mouth is bloodied and my cheek is burning.

"Next time it'll be with this," I say, lifting the hammer in the air, totally alien to myself now. "Speak and tell me." She doesn't react. "Tell me!" I shout and I bring the hammer crashing into the wall just above her head. That makes her move – like never before. She curls into a ball. I don't know what I'm doing, but I keep thinking of Jennie. In pain. "You keep quiet then," I say. I walk to the bedside table. "Keep quiet if that's what you want."

Jennie in pain.

I swing the hammer repeatedly. The lamp, the picture frame, the telephone – they all crumble and pieces go flying.

Jennie in pain.

I hit the bed, I crawl over it and I hit the other bedside table. I move over to the wardrobe that's opposite.

Jennie in pain.

"Here," I point, "have you got something of Jennie's hidden in here? Well, do you?" My hand and the hammer collide with the doors. The wood shatters. I pull off what's left of the doors and start smacking everything inside.

"Please," I hear her say, sobbing. "Please, no."

Jennie in pain.

I pull all the clothes out and throw them across the bed. "Is this Jennie's?" She doesn't answer. "Is it?" I pull out the

246

last item of clothing: a dress. As I pull, the plastic hanger breaks and falls to the ground.

Jennie in pain.

"You like this?" I say, holding up the dress. I start tearing it. Then I pick up more clothes that I've dropped onto the bed and floor and I start tearing at them too. She sobs even more. "Please" escapes from her mouth between gasps for air.

Jennie in pain.

"Tell me and I'll stop." I'm still tearing at them. "Tell me and I'll stop!"

"No!" she wails, and she gets up and charges towards me. She grabs me by the neck. Her nails dig into my skin and I flinch. She's stepping on my feet, time and time again. Her arms start to flail and she connects strike after strike. My eyes search the room. All I can see that makes any sense is the hammer. One hit and she'll be out like a light.

But I'd kill her. No, I can't. I've got to regain control. The clothes: I can use the clothes. Restrain her.

I take the material that's in my hands and wrap a jumper around her neck. I squeeze. "Tell me," I say again. "Tell me." I'm almost pleading with her. Don't make me do this. The energy is leaving her. She's not hitting me any more and falls to the ground. I don't let go. "Tell me," I say a final time; it sounds like a whine. There are tears in my eyes. I'm covered in sweat.

With my arms still strangling her, I look up at the ceiling. It's like my vision slingshots back on me; I find that I'm looking down on myself. The angle gives me a clear view: I'm strangling a woman; her life's beginning to subside. I'm holding on with all my strength. And I recognise, as clearly as I can see what I'm doing to her, that it's all wrong. I can't kill her.

What the hell am I doing? I scream. My own scream is

much louder than hers.

I stop myself. I can't do it. I release her, pick up the hammer and hurl it at the window. It cracks but doesn't shatter.

I look at her as she lies on the floor, leave the room and stumble down the stairs. I pull open the front door and don't bother to close it behind me. It only takes me thirty seconds to be in the car and out of the street.

Chapter Twenty-Five

It didn't take long for DS Nielsen to hear about a madman terrorising a couple, the Wongs, ransacking their house, assaulting Mrs Wong. She knew instantly who the madman was.

"Nielsen," the voice had boomed down the phone. He didn't need to say any more – she knew who it was – but he did. "DCI Morgan here. Those chinks you were talking about. Find out what the fuck's happened. The woman's been attacked. In her home."

The goose bumps emerged across Nielsen's back. "When? By whom?"

"Seems like your lonely friend couldn't wait for you to do your homework."

"Fuck." Surprise, despite all he'd done, filled her voice. He was out of control and had to be stopped.

"John fucking Simmons. Seems like your new best buddy might be a little dangerous after all." He sounded smug but with an undertone of fury as well. He spoke slowly. "Speak to them, find Simmons and bring him in. Their place will be buzzing with uniforms, but you get over there and you take over. Do you understand?"

"Yes, sir."

"Get that Simmons prick once and for all."

"I'll need a warrant for his house."

"Already done. Two hours. They'll call you. And Nielsen. Trust a wacko again, fuck up again, go off on a tangent again, and you're done, you hear me?"

It wasn't a question. He hung up the phone, didn't give her time to respond.

Nielsen slammed her phone down. "Fuck."

She lifted up her warrant card wallet as she slid her handbag off the back of her chair. Her coat over her shoulders, she made her way out of the office, down the detectives' corridor, past Morgan's office where she saw him follow her with his eyes as she went by, down the stairs, out the door, through the foyer where she'd first met John Simmons, out of the station's main entrance, and into her car. It wouldn't be a long journey – she'd make sure of that.

*

Just like Kate Nielsen, Sam Cook hadn't slept the previous night. He'd finished interviewing Rod Taylor with Nielsen, convinced as much as they could be that Taylor was telling the truth, drunk coffee and ploughed through more paperwork. He'd woken Fiona Redding when he called her before seven that morning. It was her day off and she agreed to meet him.

Fiona Redding was a short lady, about thirty, and she had large brown eyes. Her skin was tanned and she'd clearly spent time making herself presentable before Sam had arrived.

"John and I weren't together that long," she said. "About two months, all told. I was looking for fun, he wanted more than that. He was a nice guy, but he was a bit too serious for me. A bit too into it, if you know what I mean."

They were standing in her kitchen. Sam had declined Fiona's offer of coffee and was leaning on a sideboard while Fiona was slicing vegetables for the stew she was preparing for the evening's dinner, ready for when her husband returned from work. She'd married a year after splitting up with John.

"Did any of his behaviour ever concern you?" Sam asked.

"John wanted what I wouldn't give him. It was as simple as that. He wanted more than a fling. I wasn't looking for anything serious. Yes, I changed not long after that, but at the time that was me. You know, I remember when he introduced me to his mother. She thought I was some kind of serious girlfriend. She mentioned something about when we get married this or that would happen. It was too much for me. *He* was too much. So I bailed. Yes, I hurt him, but that's life. He was a decent guy though. He never did anything that wasn't charming."

Sam told Fiona Redding he'd be in touch if anything else came up; that maybe DS Kate Nielsen would make contact soon.

*

Nielsen found Mrs Wong sitting in the lounge with Mr Wong by her side holding onto her, as if for dear life. Every few seconds he rubbed the sides of her arms, ready only to loosen his grip for the slightest amount of time. They looked up at her when she said their names; they hadn't seen her enter. Other officers were still gathering evidence from around the property.

"Mr and Mrs Wong, my name is DS Kate Nielsen. I'm sorry to trouble you, but it's important we speak."

"It's okay," Mr Wong answered. "What can we do for you?"

"May I?" she asked, pointing at one of the dining table's chairs.

"Please," he said, after taking a quick look at what she wanted.

"So Mrs Wong, you know the man who broke in here?"

Her husband jumped in. "It was the same man as the other day. The same man from the theatre."

251

"And did he make the mess in here?"

Mr Wong again: "All over the house. Not only in here. It's in the kitchen, it's in here, in the hall, under the stairs, on the stairs, at the top of the stairs and in the bedroom. The bedroom's ruined. And he threatened my wife. He used a hammer, for God's sake."

"Did he actually *use* the hammer, Mrs Wong?" Nielsen had got her notepad out and had begun scribbling some notes down – key points she'd most likely need to refer to when she caught up with John Simmons. She was confident he'd make a mistake soon and that he'd be taken in as a result.

"Yes–"

"No, Huang. I speak now." Mrs Wong looked her husband in the eye. He was against her speaking, Nielsen could tell, and his eyes tried to communicate a message to his wife. "I okay." She turned to Nielsen, but there was anger behind Wong's eyes – he couldn't hide it; he wasn't that good. "He use hammer, yes. But he no use on me." Immediately, Nielsen noted the difference in their accents. "He hit pictures and flowerpot and wardrobe. But he no hit me. For moment, I think he will. He take it high above head and look like he mean to hit me. Look very angry. When I say him I don't know this woman he look for, then he look very angry. He scare me. But there come time when I see in his eye. I see he angry, but I see he no killer. He no going hurt me. So I fight him. I scratch skin, hurt foot, hit. Then he take clothes round my throat and I think for moment maybe I wrong. Maybe he kill me after all. But no. He no kill me. He scream. He look up at ceiling and he scream. And he run fast from house."

"Did he take anything?"

"I no think so. Maybe, but I no see. Maybe, but I no think so."

"Was he looking for anything? Did he ask you for anything?"

"No, no. Just where Jennie? And he tell me about London. We go three days ago. He tell me where we go. Like he know. Like he follow us more than just at theatre. How this man be like this?"

Nielsen didn't know if she should defend John Simmons' actions or acknowledge that he'd done wrong. Criticising him would make her feel better, though, for putting the Wongs in a position where John could come after them and turn them into the innocent ones. She was angry at herself for not doing more about it when John came to her, for not making absolutely sure that he wouldn't do something irrational, something stupid like this.

"He's very scared," Nielsen said. "He thinks that someone has kidnapped his girlfriend. He thinks she lives here."

"But we already told him," Mr Wong added. "We've lived here for two years. No Jennie lives here. Just us."

Nielsen nodded her head. She had wanted to believe John Simmons; she really had. "I know. I can see that." I know that now, she thought.

*

Nielsen had left the Wongs downstairs to continue consoling themselves, with the promise that they'd get to the station in the coming days, soon, when they'd managed to calm down, to finalise their statements. She stood upstairs in the bedroom. In the room where the violence had broken out. Where John Simmons had become the criminal, where he had done wrong, where he had made all her doubts front and centre and true. She looked at the clothes that were everywhere, at the smashed lamp and the telephone on the floor, at the wardrobe doors hanging from their hinges and splintered to pieces. She looked at the cracked window. And on the floor in front of the window, the hammer – which she'd instructed while en route to the crime scene not be removed until she arrived and saw it. Saw it to confirm to herself a truth with which she was struggling to come to terms: that John Simmons had lied to her again, after she thought she'd got through to him, that he'd taken a deadly weapon to this house, premeditated, and that he'd used it. That he'd ignored her and taken the law into his own hands.

She reached into her pocket and pulled out her mobile phone. She felt so dejected; defeated almost. She didn't care about many things – had little care for herself – but she'd given this man her trust and he'd abused it. Another man had done that to her. She could have kept Simmons locked up after the theatre incident and now she wished she had. She could have pursued the wasting-police-time angle and now she wished she had. But she'd had faith in him, for some stupid reason. Misguided faith and she'd given him a break, a break that led to this and made her look like a fool. Again.

She found the number in the phone's memory. "It's me," she said.

The voice on the other end said, "And?"

"He's done them over pretty well. Pushed it too far. Even though it's quite clear this Wong guy is Mr Dominant. Whatever, they've definitely been well and truly on the receiving end."

"Now, aren't you glad you had me to tell you how to behave?"

She wanted to punch him. The smug voice, the smug face, the mug.

"Can you press for the warrant to be ready quicker?"

"Done." With that DCI Morgan clicked off.

Nielsen returned downstairs to find Wong standing

over his wife. She bade them goodbye and left, with Wong showing her out.

As soon as the front door closed, Mr Wong went back into the living room. He walked over to his wife. She stood up. As quickly as an eye blinks, he brought an open hand against her cheek. "That," he said through gritted teeth, "is for interrupting me and embarrassing me. Don't fucking embarrass me again. They've got to help us."

"But Huang—"

"Do not," he growled, "fuck that up!"

*

As soon as Nielsen had left the Wong household, she'd dialled Sam's mobile. He'd just finished with Fiona Redding, gave a brief progress report.

"I'm going to need you to help me take Simmons down. Waiting on the warrant for his arrest and to search his home."

"When'll it be ready?"

"Hopefully within thirty minutes," she answered. "I'm expecting a call to confirm."

"So are we moving in hard or proceeding lightly?"

"Whatever's necessary. This has gone too far. We need to end it today."

She told Sam to meet her back at the station. She'd collect the warrant en route.

It was, in fact, only twenty minutes before the call came through: the warrant was ready. Nielsen got it and was back at the station just minutes after Sam had arrived there. They met in the car park. She told him to wait. She had someone to see first. One last stop.

*

255

She'd made wrong judgement calls before – one in particular that cost her dearly, almost cost her her life, affected her still – but this one stung more than anything else. Was it because it was fresher? Could that have been why?

She'd put her faith in John Simmons, almost went against Morgan's commands, was sure she could help. And his single act of violence had destroyed that faith.

Innocent people, victims, those in need – they don't do this kind of thing.

Or was it the work of a desperate man, one who didn't know which way to turn any more?

The only thing she understood was that nothing was clear.

From now on she'd play the safe card: she'd bring John Simmons in, no questions asked, and figure out the rest later.

She knocked on the door. Like a child, she didn't want to enter. Too much to face, too much shame.

"Come." The deep gruff voice again. It always had that booming quality about it.

As she inched round the door, Morgan's eyes lifted and his eyebrows rose. He was standing behind his desk. She could detect the smugness in him – his face, his whole demeanour. And that was mixed with anger. She wanted to hit him for it. She wanted to slap him and tell him to fuck his job and laugh at how pathetic he was. But she didn't; she couldn't.

She had to see this through. After that, she wasn't so sure. Maybe this was the beginning of the end for her.

"Take a seat." He signalled to one of the two seats on the opposite side of his desk. He only ever did this – asked someone to sit – when he wanted them to squirm, to make them wait for his onslaught. Only had time for his staff when he wanted them to realise how much better he was at the job than them. Better from behind a desk, that is.

Nielsen wasn't willing to let this go on any longer than was necessary. She sat and he said, "And?"

"We have the warrant. Ready to move in."

He sat down, placed his feet on the desk and stretched his arms behind his back. Behind him on the wall was a shelf on top of which a row of certificates was displayed. Above them were a few photo frames: his wife and children on holiday with him in various places, always heavily tanned, surrounded by blinding sunshine and full of fake smiles. Photo smiles. Nielsen knew that kind of smile well.

"So, do you have any idea where your new-found friend might be? He'd have to be the craziest bastard alive to be back at his home right now."

She wanted to shout, "He's not my fucking friend, you sad son of a bitch!" But she didn't. "No," she said. "I have to hope he's at home, but you're right, I doubt he's there. If he's not, we'll look for clues, for family, friends, any sign of relationships we can find in his home. He doesn't strike me as…" She paused, leaned back in her chair.

"As?"

"He doesn't strike me as someone who makes a habit of doing this sort of thing. I'm still not convinced this was deliberate."

"Well, that makes it—"

"No, listen, please." To her surprise, Morgan cut his sentence short and motioned for her to go on. "By that I mean he won't have a place to hide. He won't know what to do."

"Maybe." Morgan gave a thoughtful pose, as if he were considering something of the utmost importance. "To tell you the truth, I don't care."

Nielsen waited for more. None came, so she said, "Why did you call me back here?" She'd received a text message of all things while collecting the warrant.

"Because you've fucked up enough and I wasn't sure a phone call would spell it out clearly enough to you. I thought maybe face to face would make more sense to that tiny brain of yours. I want him brought in. Whether you hurt him or he hurts you, or you feel sad about how this has worked out or whatever, just get him. Do one little thing right and stop being a tosser. This sad fuck's already taken up too much of my time." He clasped his hands together behind his head. Paused. "And so have you. Get up, get out and redeem yourself." He put his feet back on the floor and started to read some of the papers on his desk. "Now we're done." Nielsen's signal that the meeting – the chat, the telling off, whatever you want to call it – was over.

*

"I'm driving," she said.

They got into her car, Sam in the passenger seat, the warrant in his hands.

"He might be delusional," Sam said when Nielsen had finished briefing him on all she knew about the John Simmons and Mrs Wong incident.

"It's possible." She wanted to believe that. She wanted to believe that all this could be sorted out by simply saying John Simmons had made up his story. "But I'm not sure that feels right." Feelings again; hunches. She'd said it earlier – to hell with them – and here she was again listening to them. "He's very believable, if he is out of his mind. And this attacking Mrs Wong. Even I could tell she's helpless. Her husband's the bully, that's obvious."

"Man with nothing to lose then."

"Maybe. Sooner or later you're going to snap when you don't know what to do. And we don't know that he knew Mrs Wong was there before he entered the house. Then again, maybe he wanted to scare her. I don't know."

"Just like at the theatre. Scare the hell out of someone enjoying a show."

"The discovery of Jennie Michaels at the leisure centre proved a Michelle Keating has gone missing or at least isn't around at the moment. We just have to find out whether Simmons did have a relationship with her and whether Simmons is somehow involved in her disappearance, if her disappearance is somehow sinister."

A left-hand turn and they entered Woodham Close. Nielsen drove slowly, passed three houses, four, five, then said, "That one." She pointed to the sixth on the right, kept the car rolling. "That's the one."

She parked the car outside the tenth house along. They got out and started walking towards John Simmons' home, no hesitation in their steps. Nielsen walked on the left, Sam on the right and two steps behind her. They didn't speak. The time for talking had passed and now all their focus had to be on the action ahead. All focus, for neither had the desire for anything to go wrong, and despite evidence to the contrary Nielsen still wouldn't ignore the possibility that John Simmons might not be a dangerous man, despite her DCI insulting her over it, despite much of the evidence pointing the other way; but she'd learned that at the moment of action trust was the last thing you gave a suspect. She'd learned that the hard way.

It was a small house. A low black gate, a minute front garden, a flowerbed the size of a doormat. A short path led to the front door. The wooden front door had the number six on it in gold-coloured metal and there were three central frosted-glass panes. There was a knocker – very old fashioned. Nielsen pulled it away from the door and pushed it against the wood five times. The vibrations travelled up her arm.

They waited on the doorstep for thirty seconds. No answer. So Nielsen knocked again, louder this time, with more force, and she called, "John Simmons. Police. Open the door. We have a warrant for your arrest."

Another thirty seconds and still no answer forthcoming. Nielsen nodded to Sam. He removed a baton from under his coat and smashed one of the glass panels. Access into the house from here was easy. He reached through, round and released the lock. The door opened.

"John Simmons," she repeated as she stepped inside. "Police."

There was no answer as they stepped over the mail and moved deeper into the shallow hallway.

"John," she said, good volume still. "Kate Nielsen here. Come out so that we can talk about this."

Sam gave her a look, one that said we don't normally do it like that, then he shrugged it off.

"You take this floor," she whispered. "I'll do upstairs."

Nielsen left Sam in the hallway, nothing surrounding him but peeling wallpaper. She took the stairs two at a time. At the head of the stairs, a door. She burst through it. No point in giving him time if he is here, she thought. The bathroom. All blue, a couple of pictures of boats. Nothing in here.

So she was back on the landing and took the first door on her left. Bedroom. A double bed, television facing it, curtains still not drawn. No wardrobe, just drawers. Nothing else.

A couple of quick steps and she lunged through the final door. Also on the left, it opened with ease. Curtains open, a view of the street in front of the house. A desk covered in papers. A phone on a small table by its side.

On the wall were film posters. They weren't framed; just tacked on and not straight. Really tacky, Nielsen thought. She wondered whether her young niece and nephew could do a better job.

"Where are you, John Simmons?" she said to herself.

Sam walked into the room. She didn't bother to turn around.

"He's not been here today," he said. "Post's on the floor."

Sam went to the car to radio for uniform support. "Let's get them to wait here and we'll get on looking elsewhere," Nielsen had said.

She'd moved into the living room. Her phone rang. She removed it and looked at the screen. Number not recognised.

"Hello."

No response. No voice. Nothing.

"Hello," she repeated.

The call cut off.

She put the phone back in her pocket and started looking at the books on the shelf.

Ringing once again. She removed the phone and answered, a little more force in her tone this time. "Hello."

The voice that spoke to her sounded like it was nervous and uncertain. "You're in my house. You were in my mum's house too."

"John?" She was out of the room and out of the house in five seconds. She jogged down the path and stood in the road. She looked in both directions as John Simmons spoke. Sam, in the car and speaking on the radio, noticed her.

"I've done nothing wrong," he whispered. "You've got to believe me."

"I'm simply going where all the evidence takes me, John." She wasn't going to hold back; she'd hit him hard with what she saw. He sounded shaky, so maybe this was the best chance she'd have to break him. "And right now it's taking me to believe that you have more involvement in all this than you claim."

"I've done nothing," he said, "except what needs to be

261

done to find Jennie."

"Your girlfriend?" She kept looking left and right. Could see nothing out of sorts.

"Yes, you know that. I told you. You have to believe… believe she's real."

"You mean Michelle Keating?"

"I don't know. I really don't."

"Your girlfriend, who doesn't live where you say she lives, who doesn't work where you say she works and who isn't the person you say she is. The gym membership showed us that, didn't it? It's like she's vanished into thin air and hasn't left a trace of a life behind. Explain that then."

"But she has a life. With me! She *has* vanished."

"Taken by a monster?"

"Jennie?"

"You mean Michelle."

"How am I supposed to know? You can't think… Look, I… Please believe me."

"Is she dead, John?"

"No."

Nielsen started walking down the road. Then louder: "Is she dead?"

"I don't know!"

"Is she dead?"

"I can't believe that."

"Have you killed her?"

"No! No!"

She looked behind bushes, in gardens. "You haven't helped yourself. I told you, I told you to stay put and give me time. That's all I asked. But then you cut off all contact and went on a rampage. Just some fucking time is all I asked for!"

"I couldn't wait. I couldn't sit on my backside. Can't you see that? We're running out of time!"

She kept walking. "Where are you now?"

"You know I can't tell you that."

"Are you outside? Down the road? Can you see me now?"

"I'm gone. You won't find me."

"You have to turn yourself in."

"That's the kind of thing you say to a suspect."

She came to the end of the road. Looked both ways into the main road. "You attacked that Wong woman. You broke into her home and went at her with a fucking hammer."

"I know what I've done. And you know what? I don't regret it. I did what needed to be done – they're guilty. So if that means I'm on my own, then I guess I'm on my own. You won't let me find Jennie if I tell you where I am, will you? And I'm going to find her. I will."

She looked back in the direction of the house. Sam was running towards her. "Test me then. Tell me where you are and see me. We'll talk, I'll listen and we'll sort everything out."

"I know what you really mean. You'll take me in. You'll charge me with something. You know, I didn't mean to hurt her."

"Who? Jennie Michaels?"

"No, not Jennie!" he snapped. "The Wong woman! When I broke in, I didn't think they were home."

"It's over, John."

"No, it's not. You have to help me find her."

"I think you know more than you're letting on, John. If she's dead, I need to know. If she's dead, she needs to be laid to rest. Once and for all."

"I haven't hurt her. I went into the building. I bought her a coffee. She was gone when I got back, I swear."

Sam arrived by Nielsen's side. Stopped; he knew straight away what was going on.

"Now listen to me." Nielsen flipped her hair back with

her hand. "You will tell me where you are, I will pick you up and we will go to the station and end all this. You can tell me anything and everything. I will listen to *every* word. I *will* pay attention."

"But you're not listening now."

"I'll help you in any way I can." There was no way she would, if he was guilty. "But I can only help you if from this moment on you are one hundred per cent honest with me. Put your trust in me, turn yourself in and you'll get through this. You have my word. But if you don't–"

"Jennie's been taken. Don't you see that?"

"Right now, John, Jennie Michaels isn't even a person! Show me otherwise, would you? I've tracked down every Michelle Keating in this area and they're not her either. So where is she?"

"She exists. She's my girlfriend. She was with me only days ago. I love her. We're going to spend the rest of our lives together." Silence for a moment. Then: "You've stopped looking for her, haven't you? You don't sound the same any more. You don't believe me any more."

"It's me, John. I'm the same person as before. Come and see for yourself."

Pause.

"I didn't hurt Jennie. The answer lies with the Wongs."

Nielsen had had enough of not getting anywhere. "Well, I think the answer lies with you."

Pause. A long pause. Just breathing.

"John."

Still nothing.

Louder: "John."

"The Wongs."

The phone clicked off. He was gone.

*

The phone call had knocked Nielsen out of her comfort zone; she liked to be in control, she liked to know what was coming, but now she was worried she'd pushed John Simmons too much. She hadn't controlled the tone of the conversation; she hadn't led Simmons where she'd wanted to. She was angry at herself for, she thought, messing it up and letting her emotions take over. Now she might not be able to track him down.

After the call, she and Sam continued to search the house. Then, when the uniforms arrived, they returned to the station. Nielsen found herself looking over her shoulder the whole journey while Sam drove: she was looking at people on pavements, in cars, at bus stops, at pedestrian crossings. She wanted to catch sight of John Simmons.

She didn't.

They spent the rest of the day on calls, searching databases, the internet, documents and drinking coffee. Nielsen was sitting alone in the office when she was brought to reality by Sam as he re-entered.

"I wondered if you'd still be here," he said. "Thought you might finally have succumbed to exhaustion."

"What?" she asked, snapping out of her daze. "Oh, yeah. Tempted, to be honest with you. Worried if I stop I won't be able to start again."

"You know, while I understand the suggestion's crazy, you really should go home."

She ignored him. "You haven't gone home yourself. Why's that?"

"I was about to," he said, and he left it at that. He sat at his desk and smiled at her.

"What?" she asked, noticing, then immediately defensive.

"You're a curiosity. It's gone half ten and you're still here. You didn't sleep last night. Is the work really still everything to you? No boyfriend to give your attention to?"

"Very funny."

"I'm serious."

"Well, I think you knew the answer to that one before you even asked it. Besides, where would we get the time?"

"Oh, so you're assuming, are you, that I haven't got a girlfriend? A fiancée even."

Nielsen shrugged her shoulders and let out a short laugh. "I guess I am."

"Well, I'm offended," Sam said and lent back in his chair. "I could be fighting them off."

She paused, for a moment wondering if she'd actually offended him. Then she saw through the facade: "Bloody right, though, aren't I?"

He didn't say a word; simply nodded and raised his eyebrows.

A heavy silence filled the air for the briefest of moments, then he said, "Sad lonely buggers, only able to fill our lives with work and the paperwork that comes hand in hand with it."

"Pathetic indeed," Nielsen confirmed.

"Pathetic and sad," he added. "So, my pathetic and sad compadre, what do you say we keep home on hold for a while and go and get a bite to eat. Pub down the road serves till eleven. We could just make it."

"No," her automatic response. Then she realised she hadn't even thought about what he'd asked, hadn't given herself the chance to consider whether she'd like to go or not. Stupid cow: guy trying to be nice and she shields off his attack.

Fortunately for her, he was persistent. "You're telling me some greasy chips wouldn't fill that hole you've got inside you from lack of food, lack of sleep and dead bodies? You've got to be kidding me."

"Give me two minutes," she said, smiling and rising. She

quickly left the room, not allowing herself time to change her mind.

She went down the corridor and into the ladies' toilets. She didn't need to go but felt she needed something to make what was to come feel more natural – some kind of encouragement to get herself off her backside, kick her life into gear, do something normal for once.

She plugged the drain and filled the sink with warm water. After testing the temperature, she splashed three handfuls of water onto her face. No make-up to distort. She wiped the sleep from her eyes and looked at herself in the mirror. It wasn't a sight she liked to look at. Hers wasn't a life she liked to be a part of. But she knew only one thing – was confident about only one thing – and that was catching criminals and bringing them to justice; it was the one thing in her life that brought her any kind of satisfaction, even though it also brought her feelings of animosity, regret and bitterness. She hated doing the job, no matter what rush she occasionally got from it, but, despite the second thoughts she'd had earlier, she was quite sure she'd never be able to bring herself to stop. She couldn't explain how she knew.

"Do something normal, enjoy yourself, relax," she said as she peered into her eyes in the reflection.

When she emerged from the bathroom, Sam was waiting in the corridor, holding her coat and handbag. "Madame," he said as he held the coat up so that she could slip into it.

"My computer–"

"It's off. Relax, work's over now."

"Where's this pub you spoke of?"

"End of Hill Street. Few minutes, that's all."

They walked in silence, not a word between them for the hundred and fifty metres they had to travel along to get to the pub.

Nielsen was pleased to see it wasn't busy, so, as they

entered, they had the pick of six tables. They sat at the table nearest the largest window that looked out onto the main road, Nielsen leading the way. She placed her coat on the back of her chair, ushered Sam away when he looked like he was going to come round to her side of the table and hold out her chair, and put her handbag on the floor.

"You know," Sam began, "doing that's seen as unlucky in some countries."

"Doing what?"

"Putting a handbag on the floor. It means you're going to be poor. Apparently."

"Already am. I'm on a copper's salary, remember, and I, like you, am a pathetic, sad human being who lives alone. No other bugger to help pay for the electricity. Chance would be a fine thing."

"Still, that's what they say."

"So where do you suggest I put it then?" she asked with a smile. "I could use it as a napkin, I suppose. It wasn't expensive – a bit of Bolognese sauce might do it good. Really bring out the colour."

Sam didn't know what to say, couldn't tell if he'd wound her up or if she was just joking. The smile, it could be misleading.

Nielsen broke the silence. "So where did you hear about that then?"

"Radio, I think. It's what they think in parts of Europe."

"Well, not in this one fortunately. Anyway, let's pick before they shut the kitchen."

She took a menu and Sam did the same. Shortly after, a waitress came to greet them. She had curly blonde hair, looked like she was fifteen, had braces on her teeth and spoke with a lisp. They gave her their orders: for Nielsen, a ham and cheese toasted baguette and a gin and tonic; for Sam, sirloin steak and chips and a bottle of Stella Artois.

They didn't speak while they waited for their drinks, each willing the other to begin, each smiling when eye contact was made, both failing to find the words that the other craved to hear. It was crazy to feel embarrassed, Nielsen thought – Sam too – but she felt like she was sixteen again and on a first date.

"So what do you do for fun?" he asked when they started drinking their drinks.

"What?"

"Hobbies. What are your hobbies? You do have some, don't you?"

"Oh God," she said, putting her head on the table in an overly exaggerated way. "Listen to us. We're work colleagues, adults for God's sake, and we're behaving like bloody babies."

He laughed. She laughed.

"What, you think I'm not interested in your hobbies?" he asked.

"Well, I'm certainly not interested in yours."

"True. Very true."

They downed the remainder of their drinks; unquenchable thirsts from their work.

"So when do you think this is all going to end?"

This time she didn't have to ask what he meant. "We've got no idea who he is. Always wears gloves, always uses condoms, cars are always used once and abandoned. Clean inside when they're searched. So I don't know. It's like he could go on and on. We've got to wait for him to make a mistake."

"You speak as if John Simmons isn't our number one suspect."

"That's because I still don't know. I'm as confused now as I was yesterday and the day before. Every day. I just don't know what to think. Maybe he did it. Maybe Michelle

269

Keating is real and maybe it's him who's going around taking these women. But, then again, maybe it isn't him. He just doesn't seem the type. Or maybe she's not even his girlfriend. There are just too many possibilities. Makes my head spin. I can't stop thinking, why would he have come to us in the first place if it wasn't real and it's him doing it all?"

"Maybe it's a game to him."

"But his concern," she said as she shook her head, "his concern seemed so real."

"Everyone can act. Some better than others. Or maybe he's just nuts."

"The nuts argument. Morgan's rather keen on that one himself."

She went over everything she knew, everything she'd experienced during the past week, and asked Sam what he thought. It couldn't hurt, she decided, to let someone else take some of the pressure. And he was a good cop. He could help her.

The one thing they were both certain about: they weren't certain about anything – John Simmons, Jennie Michaels, Michelle Keating, the other women. "Ten now," Nielsen confirmed. "Eleven, if we believe Jennie Michaels as Michelle Keating is dead. And what if he doesn't stop? What if we can't stop him?"

"We always ask what if, Kate? That's part of being a cop. In this case, what if we don't catch the guy? What if John Simmons killed Michelle Keating? What if she doesn't exist? What if she does but isn't part of this serial? What if the guy behind it is someone we know and it's happening right under our noses? What if we never find him?" He let out a snort. "Hey, what if it's me, you know what I'm saying?"

Nielsen nodded her head.

"We'll never know answers to speculative questions,

Kate, not until the guy's in cuffs and behind bars telling us why he did it. So don't focus on the asking of the questions; let's focus on finding the answers."

Of course she knew he was right. If she weren't so tired, it was likely she would have been the one saying those very things. But her mind was aching, her body was drained and she was fatigued like never before. Plus the twinges from her hip were incessant.

She couldn't keep looking into dead faces, seeing the relatives of dead girls, hoping somehow this would end. She had to find a way.

"Well, here's one action: I'll get to the Wongs. This whole thing about going to the theatre where Simmons says he was taking Jennie Michaels. The Wongs have been treated like the victims so far, given the respect and the distance. And maybe that's been the right thing. But now I think perhaps it's time for them to start answering the blindingly obvious questions. Like why did they go to that theatre? The question, if John Simmons is to be believed, that no doubt he'd have been screaming at Mrs Wong when he stood in front of her with a hammer in his hand. You know, the image of it makes me sick. Whatever his involvement, he's a little bastard."

"Doesn't make any sense why the Wongs would go there. Could be a coincidence."

"Hasn't made sense since day one, Sam. Nothing has."

Their food arrived and they returned to their silence. At times, Nielsen thought Sam wanted to say things to her, start more mini-conversations. At times, he thought she wanted to speak.

They didn't. They ate, paid and left. "Good night," they both said as they went their separate ways. They'd see each other in the morning.

*

While Nielsen was walking to her car, she checked her mobile and had a missed call. Hadn't heard it ringing during supper.

She didn't recognise the number, dialled voicemail, hoped there'd be a message.

There was. The voice spoke in a whisper. It was breathy. The woman on the line didn't introduce herself, but Nielsen knew who it was.

"He hit me," she said. "He hit me, not first time. And…" Now the pause came. Then: "Detective, I scared. I scared of man who come after me with hammer. But I also scared of home. Huang. Is more to say. I scared, Detective. Please phone."

Mrs Wong didn't leave a number, but Nielsen pulled the notepad out of her bag and retrieved it. She dialled Mrs Wong's mobile number. A pause and then the ringing. She thought of the fear in the woman's voice. She'd said she'd been hit, but by whom? John Simmons? If that's what she meant, Nielsen was already aware of that. Or by her husband? Then was this just an exaggeration of a spousal bust-up in light of their situation with Simmons, the tensions that would undoubtedly be caused, or was it more?

The ringing continued, but the phone wasn't picked up. Nielsen contemplated calling the house number she had written down, but then she heard DCI Morgan's voice after Wong complained, which he no doubt would, the result of being woken at well past midnight. "First we let that wacko smash his place up, then you think you can wake him up. Are you out of that tiny head of yours? The fucking morning, Nielsen, why didn't you call in the fucking morning? It's when people get up. Always bother them in daylight."

So she'd leave it till the morning, bright and early.

Nielsen pulled up outside her home fifteen minutes later. Her eyes were heavy. She'd yawned several times in the past couple of minutes. She thought that sleep might come on quickly; that she wouldn't have to spend hours staring at the ceiling this time. For once, she would welcome the chance to crawl into bed.

She got out of the car and locked the door. Approached her front door. Pulled the key out of her pocket. Tried to put it into the door lock.

Couldn't. Froze when she realised the lock had been drilled out and was no longer there.

Instantly awake, she removed her folded baton from her handbag. Extended it. Pushed the door lightly with her fingers. It crept open.

Inside it was dark. Limited light from the street lamps illuminated her path. She stepped forwards. Her breathing was trembling. She didn't know what to expect, wasn't sure whether to turn the lights on.

She poked her head around the kitchen doorway. Nothing.

She continued down the hallway. A slight turn to the left. The living room door was closed. She never shut it.

She swallowed hard and braced herself. She raised the baton and, with the other hand, slowly pressed on the door handle. She opened it only a few inches. Reached her hand onto the light switch, which was on the wall by the door. Counted down from three in her head.

Three. Two. One.

Switched the light on and pushed at pace through the door with her shoulder and hip. Grimaced through the pain. Screamed at the sight that lay before her eyes when she'd adjusted to the light.

The mobile phone sat on the dining table. It had been set to silent mode. She wouldn't hear it.

The words. He'd heard the words.

Mr Wong was sitting on the bed, a newspaper open in his hands. His wife was taking a shower. The bathroom was filled with mist and, when she got out of the shower, she used the towel to wipe the mirror clear. She put her hand to her cheek, took a look at his handiwork. The touch alone stung.

Despite her looks, about which her husband reminded her regularly, she still took great care when applying her eye and face creams.

When she brushed her teeth, she left the bathroom, switching off the light. She walked into the bedroom and saw her husband. She paused; she wasn't expecting him to be here.

*

Nielsen had her mobile in her hand, even though her whole arm trembled relentlessly. She dialled 999. She identified herself, asked for help when she was patched through to the call centre. Asked for everybody to be sent.

In front of her, on her sofa, sat Mark Sampson. His eyes were open. His arms were spread out either side of his body as if he were reaching for both armrests. His feet were planted on the floor. His head was leaning back against the top of the back of the sofa.

His throat had been cut. Nielsen could see the gaping wound. His black T-shirt was covered in blood. His black trousers and trainers were also covered in blood. Nielsen took a closer look. A gaping wound in each thigh as well.

Blood had been painted onto the beige sofa, every inch of it. Pools of blood encircled where he sat. Blood was sprayed on the walls.

Nielsen turned around. There was worse to come.

*

"Refreshing shower?" he asked, peering over the top corner of the paper, which he folded down beneath his finger.

She nodded, didn't dare speak, not when he was in one of his moods.

"Stand there," he said, indicating with his head the space at the end of the bed, dropping the paper onto the floor. She did as he instructed.

The words.

"Why did you leave me?" he asked.

She took a step back. Not this, she thought. Not again. She thought this was over.

"Why?" he said slowly.

"Huang, I no want speak about this. You know past is past."

"Past is past," he said, mocking her accent. "You know, I tried to have something normal with you, but you took that away from us when you, *you*, fucked Robert Chan. You took away *my* normal life."

She didn't understand him.

She'd left him, seven years before. Prior to that they'd managed thirteen years together. Thirteen years of what he'd called normality. First his mother, then the isolation, then his wife. The day she left, the normality was gone forever.

Eleven months later, she came back to him, realising her mistake, she'd said, that Huang Wong was the man she loved, not Robert Chan, that she was a better person than her passions had forced her to momentarily be. He could no

275

longer hold the thoughts at bay, no longer resist the desire to fight back, no longer be normal. He took her back and, as he did so, he knew that it would only be a matter of time before he would begin. To everyone on the outside things would appear normal, but that would be far from the truth. He just needed time.

The words.

*

Nielsen was sitting on the pavement curb outside her home when the first police car arrived. She clutched hold of her mobile phone. She pressed her knees into her chest and wrapped her arms around them, trying to keep warm. She gently rocked back and forth.

The front door behind her was open. The first two officers charged past her and into the house. A second car arrived, shortly followed by an ambulance.

She'd called Sam as soon as she'd come outside. After she'd vomited on her carpet. After she couldn't take it any longer. He arrived next. After him two more police cars came, their sirens lighting up the darkness.

Sam put his arm around her. He asked if she was okay. She didn't answer. Didn't answer for a long time.

Finally, she said, "Why me again?"

"He's sick, Kate. Simmons or whoever it is, he's sick. We'll get him."

"He's coming after me, just like Mike Butcher."

"You don't know that." He held her more tightly.

She pulled away from him. "Yes, I do. It's starting all over again."

Sam's skin started to crawl. "Why are you saying that? You've got to be strong, Kate. You can beat this guy. *We* can beat him."

Nielsen turned towards the house. "Take a look for yourself, then you'll see."

Sam entered the house. He passed two uniformed officers and entered the living room. It was a mess. He swallowed hard at the view and the rancid smell. Then he understood what Kate had meant, why she'd said, 'He's coming after me'.

The back of the door. 'Kate' fingered on it in blood.

*

"Put the towel on the bed," he said. His stomach was rising and falling faster than usual and his head felt bloated. He wanted to puncture it, but he had a plan to execute. He'd decided that now was the time.

She did as he commanded.

He looked at her naked body and grimaced. He couldn't believe he'd married this woman, couldn't believe he'd chosen her to help him be normal. He saw her body shaking and, finally, he smiled. He knew how it was going to be.

"Dance for me," he said.

She didn't want to, shook her head.

"Now," he said.

"Huang, I no—"

He spoke slowly but meaningfully: "Do it now." And she was consumed by fear, more than ever in her life, more than the day she'd walked out, and confirmed then cemented in him his reason to hate women forever.

She moved from left to right, fumbled really. Moved awkwardly and her figure did nothing for him. Disgust on his face.

"Lie down," he commanded.

She walked round her side of the bed and lay down gently.

"Open your legs."

"Huang–"

With a volume unlike anything she'd ever heard: "Open your fucking legs!"

She didn't want to, but she did. Had no choice.

He stood up. He faced the wall. Without peering back at her, he removed his dressing gown, pyjama top and bottoms. Momentarily, he stood there naked. He stretched his arms. His shoulder muscles protruded through his skin.

"Why did you leave me?" he asked.

This, she thought. This the reason. Hit too much.

"Why did you come back to me?" Silence. "My mother left my father. She never came back." He hadn't spoken to her about his parents, had said they were dead.

"Huang–"

"I hate them both. Equally." Now he turned, made eye contact. "And you, what did you do?"

She didn't answer and he didn't ask again. He walked round to the foot of the bed, climbed on top and moved himself forwards on his knees.

"Why?" he growled as he moved over her body, sniffing her scent from foot to where he came to a stop at shoulder level.

They hadn't had sex for almost a year. "You fucked Robert Chan. You did that to me, and look at you, nothing to look at. First her, then you."

The words.

"And now you fuck me with that detective."

Upon hearing the words, Mrs Wong tried to move, realising he knew about her phone call, tried to get off the bed, but his body cradled over her, holding her down like a spider clamping its prey.

His right hand moved towards his penis, clutched it and put it inside her. She squirmed.

"What did you think?" he said as he moved slowly, very

slowly, backwards and forwards.

The woman underneath him was crying silent tears.

He didn't rush – kept to a steady pace. "You fucking women are all the same. I've been waiting for over six years to do this." He stopped. "No, actually, come to think of it, it's been thirty-one years since the thought first entered my mind."

Suddenly, he thrust as hard as he could. The woman underneath him gasped, bit her lip. He kept thrusting as his hands wound around her neck. The fat made him spread his hands wider than was comfortable. But he kept pushing with ferocious might, managing to squeeze his fingers until he saw the breath leave his wife's body.

He'd finished before she died.

Chapter Twenty-Six

The following morning Kate Nielsen stood in front of the door that John Simmons had been in front of too often recently. She'd managed about two hours of sleep before giving up and getting up. She'd relied on Sam too much since yesterday. He'd taken her home last night, comforted her and cared for her. He'd slept on the sofa, given his bed to her.

And he'd done a good job. He'd managed to help her relax. Put the fire on, talked to her, given her cups of tea. Some brandy too.

But now she wanted to be alone.

It wasn't the dead body that had shaken her up so badly. It wasn't the fact that there had been a dead body in her house. Rather it was the unknown, just like the night with Mike Butcher. She didn't know who this man was, but he knew her. She didn't know how to find him, despite trying desperately, yet he had found a way into her home. And he'd brought death in there as an indication of what she should expect personally.

But she'd quickly realised: death is not as painful as rape. She'd filled her night hours wisely sorting out her head. You can't scare me any more, she thought, unaware of who the thoughts were for.

The night before she hadn't revealed details of the things flooding her mind to Sam, but what he said had helped her cope. The fact that he was sleeping in the next room helped her relax too. The more she thought about Mike Butcher and what he'd done to her, the less of a threat she found some blood on a door. For a time even, she found herself feeling more determined. Nothing, nothing whatsoever, could be as devastating as rape. Nothing, she thought, as she closed her eyes.

Twice she'd awoken during the night because of the sight of stockings being stuffed into her mouth. She didn't go back to sleep after that.

She got up, quietly so that she didn't wake Sam up. She left his flat with a single thought: today, she determined, we'll find him. And if not today, then tomorrow. But we'll find him. Not the other way around, of that she was sure.

So she was standing in front of the door. She had decided to act on last night's phone message.

She rang the Wongs' doorbell. Shortly after, looking through the glass, she made out the figure of a slender man approaching. He had dark hair and was wearing dark clothing. The door was unlocked from the inside and then pulled open.

"Yes," he said.

"Mr Wong, you may remember me. I'm Detective Sergeant Kate Nielsen. Can I have some time please?"

"Sure," Mr Wong said. "Come in," he added, stepping aside.

As Nielsen passed him and entered the hallway, he could barely keep the smile from his face. He inhaled deeply.

Still a mess, Nielsen observed, the result of John Simmons' visit – although she wasn't aware of an official reason why the place couldn't have been straightened up. Papers were piled high and broken frames were leaning against the walls.

Mr Wong led her into the lounge, where there were even more piles of paper. He saw Nielsen looking at them. "Yes, a mess. We haven't got round to tidying up."

"Is your wife home at the moment?"

"No," he answered. Not in the sense you're thinking, anyway. "She's still very shaken, so she's gone for a few days' break to friends. You know, Detective, I'm growing incredibly tired of this man bothering us all the time. How he could follow us to London like that, ruin our lovely day at the theatre, break in here and assault my wife is beyond me."

"I understand that," Nielsen answered, trying to read the man before her. "I would be too if I were in your shoes. I'm here to try to help see an end to this. I want to figure out what's going on."

Wong nodded and looked at her for a little too long. He wondered how she'd reacted last night, if she'd appreciated his little gesture. She was well and truly in the game now. It was coming. Anticipation was building up so much within him that he could feel the saliva increasing in his mouth. "Can I get you a drink?" he asked, an opportunity to begin, even though sooner than he'd expected. "Then we can talk properly."

She stared back, also for a little too long, but she didn't care if she made him uncomfortable. "Coffee would be great, thanks. White, one sugar."

"Please, take a seat. I'll be as quick as I can."

She sat down as Wong left. When he was out of the room, she heard him opening cupboards, the clang of porcelain. She looked around the lounge-diner, saw nothing but mess, thought for a moment. Got off her feet and walked over to some drawers that were open a fraction. Started looking inside, the occasional glimpse over her shoulder. She still heard noises from the kitchen.

Her plan was to speak to Wong, to see what he had to say about John Simmons, Jennie Michaels, Michelle Keating, the whole situation. After that, and only after, she'd drop the bombshell on him: his wife's message. She'd find out why it had been sent, just what Mrs Wong had meant. She wanted to gauge his responses carefully. He came across as calmness personified, a man genuinely frustrated by a bothersome individual. But she didn't know who to trust any more, so she wouldn't trust him completely. If she felt it necessary, she'd take him in. Of course, she wouldn't let him know that until she was ready for it to happen.

Some more drawers, already open. Looking. Some shelves on the wall. She took a closer look. Books reveal the kind of person, she once heard. Soppy romance and violent thriller. Knocked into one of the many piles that were at her feet, felt the paper fall into an even bigger mess. The next pile tumbled as well. Knelt down to shuffle the pages together again. Restacked the pile. She moved to the rest, picked up a stack of papers and flicked through them. Then another. And another.

She didn't hear Wong as he re-entered the room. She didn't know that he saw what she was holding. "Can I help you?"

She stood up, spun around. Searching her mind quickly for a response, she heard Morgan's booming voice admonishing her behaviour here.

"I, uh–"

"Your coffee," he said holding out a cup, a twisted smile on his face. He took a step closer, too close, and handed it to her. She took it from him. It wasn't hot. She looked down. No liquid inside it. Paper.

She pulled it out. A picture. A face she recognised, only changed.

Jennie Michaels. Michelle Keating. Blood. Black eye. Broken nose.

Nose like mush.

She only felt the blood when it trickled down her head and the sharp pain caused by Wong bringing his coffee cup, and its scalding contents, to her forehead.

She fell to the ground.

Chapter Twenty-Seven

Sam had woken up expecting to make Nielsen some breakfast. He hadn't expected her to jump straight back into the job.

He was surprised when he found a note from her on his kitchen table: "Chasing lead at Wongs. Will check out Simmons' house again after. Meet you at station at lunch."

He made a coffee, sat down, logged on to his laptop in the kitchen and began searching. He'd work from home this morning. He scanned the day's news stories, trying to unearth more links.

His mobile rang. He half expected it to be Nielsen, was disappointed when he saw who it actually was.

"How is she?" DCI Morgan asked. Could Sam detect a hint of sympathy in the man's tone? He could hardly believe it.

"Like nothing's happened. Back on the case."

"What do you mean back on the case?"

"The Wongs. Gone to press them on all these coincidences, no doubt."

"Like fuck she has." All sympathy gone. Back to normal. Voice raised: "They're the ones this Simmons prick has bashed around and you want to stick a rod up their arse. You're supposed to be keeping an eye on her. It's only been a night and already she's pushing it. Bloody woman. Bloody women!"

"It's just her way of dealing with things. She obviously wants to get on as if nothing's happened."

"She can't go in there shooting her tossing mouth off. They complain, I get it up the arse, and you'll both get it, her up both holes. Get what I'm saying? So get off your arse, stop being a lazy shit and stop her. I told you she's fucked this up enough and I don't want her left alone to make it worse. Surely the two of you can't fuck it up any more."

"Sure," Sam answered, even though Morgan was still speaking.

"Fucking morons! I work with a bunch of fucking penguins! Like penguins in the fucking desert!" The line went dead.

As he stood up, Sam smiled at the thought of Morgan rambling to himself about them for the next ten minutes. Penguins in a fucking desert.

*

He's got me and I'm helpless. I agreed to this. I've signed my death warrant all in the name of a job. He's supposed to be here. He's supposed to help me.

I've been hit in the face. The pain in my right cheekbone is unbearable. I can feel my eye starting to swell up. I'm lying on the ground and I can't move. The part of my brain that's supposed to tell my body to move, to get up, to resist, to do whatever the fuck it is I have to do to get out of here alive, is dormant, it's gone away, it's fucked off when I need it most. My body is paralysed – because of fear, or because I've banged my head on something, or because I no longer have control of my bodily functions, I don't know – and all I can do is look up at him, blurred though he is in my vision, and wait for the next thing he's going to do.

He's stroking his groin and smiling as he kneels down over me.

I manage to get out, "Please."

It's a plea that falls on deaf ears. He doesn't so much as pause, doesn't show any indication that he's heard me, as he unzips and readies himself for what he's been waiting for since the last one.

"Please," I repeat. My voice is hoarse and now I'm not even sure if he can hear me, so weak and soft is my attempt to speak.

He kicks his jeans off. His boxers remain around his ankles.

He lies on top of me. Tears at my stockings. Stuffs them in my mouth.

He's inside me. I can't bear how he feels down there. I'm being invaded in a way I never imagined. Tears are streaming down my face. Tears because I can't do anything about this, because this sick bastard is where only a loved one should go. Tears because I want to die.

"Please," I say one last time, but this time there's no volume to my words.

He's rocking backwards and forwards. He's moving faster. He's pushing harder. I bite on the stockings to try to get my mind off what's going on. It doesn't work. I want to kill this man. I want revenge. I want to see him suffer and squirm and succumb to my power, not the other way round.

But that's not going to happen.

When he's finished with me and when he kills me, these are the things I will think of. He might not know it, but I will win in my mind. I will be defiant and I will not leave showing fear.

Will them away I may, but I can't stop the tears. These fucking tears that mix with his sweat as it drips on my face. I look him in the eye, but he doesn't return the look. In fact, he's avoiding looking at me. I can see now – he's ashamed. Ashamed at what he's doing. Yet he carries on, harder, rougher, and now his head drops next to my neck and shoulder. He hides from me. I feel his teeth bite into my neck. I open my mouth to scream, but no sound escapes. Nothing, just stillness.

Nielsen came to, woken up from her nightmare and dumped into a new one. The back of her head was throbbing. When her eyes opened and she got away from the images that had haunted her for four years, she saw Wong sitting on the sofa, his hands clasped together, his chin resting on them, his gaze fixed on her.

She was tied to a dining table chair, her hands wrapped behind her back and round its support. She tried to shake herself free, but her hands were locked in place. She heard the jangle of metal and knew that Wong had tied her hands together with her own handcuffs.

"Untie me now," she said, determined, more than she'd felt in a long time. It was as if the blow to her head had rejuvenated her and she was ready to get back on her feet, end this thing.

"It can't last forever," Wong said, keeping his eyes locked on her. "I knew that from the beginning."

"I said untie me now."

"Be quiet," he said.

"This is a police officer giving you an order."

"Be quiet, you piece of meat!" he shouted, suddenly on his feet, a wild animal, lunging towards her, grabbing her by the shoulders, shaking her, shaking her so hard she thought her insides might fall out. "Fucking woman and you think you can tell me what to do!"

As quickly as he'd leapt towards her, he released her and walked out of the room. She heard him run upstairs and then heard him rummaging through something. Metallic sounds.

He returned moments later with a curved knife. "Look," Nielsen said, wincing, holding down the sick that wanted to escape, "whatever has happened, we can still end this peacefully. We can still make this right. Untie me and let's talk."

He ignored her.

"Speak to me," she tried again. Had to try harder. "Speak to me and let me help you."

Still no answer. He was working out the final stages of his impromptu plan.

288

"I can help you. Let me."

Being calm wasn't helping. When it was clear that no response was forthcoming, she decided on the ballsy approach: "Why do you have a picture of Michelle Keating?" He didn't answer. "Why?" she asked louder. Then really loud: "Did you kill Mark Sampson and the other women as well? Did you? Speak to me, you murdering son of a bitch!"

He spun around and leapt towards her again. Grabbed her by the chin and squeezed hard, so hard she thought her teeth might fall out. The butterflies – not the ones that come from excitement, but the ones that dwell deep inside, the result of fear – ran amuck, and now it was clear to her that he might extinguish her life at any time.

"Let go of me," she said through gritted teeth – gritted because she couldn't open her mouth any wider. His grip only increased in force.

"Do you know what pleasure is, Detective? I was robbed of it when I was eleven years old. Then, once again, when my whore of a wife left me."

He was right in front of her. Now she knew she would be number twelve.

"This," he said indicating the tied-up Nielsen before him," this gives me pleasure. I like to prepare, you know, like I did with Michelle. I made an exception once. It didn't go so well. I've been planning your end for a couple of days now, but I must say this opportunity today is unexpected. I didn't think you'd be stupid enough to walk into my home alone, especially after you received that phone call from her. But I'll thank you and take the opportunity with open arms." He licked her face. "Oh, you're a hot one. This is going to be something. I thought I'd have longer, you know, before it came to this. Thought I could play with you longer. I could've if you'd have followed where I was leading you. After I'd led that crazy bastard to the theatre, why didn't you think he was mad, like you were supposed to? After he tried to run you over, why not then?"

"He didn't," she managed to say. He hadn't released his grip. "You did."

He put some of her hair into his mouth and pulled hard. He let go of her jaw and she cried out. He stood up.

"There, there. Get ready because it's going to get far better than that."

"Where is your wife?"

"She shouldn't have called you. Besides, she was always done for. Her time would have come sooner or later. She made me look normal. She gave me the cover I needed. Only reason I ever took the bitch back."

"What have you done to her?"

"What I wanted to do years ago. You know what? It feels even better than I thought it would. You aware that that bitch left me? Seven years ago. That repulsive little beast fucked someone else. Of course, she wasn't quite as repulsive back then."

He walked back to her, the knife in his hand. With his other hand, he took hold of a clump of her hair.

"Let go," she said, but her voice cracked and tears welled up in her eyes. Without wanting to, she had given Wong every sign that he was winning, that he'd induced in her the greatest fear possible, that he could have his way with her just like he had with the other eleven women, Michelle Keating the latest.

His wife was number twelve.

"You're going to die, you know that?" Number thirteen. "I decided you'd be the last one, but I don't want to stop yet. Last night's fun with that silly little boy was only supposed to be the beginning. And now you've fucked that up for me, so it's going to be painful, I promise you." He put the knife on the floor, moved his head closer to hers so that their eyes were only an inch apart. "I like to plan fully. I like control. Women don't control me, I control them. Oh, I've been looking forward to this, darlin'." He was drooling like a dog. He planted his lips on hers, his hand again locked around her chin, further up so that her jaw was becoming numb.

She closed her eyes, but the tears still found a way through. She didn't want to see him, even though she could feel him.

And then she felt him somewhere else: his hand was on her leg, moving upwards, moving closer to her groin. She squealed when she realised the last man to touch her so intimately had been Mike Butcher. And now him.

"Mm, two in a row. Her up there and you down here. If I've got to go out, might as well go out with a bang." His claw moved in and pressed hard, too hard, and her body convulsed. His hands explored her. She tried to scream, but he held her too tightly. "The first touch is always the best." He shivered. "Oh, I've been dreaming about this. I've been so close before. You're everything I dreamed you'd be."

His head moved back a few inches as his hand pressed harder and harder, so she let out a scream so loud that eardrums could burst, a scream so loud that Wong planted a backhand across her cheek, cutting the shriek off.

"You like it rough?" he asked. "I like it rough too." And he hit her with another backhand, this one across the other cheek. He gave her two more and she became woozy, was unable to see clearly.

He pulled at her hair and tore her blouse open. Now he was growling. "Black bra. Naughty girl." Then more laughter – a sick laugh, guttural, deep. His hands squeezed both breasts at the same time. Hurt her. "You know, with the first one, I made a big mistake. Back then I reckoned what I was doing was like a second marriage. I took someone who could have been my bride if I were starting out again.

She made me want her. So young and beautiful. She might have made me normal again. But then she showed me she was also a dirty fucking whore. So that was it; I was ready to take. They were my objects, my play things. Fucking toys there to fulfil one purpose."

Nielsen wanted it to be over, almost wished it would be, but there was a resoluteness that remained in the back of her mind. In any way, if the opportunity arose, she wouldn't let that dream, her past, become a reality again.

One hand remained on her breast; the other returned to her groin. "And once you have one like that, you want another and another and another. Then I wanted you."

She'd been invaded before – it couldn't happen again. His head returned, lips first, she thought for another kiss. She opened her mouth, lifted her head an inch or two, and brought her mouth closed over his nose. She bit, bit and gnawed, and wouldn't let go. His hands came away from her breast and groin and he seemed to run on the spot for a moment. She heard his agony, a shout of incomprehensible words as she tasted blood, and then she felt a blow to her ribs, then to her hip. The combination of the blows was enough to make her release Wong's nose.

He gripped her neck, squeezed for all his worth – she could hear the effort in his breathing. Her breath was quickly leaving her. She couldn't get him off, despite shaking as much as she could. She couldn't do anything, was helpless. She could see the knife, wanted to grab it, couldn't. She was aware of a kind of fading, a sense of loss, a feeling of being overcome, of switching off. Then her eyes closing.

It was almost over.

So this is death, she thought. Death's approaching.

And it was: it was coming for her, open-armed. She couldn't hold it off any more; he was too strong and she was too weak.

Drifting, leaving, almost there now. Not much longer. Her head tilting forwards, her body drooping, becoming lifeless.

And then release: nothing.

*

Sam was ten minutes away from Sanders Road. He was in the Volvo, a sign on the pavement announcing road works ahead, a queue in front of him. He could see the workmen, could see the temporary traffic lights that changed from green to red within seconds when his side was given the briefest of moments to advance, that seemed to let dozens of cars through from the other side.

He kept glancing at his watch. Kept thinking this was all a waste of time. He kept thinking that Nielsen would be back at the station before he'd even get there.

*

Release: nothing.

Wong had let go, although Nielsen, almost unconscious, wasn't aware of being given her life back, wasn't aware of the body that lunged at Wong, wasn't aware of Wong hitting the ground, wasn't aware of the tussle that ensued at her feet, wasn't aware that fist after fist hit Wong's face, chest and stomach. She wasn't aware of being untied, the knife cutting her free. She wasn't aware of being lifted up and placed on the sofa. And she wasn't aware of the voice calling the police.

*

Sam heard the call on his radio. Bile immediately appeared in his mouth.

"Fuck," he said, swallowing.

He pulled the car onto the pavement, no siren to hand, and accelerated, the car catching the wall and scraping along it as he drove. He kept on the pavement until he reached the front of the queue, rejoined the road and sped past the traffic lights, the window down, his head half out, screaming at other drivers, telling them who he was, little did they care. He sounded his horn repeatedly and swerved in and out of cars, took corners so sharply that he skidded, and arrived at the Wong residence only minutes later.

Leaving the car door open, he charged along the path to find the front door wide open. He ran into the hallway and screamed, "Kate!"

"In here," he heard a man's voice; he didn't recognise it.

He ran into the lounge and saw Nielsen lying on the sofa, her eyes closed, a man kneeling on the floor by her, and Wong on the floor, handcuffs forcing his hands behind his back.

"Kate," Sam said and leapt to her. He heard more noise outside and then footsteps inside. Officers and paramedics appeared. "Kate, it's going to be all right," he said, stepping back while looking at the mess – the blood, the bruises – on her face, giving the medics room to work.

He looked towards the man who was on his knees, then at Wong, then back at the kneeling man. He smiled and let a gust of air escape his lungs.

"Good job you were here, John."

Chapter Twenty-Eight

He's got me and I'm helpless. I agreed to this. I've signed my death warrant all in the name of a job. He's supposed to be here. He's supposed to help me.

I've been hit in the face. The pain in my right cheekbone is unbearable. I can feel my eye starting to swell up. I'm lying on the ground and I can't move. The part of my brain that's supposed to tell my body to move, to get up, to resist, to do whatever the fuck it is I have to do to get out of here alive, is dormant, it's gone away, it's fucked off when I need it most. My body is paralysed – because of fear, or because I've banged my head on something, or because I no longer have control of my bodily functions, I don't know – and all I can do is look up at him, blurred though he is in my vision, and wait for the next thing he's going to do.

He's stroking his groin and smiling as he kneels down over me.

I manage to get out, "Please."

It's a plea that falls on deaf ears. He doesn't so much as pause, doesn't show any indication that he's heard me, as he unzips and readies himself for what he's been waiting for since the last one.

"Please," I repeat. My voice is hoarse and now I'm not even sure if he can hear me, so weak and soft is my attempt to speak.

He kicks his jeans off. His boxers remain around his ankles.

He lies on top of me. Tears at my stockings. Stuffs them in my mouth.

He's inside me. I can't bear how he feels down there. I'm being invaded in a way I never imagined. Tears are streaming down my face. Tears because I can't do anything about this, because this sick bastard is where only a loved one should go. Tears because I want to die.

"Please," I say one last time, but this time there's no volume to my words.

He's rocking backwards and forwards. He's moving faster. He's pushing harder. I bite on the stockings to try to get my mind off what's going on. It doesn't work. I want to kill this man. I want revenge. I want to see him suffer and squirm and succumb to my power, not the other way round.

But that's not going to happen.

When he's finished with me and when he kills me, these are the things I will think of. He might not know it, but I will win in my mind. I will be defiant and I will not leave showing fear.

Will them away I may, but I can't stop the tears. These fucking tears that mix with his sweat as it drips on my face. I look him in the eye, but he doesn't return the look. In fact, he's avoiding looking at me. I can see now – he's ashamed. Ashamed at what he's doing. Yet he carries on, harder, rougher, and now his head drops next to my neck and shoulder. He hides from me. I feel his teeth bite into my neck. I open my mouth to scream, but no sound escapes. Nothing, just stillness.

And then the reality of what he's doing comes: he comes. His head lifts up and he presses his bodyweight up by using his shoulders. He is released. And I stare right at him, though he won't look into my eyes. Yes, the tears are still there, but there's no fear in my eyes any more. Only disgust; I realise how pathetic he is. He looks so small.

His body slowly loosens and it happens: our eyes met. For a moment we look at one another, both trying to give nothing away, both failing. Me: hatred; he: guilt.

The courage is there instantly and I want him to know it. While he is still inside me, I open my mouth and scream. Scream so loudly that strangers a hundred miles off can hear. The scream lasts and lasts, only ending when every ounce of air escapes from my lungs.

He looks down at me. A tear falls from his cheek. It lands on *my face. With my one good eye I call him a million words.*

His left hand holds his body in position; his right hand goes behind his back. From an invisible pair of trousers, from under an invisible belt, he takes it. The gun. He brings it round to my face and I hold steadfast: I show no fear, no desperation. I won't close my eyes.

He puts his finger on the trigger. We are still as one. Now is the time.

As he begins squeezing the trigger, he turns the barrel of the gun towards his head. He fires and his face blows apart. He is inside me and I'm covered in pieces of him.

And that's when I smile.

Kate Nielsen woke up with a start. She wasn't covered in sweat, not this time, not like every other time. It may have startled her, just as it always did, but for the first time the dream had an ending. An ending that had evaded her for four years. Maybe now the nights would bring with them some peace.

Unknowingly, she'd been awoken by the phone ringing. It took several seconds before the noise entered her consciousness. She answered.

"Are you all right, Kate?"

The voice calmed her. "Sam. Morning. I'm fine. Just fine."

"Sleep well?"

"You know what? Better than usual. That dream, you remember?" She'd told Sam about it after Wong had been cuffed, after he'd been taken away, after his wife's body had been removed from the upstairs bedroom, after Sam had sat with her in the hospital while she healed, after he'd asked her out on an official date, after they'd decided to see more of each other. "It ended this time. You know, it's never had an ending before. Whether it comes back or not, after today I'll feel a hell of a lot better about it. All this stuff with John

Simmons, it's helped me realise there can be closure. And even if it's not ideal or good news, it can satisfy in its own way."

"Good, I'm glad."

"Me too. You know, I'm glad I said yes to you." She lay back down and smiled. "And I'm glad I told you. The guy in the dream has hurt me so many times, too many times, and you know how I got him back?"

"How's that?"

"I watched him shoot himself square in the face."

"In the face?"

"That's right."

"Just a dream. Don't let it worry you any more."

"It doesn't and I won't." She placed the receiver on her chest. Then to herself: "Not any more."

They finished speaking and ten minutes later, after Nielsen had wrestled herself out of the warm bed and freshened up in the bathroom, the doorbell rang. She headed downstairs and opened the door. It was Sam.

She gave him a hug and led him to the kitchen where she dished up coffee and croissants. During the past two weeks, since they'd first gone out to dinner, confided in one another and enjoyed each other, they'd repeated this ritual every two days: coffee-and-croissants mornings. Suddenly, Nielsen's days didn't seem so empty, void and meaningless.

"Paper," Sam said, tossing it on the table so that it landed in prime position for Nielsen.

"The beautiful tabloid," her response, and she left it alone.

After they ate their croissants and drank their coffees, they kissed, a long, slow kiss.

The kissing ceased but recommenced in seconds. Over his shoulder, Sam looked at his watch. He pulled back from the embrace. "I'm going to be late."

"So take the day off." Nielsen had been signed off – needed

time for the physical wounds to recover; the psychological, she'd started to deal with sooner than expected, much to everyone's surprise. She'd take one more week off and then she thought she'd be ready to return.

He kissed her again, even more passionately than before, if that was possible. When they parted: "If only."

"I know. If only. I'll have a meal ready at six."

"I won't be late."

Sam left and Nielsen bolted the door. She turned around and smiled. Leaned back against the door and felt content; content like she thought she'd never feel again. Happy, safe, secure.

She returned to the kitchen, refilled her coffee cup, sat down and opened the paper. She wasn't on the front page – not any more, not five weeks after she'd almost died at Wong's hands. In fact, her story had been relegated to page five today and was no longer featured every day.

She read the story, read it and felt appeased that it was over, that the mystery of Michelle Keating's disappearance had been solved, however terrible the outcome, that John Simmons could finally put the memory of the woman he knew as Jennie Michaels and her tragedy behind him, that eleven families could put their loved ones to rest, and rest themselves. And she said a quiet prayer, thankful for John Simmons, thankful for him coming into her life, for him being the persistent nuisance that he was, for ultimately saving her life.

She was brought out of the article by the ringing of her mobile. She recognised the number instantly.

She picked up. "John, how are you doing?"

"How else?" He didn't say anything further. He still sounded deflated.

"I know," the only thing Nielsen could think to say. He felt the way she'd felt for four years.

"And how are you feeling?" he enquired.

"Recovering, thanks. Getting better every day."

"I keep thinking…"

"Yes?"

"I'll never get over this, you know. I was going to propose to her. She was going to be my wife. She would have said yes, I know it."

"I'm sure she would have. And I'm sure you would have been very happy together. You're a good man."

"We would have been. If only…"

"You can't blame yourself, John. You couldn't have predicted what was going to happen. She was a woman with a past. A past she'd kept secret from everyone."

John laughed in a self-deprecating way. "If she'd have said yes, just think, I could have been marrying someone whose name I didn't even know. Jennie Michaels. I feel so stupid."

"There's nothing to feel stupid about, John. Michelle Keating, Jennie Michaels, whatever name you'd have known her as, you couldn't have known the truth. She was a woman with a past she wanted to escape. And she thought the Wongs were the people to help her. What she didn't realise was that Wong saw an opportunity with her when she asked to be his tenant. He was looking for women to kill, John. And a woman in hiding is an easy victim. It's that simple. No one knew she was there and that was attractive to him. She wasn't any the wiser. Just like his wife; they were both in the dark about who he was and what he was doing."

"But if Jennie hadn't been running from her ex? Or if she'd just have been honest with me, maybe she'd still be here and not strangled then dumped in some filthy alleyway. Jennie, Michelle, I don't know what to call her any more. But maybe I could have helped her."

"Maybe." Nielsen paused. "But there's no way you

should blame yourself." Maybe I could have helped her, she thought, thinking the conclusion might have been different if Morgan had let her put Jennie Michaels' picture on television when she'd first asked, or if she'd gone ahead and done it regardless. "She changed her name and she didn't want to be registered as Wong's tenant because she didn't want her ex to find her. Some women will do anything to get away from an abusive ex who won't take no for an answer. As soon as she moved down here and didn't register anywhere with her real name, she gave Wong an open invitation to do with her as he pleased. No one could have predicted what would happen and no one could have stopped it."

"You're right. Of course you are. But I just wish things were different. There was something special there. We could have made it work. I've never felt that way about someone before and I know it – I never will again. It could have all been prevented if she hadn't cancelled her old phone number the day we were travelling to London, or at least told me she was getting a new number. Her ex wouldn't have found her that way and the police wouldn't have thought I was crazy. Why'd she have to be so bloody careful?"

"Too careful. She thought her ex had got her number from her brother, Tom, and that cancelling it was her only option. And she couldn't tell a soul. Like I said, women running from something are always extremely careful."

"Too careful, yes. We could have traced her if her phone number hadn't been disabled. We could have found her, Detective."

"Kate, you know that. Remember to always call me Kate."

"Kate. Thank you. You know, sometimes you just need to hear a familiar voice."

"Oh, I know," she responded. "I know that *too* well. Any time, John. I'll be a familiar voice any time."

"You're a good person. You helped me and, while this

didn't end out the way I wanted it to, one thing's for sure. You're a damned good cop and you've got to keep on helping people."

"Yes," she said, "so people keep telling me. I will, John, I'll press on." She sighed. "I'll keep trying. Things are getting better."

"Good luck."

"Thanks, John, and any time, you hear?"

"Any time."

The call ended. Nielsen looked down at the paper. Her eyes returned to the headline: 'Promotion honour for hero cop'. Work hadn't made her smile for years, but she smiled. She smiled because she knew that with every end comes a new beginning.

The past was the past. She was strong enough to see that. Now for the beginning.

About the Author

After studying literature, linguistics and Spanish at university, Karl Vadaszffy trained as an English teacher and actor. He has edited magazines, taught English as a foreign language in Poland and taught English, Media Studies and Drama in secondary schools in England.

Working in schools in Hertfordshire, UK, he became Head of Year when he was only 25 and a Head of English at 26. He is currently the Head of English, Drama and Media Studies at an Ofsted 'outstanding-rated' Catholic school in Hertfordshire.

Karl currently juggles his teaching responsibilities with work as a freelance journalist. His articles regularly appear in ten industry-leading magazines that cover the automotive, aerospace, technology and travel sectors. His articles are read by over 12,000 subscribers in print, and more online.

While in a previous teaching role, Karl established The Astley Cooper School's author visits programme, which saw a number of authors, many internationally bestselling, visit the school to give talks, sign books and host workshops. These included Frederick Forsyth, Jodi Picoult, Sophie Hannah, Peter James, Darren Shan, Joanne Harris, Michael Marshall, Deborah Moggach and Elizabeth Buchan. The programme ran for three successful years until he left the school.

Karl was a competitive fencer for seven years. Fencing is in his blood; his father was Hungarian Foil Champion and three-time British Epee Champion, coached the under-21s British Olympic foil team and was the personal coach of Bruce Dickinson, lead singer of Iron Maiden, for almost thirty years. He also coached actors, including Ralph Fiennes and Robson Green, to prepare them for screen roles.

Similarly, Karl's passion for drama was inherited from his father, who also trained as an actor. Zsolt Vadaszffy trained at RADA before having a successful film and television career in the 1960s, working with actors such as Michael Caine, Sean Connery, Anthony Hopkins and Alec Guinness. Karl followed in his father's footsteps by training at the London Centre for Theatre Studies.

3057619R00158

Printed in Great Britain
by Amazon.co.uk, Ltd.,
Marston Gate.